BLOOD IS THICKER THAN BEAUJOLAIS

BLOOD IS THICKER THAN BEAUJOLAIS

Tony Aspler

HEADLINE

First published in Great Britain in 1995
by HEADLINE BOOK PUBLISHING

10 9 8 7 6 5 4 3 2 1

British Library Cataloguing in Publication Data

Aspler, Tony
  Blood is Thicker Than Beaujolais
  I.   Title
  823 [F]

ISBN 0-7472-1440-9

Typeset by Keyboard Services, Luton, Beds

Printed and bound in Great Britain by
Mackays of Chatham PLC, Chatham, Kent

HEADLINE BOOK PUBLISHING
A division of Hodder Headline PLC
338 Euston Road
London NW1 3BH

To my son, Guy

Chapter One

Beware the enterprise not launched with champagne. Remember the *Titanic*; no bottle was broken over its bow.

The thought floated through Ezra's troubled mind as he mounted the worn stone steps of the police station.

He paused before entering, allowing himself time to recall the macabre events of the morning so that he could tell his side of the story.

The squat building with its flaking mustard-coloured façade was located on the north side of the square next to Haut St Antoine's town hall. At tables under the plane trees in the main square, old men with blue berets and red faces sat on wicker chairs nursing tiny glasses of Beaujolais. The bistro on the corner was filled with truck drivers and merchants. Everything seemed in suspension just waiting for 18 November, the third Thursday of the month, when the new wine would be released.

The old men watched Ezra as he hesitated on the top step, hands deep in his heavy blue overcoat pockets. He seemed to fill the doorway, his reddish complexion accentuated by the shock of prematurely white hair that had a life of its own in the afternoon breeze. His large expanse of forehead, deeply lined, was corrugated in a frown.

Do it, he commanded himself.

Once inside his acute sense of smell, honed over twenty-two years of detecting wines' elusive fragrances, picked up the chalky smell of dampness and the more pungent scent of stale tobacco. The reception desk, he noticed, was no bigger than the one in his hotel but the uniformed gendarme pecking at a typewriter behind it was far less obliging than the owner's wife, the bosomy Madame Barrière.

On the wall above the seated cop hung a faded portrait of General de Gaulle in full military uniform.

'My name is Ezra Brant. I would like to see your senior officer,' he said in a loud voice, hoping his message would carry beyond the frosted glass doors to the inner office.

His French accent made the man look up abruptly. In the presence of public servants Ezra adopted the air of someone who had little time to spend on explanations at a low level.

'Your business?'

'It is a matter of great seriousness I wish to discuss.'

Ezra realized as soon as he had uttered the words that they sounded as pompous in French as they did in English; but they seemed to have the desired effect on the young policeman who rose from his chair, buttoned the jacket of his uniform and knocked on the glass doors. He slid them open wide enough to squeeze through without allowing Ezra a glimpse inside and closed them after him. Presently, he was back.

'Inspector Chasselas will see you,' he said, beckoning Ezra in.

As a wine writer, it pleased him that the local police chief was named after a grape variety. He made his way across the black-and-white tiled floor to the Inspector's office.

'Monsieur Brant. I am Chasselas. Sit down, please.'

Ezra found himself facing a man of medium height with a round face emphasized by a pair of moon-shaped spectacles and a half-beard. The beard was white, as if its owner had lowered his chin into a bowl of flour; but his hair, carefully styled with some substance that made it shine under the neon light, was jet black and not the dead black one usually associates with artificial colouring. It was blue-black, the colour of a revolver.

The eyes behind the tinted lenses were shrewd and challenging. The lips were thin and almost nonexistent. The manicured hands touched the lapels of his expensively cut suit.

'You speak English, Inspector.'

'A little. You are surprised. In such a tiny backwater, you are thinking. But it is expected of us. Beaujolais attracts a great deal of attention nowadays. It was not always so.'

'I only wish my French were as good as your English.'

'But your country is bilingual, is it not?'

'Officially, yes. But I didn't come here to . . .'

Chasselas held up his hand and opened a file in front of him.

'Ezra Brant, journalist from Toronto, Canada. Wife,

3

Constance Elizabeth. Residing at Hotel Sarment d'Or. I would have thought a journalist of your reputation, Monsieur Brant, would have chosen to stay at – well, there are many fine hotels in the region.'

Ezra was both flattered and annoyed. He realized that Chasselas was reading from a file the police had opened on him. The thought discomfited him but he was determined not to let it show.

'If you know that much about me, Inspector, then tell me why I'm here.'

Inspector Chasselas shrugged and pursed his lips.

'I'm listening, Monsieur.'

'I came to report a murder.'

The morning had begun badly. Ezra could not abide showers and there was no plug in the bath-tub. At breakfast in the bleak hotel dining-room, filled with dusty plants, he had watched a man at the next table spread butter and jam on his croissant and then dunk it into his coffee. On the way out the hotel porter dropped his flight bag containing two bottles of Hermitage La Chapelle 1983 presented to him by Gerard Jaboulet and inscribed on the label, 'To my friend, Ezra Brant'. Connie had compounded the disaster by telling him not to make a fuss.

They were driving north on the autoroute in a rented Citroën between Valence and Lyon when Connie had made matters worse by saying she thought the title of his new book was pretentious. '*Footsteps In My Wine* sounds like a travel guide for the inebriated. Sorry, have I said something wrong?'

A sharp November wind blew through the open window tousling Ezra's hair. Whatever the weather he always travelled with the window down. He also kept the house in North Toronto at what his friends called polar temperatures and refused to have air-conditioning in the heat of Toronto summers.

Connie pulled down the sun visor and inspected her face in the mirror. She looked tired. Sleeping in hotel beds did not agree with her. A brighter shade of lipstick might distract attention from the hollows under her eyes, she thought. Not bad for forty-eight though. She straightened her shoulder pads with her thumbs.

'Are you watching for signposts?' asked Ezra.

It was more command than question.

The Michelin Guide to Burgundy lay closed on Connie's lap. It made her queasy to read maps in a moving car. Why did he always insist that she act as his navigator? Why couldn't he work out the route before he got into the car? And would the hand of God come through the clouds and smite him if he actually stopped to ask directions when he got lost?

Connie glanced out at the lifeless vineyards that stretched up the hillsides. The vines had been cut back to regenerate in the spring. In their serried ranks they looked like arthritic black hands clutching painfully out of the brown earth.

They drove along in silence. Ezra wondered why she had agreed to accompany him on this trip. It was only the second time she had travelled with him to wine country. The last time, seven years ago, they had visited Champagne.

After two days she had become bored with the endless chalk cellars, the bottling lines, the stainless steel tanks, the continuous talk about wine as if it were the only subject worthy of attention. She had remained in the car and read while he went around doing what he had to do, vowing never to travel with him again unless it was a place where no wine was made. Like Hawaii or the Arctic. Yet Ezra could probably sniff out someone somewhere who made wine from pomegranates or fermented whale blubber.

'Where did you say we're going?' she asked.

'Haut St Antoine. It's in Morgon between Brouilly and Fleurie. I phoned Monsieur Verrier and told him we'd be there at ten.'

Both Ezra and Connie were punctual people. They had a horror of being late. They had spent the night in Tain-L'Hermitage in the Northern Rhône where Ezra had visited Jaboulet and Chapoutier, two prominent wine producers who sounded to Connie like a firm of French solicitors. At seven-thirty in the morning Ezra had wanted to get one last shot of the old chapel in the Hermitage vineyard, an excursion which had set them back almost an hour.

For Ezra, the stay in the Rhône had been a bonus. The *Toronto Examiner*, the newspaper for which he worked, had sent him to cover the Beaujolais Nouveau race. He had visited the region on several occasions but never for the release of the new wine. And this time he was to be inducted into the Confrèrie des Compagnons de Beaujolais.

'Does that mean you'll have to say nice things about their

wines?' asked Connie who had an unerring capacity to read hidden agendas.

Ezra was under no illusion as to why he as a journalist had been singled out to join the brotherhood of Beaujolais vintners but the invitation was welcome nevertheless. The whole idea of the ceremony – the costumes, the songs, the oath of allegiance to the region and the quaffing back of copious amounts of wine with the men who made it – appealed to him. It would mean another gaudy scroll for his study wall, a frivolous honour of no consequence to anyone but himself. When he tried to explain this to Connie, she repeated a phrase she had picked up from their fifteen-year-old son: 'Well, whatever blows your skirt up.'

Yet she surprised him the next day when she announced that she had decided to take a week's leave from the laboratory and join him on his trip to France. Michael could stay with his friend Justin. He seemed to be spending more time there than he did at home as it was.

Off the autoroute at Belleville the road began to wind through an endless vista of low hills hung with morning fog. The undulating land was quilted with vineyards, their geometric shapes defined by the mud tracks worn deep by tractor tyres. Clusters of squat, honey-coloured stone farmhouses with red-tiled roofs nestled in the cleavage of the hills. Church spires pointed up to a jigsaw puzzle sky.

'Where is everybody?' said Connie. 'The place looks deserted.'

'They're all in the cellars, making wine,' replied Ezra. 'That's Brouilly over there. Around the base of the Côte de Brouilly, two of the ten Beaujolais *crus.*'

'Like Mötley Crüe.'

'Pardon?'

'It's a joke, Ezra. Boy, you wine guys have one-track minds. Mötley Crüe, the group that Michael plays over and over at the threshold of pain.'

Ezra pursed his lips and breathed heavily out through his nose, a gesture, Connie had learned after eighteen years of marriage, that meant he was irritated. Not with her, but with the memory of their son disturbing his concentration while he tried to write in the office next to Michael's bedroom. She patted his hand on the gear lever and smiled to herself.

'Haut St Antoine!'

Ezra pointed at the road ahead. The clock in the church tower was striking ten.

'We don't have time to check into the hotel,' he said. 'We'll have to go straight to Verrier's.'

'Why did you have to make the appointment so early?'

'This is their busy time. He's accommodating me.'

'If you wrote for *The Wine Spectator* or *Decanter* he'd have seen you when *you* wanted.'

'You're right.'

Connie began fanning herself with the guide book.

'Here comes another hot flush. You don't know how lucky you are.'

Ezra, who had a low threshold of tolerance for conversations about other people's metabolisms, merely grunted.

8

'Now that's what I'd like,' said Connie, glancing up at a château set half-way up the hill overlooking the village. It was surrounded by a high wall with towers at each corner. Their steeply raked, conical roofs reminded her of witches' hats.

'Can you see it?'

Ezra inclined his head towards the windscreen and raised his eyes.

'The heating bills are probably astronomical but I bet he's got a great—'

'Ezra! Look out!'

The alarm in his wife's voice drew his eyes back to the road. He jammed on the brakes and the car skidded on the loose gravel. The Citroën came to a juddering halt two feet from a woman who stared quizzically through the wind-screen at him. She had red hair that lay flat on her head like a helmet. She was wearing a short-sleeved blouse and a floral print skirt. Her feet were bare. Ezra could see the goose-bumps on the flesh of her arms. Before he could say anything the woman smiled a dazed smile at him and ran her fingers along the body of the car as she moved away.

'She must be drunk!' exclaimed Connie, her knuckles white from their grip on the dashboard in front of her.

'Occupational hazard,' said Ezra, hiding his consterna-tion in humour. He felt the sweat prickling in his armpits. He looked back but the woman had disappeared.

'Pity. I could have asked her directions to Verrier's.'

He pulled into the main square. It was packed with cars. Every conceivable parking space had been taken. A game of *boules* was in progress between two avenues of plane trees. Men with glasses of wine sat smoking strong-smelling cigarettes on the stone parapet surrounding the fountain. A tricolour flag flapped in the breeze above the classical façade of a low building that proclaimed itself to be both the mayor's office and the local school.

'I thought you said they were all in the cellars squishing grapes in their socks or something,' said Connie.

'They're truck drivers and visiting wine merchants. It's one long party until the big night.'

'Charming.'

Ezra had never met Jacques Verrier before, although he had tasted his wines at shows and competitions in London and New York and had written about them in glowing terms. Verrier had a reputation among those who cared about Beaujolais for his selection of the best wines from the ten different communes. He owned a small vineyard himself from which he produced a simple Beaujolais-Villages, but his real expertise was in buying grapes and finished wines from the best properties in the region and merchandising them under his own name. Verrier's palate, they said, was the finest in Beaujolais. His operation was small, around thirty thousand cases, but his seal on a bottle was a true guarantee of quality.

Ezra had written to Verrier from Toronto asking if he might visit him and buy a twenty-litre barrel of wine for the Beaujolais race to London. It would make a good story. A dinner had been arranged at the Canadian embassy in London for the Friday night after the release. The French ambassador to the Court of St James had been invited and

so had the high-profile Canadian correspondents, enter-
tainers and business leaders living in the capital. All Ezra
had to do was to deliver Verrier's Beaujolais-Villages
Nouveau.

'You mean this is where he lives?'

Connie surveyed the vintner's ramshackle farmhouse.
The woodwork was badly in need of paint and a broken
ground-floor window was covered with cardboard. Plough-
shares rusted outside an abandoned barn whose tile roof
had collapsed inwards. The courtyard was a sea of mud.
Planks of wood had been laid as paths to the various
outbuildings. A vineyard, separated from the property by a
road and a low stone wall, rose steeply behind the house.

Ezra hid his disappointment as he picked his way through
the mud to the farmhouse door. A gaggle of geese,
marooned on the only patch of grass by the barn, honked
wildly at him.

'Wait there,' he called to Connie who had no intention of
getting out of the car until their host had invited her in.

Gingerly, he moved towards the farmhouse, pulling the
cuffs of his trousers up above his ankles. Connie could not
help laughing as she watched him. He looked even bigger
than usual as he tiptoed through the mud. She saw him
reach into his pocket as he approached the door. The
first thing he would do would be to present Verrier with
his business card, held out like a winning lottery ticket:
Ezra Brant, Wine Writer/Consultant, it read in burgundy-
coloured print, followed by their home address and telephone number. The fact that Ezra worked out of home had
been a constant bone of contention between them.

Connie had never felt the house was hers after he resigned from the Canadian Broadcasting Corporation to devote himself to his passion, wine. She was happy for him that he was doing something that he loved. But when he wasn't travelling he was always there. And it wasn't as if he confined himself to his untidy study. He held meetings in the living-room; tastings with visiting producers in the dining-room. The basement was filled with cardboard cartons. There were always bottles of wine on the sideboard and glasses in the sink. When she came home from her work at the lab, tired from long days over a microscope, she would find piles of books on every surface. Ezra had used them as weights to press labels he had soaked off the endless parade of bottles. Even their garbage was a source of embarrassment to her. The blue recycling box at the kerb bristled with empties. 'God knows what the garbage men say about us.'

To the fastidious and compulsively neat Connie, Ezra was nothing but a pack-rat. He could throw nothing away and justified himself by calling a pile of old press releases a collection. He collected everything – corkscrews, corks, 'memorable' bottles, Christmas cards from wineries, plastic bags with wine logos and wine labels. Especially wine labels. He had dozens of photograph albums filled with examples from all over the world and he vowed one day to have them all autographed by the men who made the wine. But what was worse, whenever Ezra opened a bottle he would take out a notebook and write down his impressions of the wine. Even in restaurants when they were invited out by friends. It was mortifying. Yet even worse, they could never go out to dine in Toronto without someone recognizing him and coming over to talk about wine. Thank God Michael couldn't stand the stuff even though Ezra made him smell each new glass he poured. Michael, their only child, perpetually baseball-capped and wired for rap music. How like his father he looked.

Ezra smelled the morning air. Above the smoky scent of pine he could detect a faint odour of sulphur and newly fermented wine. He lifted the brass door-knocker and let it fall. It hit the wood with a muffled thud. Somewhere inside the house a dog barked. He felt a sudden exhilaration at the prospect of meeting Verrier. The man was an artist, a poet. He looked back at the car where Connie sat waiting. He wished she shared his enthusiasm for wine. He heard a bolt being slid back on the other side of the door, the eager sound of a dog scraping its claws on a stone floor and a woman's reproachful voice.

'*Qui est là?*' she called out.

'My name is Ezra Brant,' he shouted at the door in French. 'I have an appointment with Monsieur Verrier.'

The door opened slightly and a woman's head appeared at the level of the lock. She was stooping down to restrain a large, over-friendly black Labrador by its collar. Her face was turned up to study Ezra. A disfiguring cast had riveted her left eye against her nose. She presented him with the right side of her face to diminish the effect.

'He is not here,' she said.

'Do you know where I could find him? I've come a long way to see him. I have an appointment.'

The woman placed her knee against the gap in the door
to dissuade the dog from pushing through and stood up to
her full height. She was dressed in a man's sweater which
she wore over a faded orange housecoat. She must have
been in her mid-forties, Ezra estimated, perhaps older.
Her face was gaunt and lined. An odd choice for a man who
made wines that could sing in the glass, he thought.
Perhaps the vineyard was her dowry and he had married
her for it. Why was she being so disagreeable? Surely her
husband would have told her he was expecting visitors.

The woman looked past him to the car and then nodded.
'He is down in the cellar. You go that way.'

She pointed past the barn.

Ezra could see nothing beyond the ruined barn but
when the door was closed he had no option but to find
the cellar himself. The geese hissed once more as he
passed them. He could see Connie watching him curiously
from the car. To the right of the barn the ground rose
steeply to an arched stone doorway set into the side of
the hill. He beckoned to Connie to join him. Reluctantly,
she got out of the car and stepped onto the wooden
planks.

'I'm not dressed for this, you know. How long do you
intend staying here?'

'I just have to buy the wine and maybe taste a few and
then we'll leave.'

'I know you. One hour. That's all, Ezra, and then you
can call me a cab.'

A dim light glowed through the open door as Ezra
looked down the steep stone steps that descended into the

14

cave. The familiar smell of dampness and young wine assailed his nostrils.

'Monsieur Verrier?' he called down the stairwell.

'*Oui. Entrez, entrez,*' a voice replied.

'Careful on the steps,' he said to Connie, holding her elbow. 'They look slippery.'

The cellar had been carved out of the hill and as soon as Ezra's eyes became accustomed to the gloom he could see why Verrier's living quarters were so run down. All his profits had been ploughed back into the winery. The most expensive double-jacketed stainless steel fermenting tanks gleamed in the eerie light. Filtering machines he had seen only once before at the Robert Mondavi Winery in Napa Valley stood in one corner. Everything was spotless. Ten large oval-shaped barrels, set on sturdy oak trestles above the raked gravel floor, lined one wall. Their inner rims were painted red.

Verrier was leaning against one of the barrels with a wooden mallet in his hand. He was tall, taller than Ezra but much less substantial. His florid face seemed to shine like a beacon in the half-light, accentuated by the whiteness of his smile. He wore rubber boots, a leather apron over a wool shirt, tweed trousers and an English cap, the kind Ezra had seen at elegant hatters on Bond Street.

'Good morning, you must be the famous Ezra Brant from Canada,' said the vintner in accented English.

Connie winced.

'A pleasure to meet you, Monsieur Verrier. This is my wife, Connie.'

'*Enchanté, Madame.*'

'*Comme vous êtes gentil, Monsieur.*'

'*Mais vous parlez français avec un accent Parisien, Madame.*'

'*J'ai fait mes études à la Sorbonne mais il y a vingt-sept ans.*'

'*Félicitations, Madame.*'

Verrier approached Connie and took her hand. He looked directly into her eyes and then kissed it. His fingernails, she noticed, were encrusted with dirt.

'Come, I will give you a tour. But there will be no bottling line. All my wines are bottled by the co-operative. That is my next investment.'

He led Connie along the row of barrels, one arm around her waist, the other still holding her hand. Ezra followed them, irked by the vintner's attentions to his wife.

'Each of these casks contains one hundred hectolitres of wine. That is roughly seven thousand bottles of Verrier Beaujolais-Villages.'

'And how's the 1993 vintage looking?' Ezra called after him.

Without even looking over his shoulder Verrier replied: 'Excellent, excellent. A very good year.'

Ezra had never heard a French producer confess that a year was mediocre, let alone bad. There was always some redeeming feature to be exploited even if God had sent plagues of locusts and rivers of blood during the harvest.

'Here, you must try it.'

Verrier let go of Connie and with the speed of a ferret snatched three tulip-shaped glasses hanging upside down from a rack above a wooden table. Crossing to a bin of unlabelled bottles he took one out and reached into his apron pocket for a corkscrew.

Ezra watched the bright purple Beaujolais stream out of the bottle. Verrier handed the first glass to Connie, winking as he did so. Ezra took his, swirled the wine with a practised movement of the wrist and then sniffed the bouquet. The fragrance of sun-warmed cherries filled his head. He took a mouthful and let it wash over his palate. He held it there for several seconds, sucking in air as he did and then he looked around for somewhere to spit. Verrier watched him gravely, nodding.

'On the floor, that's okay,' he said, gesturing at his feet.

Connie, too fastidious to spit, swallowed the small amount she had sipped.

'Gorgeous,' said Ezra.

'Yes, a fine vintage,' said Verrier, smiling.

Ezra could see that he was addressing his remark to Connie.

'As I mentioned in my letter I'd like to buy a small barrel of your Nouveau. For the race back to London.'

'Yes, that is possible, Monsieur. But you understand I cannot release it until Wednesday at midnight. That is the law. And you will need the papers for *les douanes*. How you say, the customs.'

He crossed to a wooden cabinet and opened a drawer. He withdrew a green form and placed it on the table.

'*L'acquit vert*. But I have no pen to write,' said Verrier.

Ezra handed him the Cross pen Connie had given him for Christmas three years ago.

'Here's my card,' said Ezra, 'with my address, etc. How much is it?'

'Verrier Beaujolais-Villages Nouveau is more expensive than the rest but then it is better. Twenty-two francs a litre. Of course, the barrel is extra. The twenty-litre size is three hundred and ninety francs. Those barrel makers, every year their prices go up.'

Like vintners, thought Ezra, but he said: 'That's fine, if you'll just make me up an invoice.'

Connie stood shifting from one foot to the other, impatient to be gone.

'If you don't mind. I'll wait for you in the car, Ezra. I'm getting a bit chilly.'

'Please, go to the house,' said Verrier. 'There is a fire. Marie-Claire will make you tea.'

'Thank you but I think I'll just read in the car,' said Connie, looking meaningfully at Ezra. 'We have to check into the hotel, remember.'

'I'll be right along, darling.'

Verrier's eyes followed her legs as she climbed the stone stairs.

'Before we finish our business perhaps you would like to try some other wines,' he said, turning his attention to Ezra when the door closed above them. 'I cannot offer you the wine of your birth as they do in Bordeaux. After all, this is Beaujolais. But Beaujolais can age too. Maybe the year of your last impure thought.'

'Delighted,' laughed Ezra, 'how about September?'

'I will get the pipette. Bring your glass with you,' said Verrier as he moved deeper into the cellar.

The ceiling was lower here and Ezra had to bend down to avoid hitting his head against the hewn granite. The floor had been cemented in this area and the barrels, set in a double tier along both walls, were smaller and newer. Chalked on the face of each was the name of the commune from which the wine came – Morgon, Moulin-à-Vent, Juliénas, St Amour, Fleurie, Chénas, Chiroubles, Brouilly, Côte de Brouilly, Regnié.

'We will start with the lightest, Chiroubles,' said Verrier, 'and work up to Moulin-à-Vent.'

Ezra thought of Connie waiting in the car.

'Perhaps just a couple. I can always come back.'

Verrier shrugged. With two blows of the wooden mallet the vintner loosened the bung on a barrel, removed it and inserted the pipette. Clamping his thumb over the aperture he withdrew a column of wine. Ezra extended his glass and Verrier lifted his thumb to allow a measure of wine to flow in.

'Chiroubles 1993. I will bottle this in the spring,' he said.

Just as Ezra was about to raise the glass to his lips he heard a woman's voice calling down from the doorway, 'Jacques, Jacques!'

The tone was urgent and fearful.

'Excuse me,' said Verrier.

With a quick motion he hammered the bung back into the barrel and moved swiftly towards the stairs. Outside the dog was barking and over the noise of the geese Ezra could hear Verrier talking to someone. He sounded angry. His voice was raised but Ezra could not hear what he was saying. Then there was silence. Ezra looked at his watch. It was 10.35 a.m.

He took out his notebook and began recording his impressions of Verrier's Beaujolais-Villages Nouveau. 'Deep purple colour. A nose of cherries with a hint of banana. Good body and concentration of fruit. Fine peppery finish. Evident acidity with a touch of tannin.' Funny, he thought, wines always taste better in the presence of the winemaker. Perhaps it's just our natural civility.

He tried the Chiroubles which had a discernible scent of violets in the bouquet. It was firmer than the first wine, better structured with a greater concentration of flavour and a longer finish. With a year or two in the bottle it would be a first-rate wine.

Still Verrier had not returned. Ezra counted the barrels and tried to calculate how much wine the vintner had in wood. He checked the name of the barrel-maker: Bernard Montreuil, *Tonnelier*. He studied the fungus-like growth on the cellar walls. He looked at his watch again and wondered whether he should leave. Connie would be getting impatient, book or no book. Finally, despairing of Verrier's return, he put the glass down on the table, slipped the notebook and pen back into his pocket and moved towards the stairs.

Just as he was about to climb upwards, the cellar behind him was illuminated by a flash of light. The sudden brilliance blinded him for a moment. Then he heard the thud of a heavy object hitting the floor.

The sound came from the inner chamber where Verrier

kept his Beaujolais *crus* with their names chalked on the barrel heads.

As Ezra ducked under the low doorway his eye was caught by a line of daylight along the ceiling which had not been there before. Above his head he could see a shaft and at the top there was a fringe of grass quivering in the wind. By the light that filtered down he could make out the slope of a steep wooden ramp leading up to the shaft. It must be a trapdoor for moving barrels in and out of the cellar, he reasoned.

As he stood staring up into the shaft he became aware of another sound. A slow glug-glug-glug. He looked down and saw he was standing in a growing puddle of wine. He looked frantically for the source. The barrel on the top row directly under the shaft had been dislodged and was spewing its contents over the cellar floor.

As he tried to roll it so that the bung hole would be upright the shaft of sunshine lit up a human foot that protruded from behind the line of barrels. Lying face down in a pool of wine was a woman in a short-sleeved blouse and a floral skirt. Her red hair could not conceal the ugly gash on her forehead. But there was a thin line of blood around the wound as if it had been painted on to make it stand out in vivid relief.

Ezra kneeled down. The woman's eyes were open. They held the same dazed expression he had caught fleetingly through his windscreen not an hour earlier on the road into Haut St Antoine.

Chapter Two

Ezra climbed the cellar stairs, pulling his weight up with the help of the wooden railing fixed to the dirt wall. His heart was pounding against his ribs and he had difficulty breathing. His first instinct was to find Connie, to make sure she was safe.

He burst through the door into the farmyard. The frosty air hurt his lungs and the sudden sunlight blinded him. He shielded his eyes and squinted towards the road where he had parked the car.

The Citroën was nowhere in sight.

Heedless of the mud that sucked at his ankles he ran across the farmyard to the gate and leaned against the stone wall, panting heavily. The air was alive with the sound of birds scavenging among the vines for the last of the unpicked berries. A church bell tolled the hour and the report of a hunter's rifle echoed off the hills behind him.

Where was Connie?

He stood on the low stone wall and looked down the road towards the village. It was deserted. The other way, towards Fleurie, the road turned sharply to the right about one hundred metres from the entrance to Verrier's property. Ezra could hear the clip-clop of a horse's hooves approaching. First the horse appeared, its neck arched to take the strain of the load it pulled. Then a man seated on an open wagon. Its bed was packed full of copper drums connected to each other with pipes and at the back was a contraption that looked like the water heater of an old steam-driven tractor. Except that there was no funnel or chimney to give off smoke or steam. The wagon's rotting floor-boards were strewn with grape skins and stalks and their original colour was lost under purple stains.

Another man was seated on the tailgate of the wagon. Ezra ran out into the road and called to them in French.

'Please help me. Have you seen a car? A black Citroën?'

The driver studied Ezra for a moment, turned his head away and spat against the stone wall. He picked up a chipped enamel cup and held it out to the man in the back who took it and scooped it into a small barrel before handing it back.

'You must tell me. I have to find my wife.'

The man grinned, showing Ezra red gums and not a single tooth. He lifted the cup and sipped it and then offered it to Ezra.

'*C'est bon*,' he said, nodding.

The man at the back of the wagon began nodding too, and smiling. He bore a marked resemblance to the driver. They must be brothers, thought Ezra, and the old collection of drums was probably a mobile still.

'Good,' repeated the driver and his brother took up the call, nodding his head in a similar manner.

'Did you see anybody?' demanded Ezra. 'On the road, did you see anyone? Monsieur Verrier? Or a woman in a black Citroën?'

'Marc de Beaujolais,' grinned the driver and hit the horse on its broad back with the reins. 'Eau de vie.'

The horse shook its matted mane and began to pull. The wagon lurched slowly past him and Ezra could smell the sweet cherry-pit fragrance of newly distilled alcohol. The man on the tailgate lifted a long bread-stick and put it to his shoulder as if it were a rifle. He aimed it at some imaginary bird and made the noise of a gunshot. The driver laughed and took another swig from his cup as the wagon moved on.

Ezra swore at them in English as they glided past him. He could feel the mud working its way into his socks. He had to find Connie. If Verrier had taken her somewhere the woman in the farmhouse might know.

He raced across the muddy forecourt and pounded on the front door of the farmhouse. The woman with the astigmatism opened the door and glared at him as if he were a complete stranger.

'Madame, I am looking for my wife. She was waiting in the car. Did you see her leave?'

The woman shook her head.

'Then where is Monsieur Verrier? He left me in the cellar and didn't come back.'

'He had business to attend to.'

'What kind of business?'

'That you must ask him yourself. He is inside.'

She opened the door to allow him to pass into the hall. It was decorated with framed certificates of honours Verrier had won in wine competitions over the years. Photographs of the winemaker smiling into the camera, arm in arm with chefs dressed in their whites and wearing toques, were given pride of place on the mantelpiece above an open fire.

The smell of roasting chicken emanated from the kitchen but above it Ezra's sensitive nose caught the musky perfume of a man's aftershave. It hung so potently in the air that Verrier must have just splashed himself with it. Yet he had never met a winemaker who used any fragrance, especially when he was tasting wine or showing it to potential buyers or wine writers. The smell of the wine was all; nothing must interfere with that.

The woman led him towards a doorway covered with a faded velvet curtain. She pulled it aside and inclined her head. Ezra could see Verrier seated at a table in the centre of a room which was obviously kept for visitors. The furniture was heavy and overstuffed giving it an air of self-important museum pieces. There were white lace doilies on the backs of chairs and roses set in pewter pots. Verrier did not move at the sound of their approach. His head was buried in his hands.

'Jacques,' the woman said, gently. 'The gentleman has come.'

Verrier looked up, startled. Immediately, he sprang to his feet and a strained smile formed on his lips.

'But Monsieur Brant, you must forgive me. What kind of host am I, abandoning you—'

'Where is my wife?' demanded Ezra.

'Your wife? But she is in your car. She said she would wait, remember.'

'She is not in my car. The car is not there.'

'Then she must have gone somewhere.'

Ezra felt like shaking him. He tried to control his mounting anger.

'Something has happened in your cellar,' he said, glancing at the woman to see if she had understood his English. 'I want you to come down there with me and tell me what is going on.'

'I don't understand. I'm sorry if I kept you waiting. I had some business I had to attend to.'

'You're coming with me right now or I am going straight to the police.'

Verrier glanced at the woman and motioned for her to leave. As he rose from the table and moved towards the door Ezra inhaled deeply. The vintner was not wearing after-shave. The perfume in the hallway was too heavy to be worn by a woman. It must have been the person Verrier had been called away to talk to. They had argued. Tempers must have flared. A warm body gives off its odours more readily than skin that is tempered by the frosty air outdoors.

'I don't understand, Monsieur Brant, but I don't want to upset Marie-Claire so I will come with you.'

'Who was the man you left me for in the cellar?' demanded Ezra, as they walked quickly down.

'A restaurateur from London. A customer. They always want bargains, the English. Now what is it you want me to see?'

'Down there,' said Ezra. 'Where you keep your *crus*.'

He followed Verrier down the stairs, past the rows of barrels, through the low doorway into the inner chamber.

'*Mon Dieu*!' Verrier cried out as he saw the spreading lake of wine on the floor. 'What did you do? You will have to pay if you caused this to happen, Monsieur.'

'Will you forget about your goddamned wine and use your eyes. Over there, man. Can't you see!'

Verrier moved the now empty barrel aside and exposed the woman's body.

His hand went to his throat and before he said another word he crossed himself.

'Whoever did this might have taken my wife. Kidnapped her. Do you understand kidnapped?'

In the half-light Ezra could see tears beginning to well up in Verrier's eyes.

The vintner nodded and then dropped to his knees. He lifted the woman's wine-soaked body into a sitting position and enfolded it in his arms. He rocked back and forth and let out a protracted groan.

'You shouldn't disturb the body,' said Ezra. 'You might destroy some evidence.'

Verrier was not listening. He continued to rock and grieve over the body.

'Who is she?'

Verrier looked up at him and the tears rolled down his cheeks.

'You must leave. This is not your business. Do not involve yourself.'

'But I am involved. My wife is missing. I was here when that body – she was dropped into your cellar. I could be a suspect.'

'Leave us alone. You go. No one knows you were here. I will tell no one.'

'I'm going to the nearest phone and call the police.'

'No,' said Verrier, fiercely. 'I will tell the police. You must say nothing.'

Ezra shook his head.

'I am going to find my wife. Then I will come back with the police. For your own good I advise you not to touch anything here.'

Verrier pressed the head of the dead woman to his chest and did not reply. Ezra turned and walked out of the cellar.

As he climbed the stairs he went over the sequence of events in his head so that he could tell the police exactly what he had seen. Verrier was not present when the body had been thrown down the trapdoor into the cellar. The English restaurateur with whom he had been arguing was on the property at the time he had discovered the body. Unless the woman with the cross-eye was a very good actress she knew nothing of what had transpired in the cellar, only that Verrier had been upset by his visitor.

Before leaving to walk back to the village Ezra decided to check the trapdoor. He made his way around the back of the barn and followed the contour of the hill to where the vineyards rose up the south-facing slope. The path was muddy and not firm enough to hold discernible footprints. To the left of the path he saw what appeared to be a square stone well about three hands high. There were two doors set closed across the top. Protruding from one of the doors was an odd-looking object which, as Ezra moved in for a closer look, he recognized as a gimlet.

It was a tool used by coopers to bore bung-holes in their barrels. It had been driven into the wood deeply enough to act as a handle. The ground around the base of the trapdoor was heavy with mud and yet there had been no mud on the woman's bare feet. This fact suggested to Ezra that she had been carried to the trapdoor. Which meant that she was either dead or unconscious when she had been dropped into the cellar.

She had hit her head on the barrel hard enough to dislodge it but there had been very little blood. A head wound in a living body would have produced masses of blood. He recalled how much blood there had been when Michael had fallen out of the pear tree in their backyard when he was ten. He had hit his head on the picnic table and Connie and he had spent two sleepless nights by his hospital bed.

The woman must have been killed before her body was abandoned in Verrier's cellar, he concluded. Her clothes and hair and general appearance showed no sign that she had struggled with her assailant. But it had all happened so fast. Not more than an hour ago he had almost run her down as he entered Haut St Antoine. She had appeared drunk then. She was obviously no stranger to Verrier and his response to finding her dead was more than just horror at the discovery of a murder victim on his property. He was grieving as though he had lost a soul-mate.

But if Verrier was not responsible, who was? And had Connie witnessed the murderer disposing of the body? If the man had been aware that Connie had seen him he would have to silence her too. Ezra had visions of the murderer breaking his way into the car and forcing her to drive to some secluded place.

A fresh wave of anxiety washed over him. He began to run towards the village. His first stop would be the police station. They would send out search parties. Connie must be found before the killer harmed her.

The cold air slapped at his face but the exertion of running made him perspire freely. His hair stuck to his forehead and his sides ached with the unaccustomed demands made upon his corpulent body.

The idea that Connie might no longer be part of his life caused him another kind of pain. It wasn't just the years they had lived together. It was the thought of a future without her that frightened him. The idea of facing the coming years without her – and without Michael, because he would surely choose to move away if his mother were no longer there – seemed bleak and forbidding.

He must get to the police as soon as possible. He quickened his pace and the ache in his side grew worse. He stopped and sat down on a distance marker, breathing heavily. If a car came he would flag it down. This was an emergency. A life depended upon it.

He looked down the road towards Haut St Antoine. He

could see the clock tower and the cluster of red-tiled roofs. Beyond the village the geometrical rows of wooden stakes that supported the vines marched across the roundness of the hills. Smoke rose from isolated farmhouses and the last few stubborn leaves clung desperately to the skeletal vine stalks.

Connie loved the smell of smoke. Except for cigars, his one pleasure. He was sure she objected to the Havana he lit up after dinner on Saturday because of the enjoyment it afforded him. He thought of all the little things that had annoyed him about her. The way she left food in open tin cans, put half-eaten chocolates back in the box and said 'Oops!' every time something went wrong. And the way she made a cup of coffee and let it sit until it was too cold to drink, only to throw it away. How ridiculous these petty irritations seemed now.

Ezra, perspiring freely in the sharp November wind, heard the sound of a car engine approaching. He dashed into the middle of the road, waving his arms frantically. The low autumn sun shone directly into his eyes making them water.

A car came hurtling around the bend and skidded to a halt in front of him. The driver wound down the window.

'Ezra, what on earth are you doing? Trying to commit suicide?'

Connie leaned out of the window. Her face registered sardonic indignation, as it did the first time she caught Michael with girlie magazines in the basement.

'Connie, thank God you're all right! Where were you? I thought...'

'I knew you'd be there all morning so I went to the village for a coffee. You look as if you've seen a ghost.'

She made a move to slide across the front seat to allow him to drive but he put up his hand.

'You drive,' he said. 'To the police station.'

'Whatever for?'

'There's been a murder.'

'And you always told me you spat the wine out.'

'For God's sake, Connie, it's not the time. Will you listen to me? It was the woman who nearly ran into the car. I found her body in Verrier's cellar.'

Connie studied his profile. Ezra's eyes were fixed on the road ahead. He was breathing heavily through his nose and his cheeks were filled with air, a sure sign that he was disturbed.

'What do you think happened?' she said as she pulled into the village square.

'Somebody dropped her body through a trapdoor. It hit a barrel but I'm sure she was dead before that.'

'What about your Mr Verrier?'

'He wasn't there. He was called away. I was alone.'

'Does he know?'

'I left him in the cellar. He asked me to leave.'

'And what do you intend to do?'

'Report it to the police, of course.'

'But you're a suspect then.'

'What do you expect me to do? Just forget about it?'

'Ezra, I didn't come to France to get mixed up in murder. This is my holiday too, remember. It's bad enough I have to

traipse around wineries with you without having to wait in
police cells as well. If you insist on getting involved I'll drop
you outside the police station but I'm going to check into
the hotel.'

'You sound just like Verrier,' said Ezra. 'He didn't want
me to get involved either.'

'You see, you'd only be meddling. Why don't we just
go to the hotel. You can freshen up, take a nice shower.
We can have lunch and then if your conscience is still
bothering you, you can go to the police. Is that our
hotel?'

At one corner of the square was a rustic old stone house
which had been converted into a restaurant. To the right
of the door was a curved archway leading into a flagstoned
courtyard above which was a hanging sign which read,
'Auberge de la Rose'. The window shutters were painted
fuchsia which contrasted with the cinnamon-coloured
walls. Wild roses had been trained up the stones and
large terracotta pots of geraniums flamed around the
courtyard.

'Oh, it's perfect, Ezra,' sighed Connie.

'We're not staying there. That's our hotel.'

He pointed to the building on the other side of the
square. It was narrow and rather dilapidated, badly in need
of paint. Great chunks of plaster had fallen away from the
façade exposing the brickwork underneath. Emblazoned
above the door was the name, Le Sarment d'Or. The glass
panel in the front door was rendered opaque by a multitude
of transfers signifying that the management accepted a

pack of international credit cards and had been highly rated by a couple of European guide books as being good value for the price.

'*Sarment* means vine shoot,' he said, as he moved sideways through the door.

'I am well aware what *sarment* means. I did graduate from the Sorbonne.'

'As you keep reminding me.'

Connie shook her head. How like Ezra to end up in such a place. He hated spending money. A hotel was only a place to sleep, he would say, how much time would they be spending there, anyway? Why waste money on hotels? Even on their honeymoon he had looked for a bargain. They had escaped Toronto's winter in February to go to Mexico. Ezra wouldn't book a hotel; he had a friend who owned a villa overlooking the ocean near Petacalco. A local woman came in to cook and clean every day. It was to be a wedding present to Ezra, two weeks in high season and no rent. The day before they arrived the woman died. The previous occupants left without cleaning up and the villa looked like the aftermath of a Mardi Gras weekend. There were no hotels available so Connie spent the first two days of her honeymoon washing floors and walls.

They carried their suitcases from the car into the tiny vestibule of Le Sarment d'Or. Ezra hated carrying things. If ever he made a lot of money he vowed he would never carry anything again. He would employ a bearer who would precede him, his own personal caddy to lug everything he required, from cases down to his small change.

'Mr and Mrs Ezra Brant,' he announced to the young woman behind the desk. 'We have a reservation.'

The woman smiled at him and bent myopically over the register. She wore an off-the-shoulder blouse with a plunging neckline that accentuated the cleavage of her breasts. Connie sniffed. She could see that the woman did not need to bend over at such an angle. The curved edge of the desk was pressing into her stomach. The same thought must have occurred to a man who had been watching her from the other side of a beaded curtain separating the front desk from the office behind. He appeared suddenly by her side, pulled her into an upright position with both hands and moved her physically aside.

What little hair he had left was parted in the centre and lay flat on his head. He was old enough to be the woman's father but the identical wedding rings they wore suggested to Ezra that they were man and wife.

When the man smiled his front tooth flashed with a star-shaped diamond. Probably thinks it makes him seem less bald, thought Connie. Why do men do that?

'I am Monsieur Barrière, the proprietor.'

The words almost rhymed in French and the man was obviously pleased with their effect because he allowed them to roll off his tongue for an unconscionable time.

'You see what you get with good check-ups, darling,' said Connie, below her breath. 'A five-carat smile.'

Ezra sniffed the air. 'The man was wearing cologne but not the same brand he had smelled in Verrier's house.

'Your passports if you please, Monsieur Brant.'

He took the two Canadian passports from the leather

travel wallet Connie had given him for his last birthday and handed them across the desk. He ran his eye along the pigeon holes with keys dangling from hooks. Some of them contained the passports of guests newly booked in. They were burgundy coloured, the new EEC documents which could have originated in any number of countries. He missed the old British passports with their stiff blue covers. His mother used to show him hers when he was a boy. It seemed so stately and impressive then.

'Many Englishmen staying here?' he asked the proprietor.

'But of course. It is the time for Beaujolais Nouveau. The English are very good customers.'

The room they were assigned was on a half-landing two flights up. It faced the street, or rather it looked directly into the gables of the house opposite. There was a black-and-white television on a simple wooden table, a chest of drawers, a writing desk with one postcard in a vinyl blotter, a full-length mirror and two single beds each with its own reading light.

'At least we have single beds,' said Connie, selecting the one further from the door. 'It doesn't look long enough for you though.'

She was in a better mood now that she was in the room, immediately making it her own by placing a photo of Michael on the writing desk, setting her digital clock next to her bed and hanging up her robe behind the bathroom door. She checked the closet and declared, 'You see, no hangers! Aren't you lucky I remembered to bring some with me.'

Ezra was not listening. He was thinking of the woman's body lying in a pool of wine that looked like blood.

He was silent throughout lunch. They ate in the hotel dining-room, ordering the *prix fixe* menu but the *volaille de bresse aux morilles* hardly made an impression on Ezra's palate. Even the accompanying bottle of Fleurie seemed flat. Mood, he knew, had a lot to do with the appreciation of wine, and in his preoccupied state nothing seemed to excite his taste-buds.

Connie tried to shake him out of his reverie by reading from her guide book. 'It says here that Beaujolais got its name from the town of Beaujeu. Did you know that?'

Ezra nodded, distracted.

'Well, apparently there was this Édouard, Sire of Beaujeu, who lived in the castle at Pouilly-le-Chatel and terrorized the neighbourhood. Pillaging and raping and all that medieval stuff. In 1400 he kidnapped Iseult de la Bessée, the beautiful daughter of the leading magistrate of Villefranche. Listen to this. "Iseult was as comely as she was chaste. She resisted the advances of Édouard who kept her locked in his castle under amorous siege. Her father appealed to the King of France for Iseult's release but the King's messenger was seized by Édouard and forced to eat the royal decree, seals and all, and was then thrown from the battlements into the moat where he broke his skull."'

'Must you, Connie, I'm trying to eat.'

'But wait. Here's the good bit. The King then sent troops to have Édouard arrested. He was brought to Paris and locked up in a tower until he surrendered the barony of Beaujeu to the crown. You see what happens when you play around? You could lose everything.'

Connie put the guide book down and sighed heavily, letting her shoulders drop in a dramatic gesture.

'You weren't listening to a word I said. I shall carve that on your tombstone. "He never listened." All right, go if you must but don't say I didn't warn you.'

Inspector Chasselas closed the file with great deliberation.

'Let us go through it once more, Monsieur Brant. Who is it that you say was murdered?'

He closed his eyes and placed the tips of his fingers together, listening. Ezra shifted his weight in the chair. This was the third time Chasselas had asked him for his account of what had happened in Jacques Verrier's cellar.

'For the third time, I didn't see the body at first. I heard it fall.'

'Who was with you?'

'I was alone.'

'Where was Monsieur Verrier? He is not in the habit of allowing strangers to wander unaccompanied through his cellars.'

'He was called away. His wife came to the cellar and said there was someone to see him.'

'His wife? Monsieur Verrier is not married. He lives with his sister.'

For some reason Ezra was relieved that the astigmatic woman who greeted him at the farmhouse was not Verrier's wife. He had expected the woman the vintner would have chosen to be as extrovert and attractive a personality as himself.

'Bear with me, Monsieur Brant. Again, the exact circumstances under which you discovered the body.'

The Inspector's eyes were still closed. Ezra felt disconcerted, trying to talk to him in this pose.

'Don't you want to take notes?'

'It is all being recorded.' He waved his hand as if it were an antenna. 'Please continue.'

Once more Ezra recounted his movements of that morning beginning with his arrival in Haut St Antoine and his near-accident with the shoeless, red-haired woman. He spoke of his fear that the killer had abducted his wife and his relief when she had found him on the road.

'Did you see the person Verrier was called away to meet?'

'No. Verrier said he was an Englishman, that's all I know.'

'When you left the cellar, did you see anyone else?' asked Chasselas.

In the inkstand on his desk was a short bayonet in its sheath, the kind that Ezra recognized as standard issue to the French special forces in Algeria. The Inspector picked it up and held it between his fingers.

'I saw two men in a horse-drawn wagon, a kind of mobile distillery. I asked them if they had seen my wife.'

'The brothers Fréjac,' said Chasselas and he made a circular motion with his finger at his temple. 'They travel from winery to winery begging for the left-over pomace to make brandy. The owners are only too happy to let them

have it. If they offer you a taste, don't accept. It can make a
hole in your stomach. And that would not be good for our
reputation,' he added with a mirthless laugh.

'Thanks for the advice.'

'And what time was it when you say you showed
Monsieur Verrier the body?'

There was a sense of indolence about the man that
began to annoy Ezra. In Toronto, having reported a
murder, he would have been bundled into a police car
and rushed back to the scene of the crime; and here he
was sitting in the Inspector's office being warned against
tasting the pomace brandy produced alfresco by a pair of
half-witted peasants.

'It must have been close to eleven o'clock.'

Chasselas rose from his desk and walked over to the
window. On the wall to his left was a large black-and-white
photograph of a port city taken from the air. It was
laminated to a thick board. In the bottom right-hand corner
written in red ink was the signature 'Chasselas' and the date
1987. Ezra recognized it as Marseilles. The Inspector
caught him looking at it.

'I took it myself. A hobby.'

'It's very good.'

'Thank you. It is not often the air is so clear.'

Chasselas pulled back the venetian blind and glanced
across the square. He reached into his waistcoat pocket and
took out a gold fob watch, snapped it open and tapped the
crystal.

'Sometimes I think it is the church clock that needs
shaking,' he said. Then he turned back to Ezra. 'It is now

ten past two, give or take a minute. Why have you only come to me now?'

'I told you. I was concerned about my wife's whereabouts. I had to make sure she was safe first.'

'And then you checked into your hotel and had a leisurely lunch. In a Frenchman I would expect that sense of priorities. But a Canadian! Where is your civic responsibility?'

Ezra felt the blood rising in his cheeks. He had nothing to say, except, 'I am here now.'

'So you are, Monsieur Brant, so you are. But where is Monsieur Verrier?'

Ezra looked up, startled.

'He said he would report the murder. He didn't want to get me involved.'

'The murder was reported to us, yes, but not by him. A woman called this office more than two hours ago but she would not give her name. We have the body in the morgue but we do not have your friend Jacques Verrier. He has disappeared.'

Chapter Three

Two and a half hours after he had entered the police station, Ezra stepped out into the fresh air once more. Apprehensive when he went in, now he was worried. The prime suspect in the death of the woman had disappeared and Verrier's flight had implicated him in the whole sordid business.

Inspector Chasselas had said that he was not to leave the village until the vintner had been caught and that he himself would remain under suspicion until the murderer confessed.

He cursed himself for not following his instincts and going straight to the police. Of course they would suspect him once he had delayed so long. Chasselas was probably thinking that he waited three hours to give Verrier time to get away and to allow himself breathing space to dream up an alibi.

He had tried to pump the Inspector for information about the woman but Chasselas had given nothing away. He was more interested in learning why Ezra had come to Haut St Antoine and what was his relationship to Verrier.

Chasselas had said that an anonymous woman had phoned the police station to inform them of the body in the cellar. If it had been Verrier's sister surely she would have given her name. In a village this size everyone must know their neighbours and be able to identify them by their voices on the telephone. But the Verriers did not have a phone in their house.

These thoughts swam through his head as he crossed the main square. He was oblivious to the old men's shouts and the thunk of the metal *boules* as they hit the ground. Oblivious to the truck drivers lounging at the bars with their anise-flavoured drinks and strong-smelling cigarettes.

No one paid much attention to the large white-haired man who moved in silent deliberation past the fountain and over the cobblestones to the entrance of Le Sarment d'Or. No one except for one man in a tight-fitting black suit with a pair of sunglasses balancing on his large bony nose. He sat at a white table between two sycamore trees on the edge of the square nursing a coffee. He watched Ezra's progress towards the hotel from behind a copy of *Le Figaro* and when his quarry had entered the building, he stood up, placed some change into the saucer next to his coffee cup and tucked the folded newspaper under his arm.

The hotel owner's wife flashed Ezra a lubricious smile as he moved by the desk but he was too preoccupied to notice. He felt heavy as he climbed the stairs. It was time to diet again but he would wait until he was back in Toronto. What was the point of forgoing the tempting cuisine of Beaujolais when it was easier to give up mediocre fare back home?

'Researching the local F and F, were we?' said Connie as he entered the room.

She was using her Bea Lillie voice, metallic and brittle. The phrase was one she employed for Ezra's seemingly tireless pursuit of out-of-the-way wineries. F and F stood for flora and fauna, a description she had coined on their Mexican honeymoon. While Connie's idea of a holiday was to install herself on a beach with a stack of books, Ezra needed other stimulations. After three hours of sand and sea he began to itch and the only respite for him was to explore the area. He needed the challenge of new things and his natural curiosity made him an intellectual pack-rat. His mind was full of bizarre facts and snippets of half-remembered poetry. It served him well for crossword puzzles and dull dinner parties but little else.

Connie was seated in front of the mirror applying the blow-dryer to her wet hair when he entered the room. He dropped down on the bed without removing his overcoat. The mattress surrendered to its natural U-shape and groaned under his weight.

'They have me down as a suspect.'

'There, didn't I tell you not to get involved?'

'They have a file on us both. For all I know, they suspect you too.'

Connie snorted. 'Wonderful. Remind me not to travel with you again. I'd be safer off in Yugoslavia.'

'And to make matters worse Verrier has disappeared,' said Ezra, glumly.

She turned off the blow-dryer.

'What do you mean, disappeared?'

'Vanished, gone, left, faded away. He must have got scared and run. The damn fool.'

'He must have had something to hide,' said Connie, switching on the dryer again. 'Guilt is a real spur.'

'He couldn't have done it,' countered Ezra, angry that she should assume Verrier's guilt. 'There was no way. When I went back to the farmhouse I found him sitting at the table in his living-room. He was wearing his rubber boots. And there was no mud on them.'

'So? He could have washed them.'

'If he washed them he wouldn't have put them back on, Connie. Remember those wooden planks from the farmhouse to the cellar, so we didn't have to walk through the mud? I checked around the back where the trapdoor was and it was just as muddy there. And Verrier knew I was in the cellar. He'd hardly try to get rid of a body knowing I was down there.'

'Then why did he run away?'

'I don't know.'

Connie stood up and crossed to the bed. She sat down on the edge next to him.

'Ezra, you've got to promise me to drop this thing. Do what you came here to do and let's leave. I don't know about you but I don't fancy spending my vacation in a French jail. Although,' she said, looking around the room, 'it might be a step up from this.'

Ezra propped himself up on one elbow and rubbed the bristles on his chin.

'Did you get a whiff of Monsieur Barrière, *le propriétaire*? He must be suffering from terminal BO. Talk about industrial strength,' said Connie, attempting to take her husband's mind off the events of the morning. 'And you'd better get a move on if we're going to be ready for your big moment.'

The induction ceremony to Les Compagnons de Beaujolais was held in a converted barn on the edge of the village within walking distance of Le Sarment d'Or.

The fraternal order, created in 1949 to celebrate the wines of the region and effect a little public relations on behalf of the wine growers, held four such gatherings every year. At these raucous, wine-filled events they invested members of the trade, prominent wine writers and show-business and sporting celebrities who had already made a contribution to their cause and those who might be flattered into doing so in the future. These seasonal bacchanals, called *tenues*, afforded the local community the opportunity to dress up in their finery and drink copious quantities of Beaujolais as they obeyed the order's heraldic injunction, *vuidons les tonneaux* – let's drain the barrels.

Ezra had carried his dinner jacket across the Atlantic specifically for the occasion. He had bought it twenty years ago and it was now coming into style again. He felt vindicated that he had resisted Connie's pressures over the years to buy a new one. It was a little tight if he did up the jacket but that did not matter since he could wear it open with a cummerbund.

'Well, how do I look?' he asked, as they stepped out of the hotel.

'The way Madame Barrière was eyeing you, I should say

not bad for an overweight, prematurely white-haired wine writer about to embark on his sixth decade,' said Connie, taking his arm.

'Thank you very much. Do you mind putting this in your handbag?'

He held out a small Polaroid camera.

'Why do you always do this to me? Look at the size of my evening bag. How am I going to get that in there?'

Ezra took the bag she held out, undid the clasp, opened it and dropped the camera inside.

'No problem.'

'What do you need a camera for anyway?'

'People always like to have photos. Especially at the event. It makes it more real somehow.'

'And who elected you Karsh of Ottawa?'

'Well, I want a record of it, so if you wouldn't mind, please take one of me when I'm up there.'

'So now I'm the official photographer.'

'All you have to do is point and snap. It's idiot-proof.'

'Thank you very much.'

There were other couples in evening dress heading to the hall and they greeted each other noisily in the street. The women held one hand to their hair against the wind and clutched their skirts with the other as they negotiated the cobblestones on high heels. The old men at the tables in the square lifted their glasses in salute and wiped their purple-stained moustaches as they passed.

Inside the vast hall, wooden chairs had been placed in rows facing a stage. To the left were circular tables set for the dinner. At a rough glance it appeared to Ezra that some four hundred people had been invited. He recognized some of the leading Beaujolais producers and shippers whom he had met on previous trips to the region and at such wine shows as Vinexpo and the New York Wine Experience. He wondered if news of the murder had leaked out and what effect it might have on the proceedings to come. In such a small community it was difficult to keep something like this quiet.

He checked the seating arrangement which had been posted on a board by the door and discovered that he and Connie were sharing a table with Dr Cyril Fournier, Paul de Blancourt, M et Mme Valéry Croix et les Mlles Philippine and Philomena, and André Morand.

'We're honoured,' said Ezra. 'André Morand is the head honcho. That's him over there.'

A brace of trumpeters in medieval garb struck up a brassy fanfare as the committee filed into the hall and marched their way to the stage with the smiling, florid-faced André Morand at their head. The fourteen members were dressed identically – round black felt hats with a green band, short black jackets with red buttons over green canvas aprons, white shirts and black shoestring ties. Around their necks, dangling from a braided red-and-green cord, hung a silver tastevin. Third from the end Ezra was surprised to see Inspector Chasselas dressed up in the costume of the Compagnons.

'That's the cop who grilled me this afternoon,' he whispered in Connie's ear.

With mock solemnity the men of Beaujolais mounted the stairs and positioned themselves on stage facing the guests below. The second man in line held above his head a two-foot high wooden statue of St Vincent. The crowd fell silent and slipped into their chairs.

'Good evening, ladies and gentlemen,' began André Morand, speaking into the microphone, his bass voice rolling around the rafter beams. 'Welcome to the one hundred and thirty-third *tenue* of Les Compagnons de Beaujolais. At each enthronement we associate our celebration with one of the twelve appellations of our glorious region. That is, of course, the ten *crus*, Beaujolais-Villages and simple Beaujolais.'

A quote from Albert Einstein flashed through Ezra's mind, 'Everything should be made as simple as possible, but not simpler.' Beaujolais was anything but simple. Would Morand make reference to what had happened in Haut St Antoine that morning?

'Tonight we are honoured to present to you the wines of Juliénas, one of my favourites, but aren't they all. But before we taste these delicious wines there is the matter of the investitures to take care of. I would ask those candidates for the brotherhood to come up on stage when their names are called. Monsieur Paul de Blancourt.'

The audience applauded as a tall, good-looking man with black hair swept back across his head, moved quickly through the aisles towards the stage. Ezra reached for Connie's evening bag, opened it and handed her the camera. Connie raised her eyes to the ceiling and made a small clucking sound with her tongue.

On stage, André Morand held out a polished vine-stock and touched de Blancourt on both shoulders with it. He then asked him to repeat the oath: 'I swear before Saint Vincent to behave as a faithful and free Compagnon de Beaujolais and to practise the virtues of such. My duty is to love our country, to work to uphold its traditions of hospitality, wisdom and good humour. To make known the beauty of its beautiful places, and the interest of its old churches and ancient châteaux, which bear witness to a past enriched by the spirit of its artists and builders. To appreciate and to disseminate the produce of our vines. Lastly, to honour the rugged wine-growers who, by their good work, have forged the prosperity and the reward of our Beaujolais homeland.'

A silver tastevin the size of a dessert bowl was produced and wine from a bottle of Juliénas was poured into it. Enough to fill two glasses Ezra estimated. De Blancourt took the tastevin with both hands and, much to the delight of the assembled guests and the Compagnons on stage, drained it at a draught. He wiped his lips with a white silk handkerchief, turned to the room and gave a little bow.

Connie dreaded to think how Ezra would behave in front of all these people. She who would rather walk barefoot across red-hot coals than get up in front of an audience.

At the conclusion of the ceremony a silver tastevin of conventional size on a green cord was hung around the man's neck. He was then presented with a scroll after which he was invited to sign the register. De Blancourt dismounted the stage waving his scroll and beaming a triumphant smile to the applause of the other guests.

'Monsieur Ezra Brant from Toronto, Canada!' intoned André Morand.

'Don't forget the photo,' whispered Ezra, as he rose and moved crab-like along the row to the aisle.

He was conscious of Inspector Chasselas' gaze on him even though he was determined not to look in his direction. He arrived on stage and kept his eyes fixed on André Morand.

'Monsieur Brant, you have distinguished yourself as a true lover of Beaujolais with your pen. You have extolled the virtues of our precious wine to your fellow Canadians. All of this makes you a man of discerning palate, good taste, great wisdom and a worthy candidate to become a Compagnon de Beaujolais.'

He touched Ezra on both shoulders with the vine-stock.

'Say after me, if you will, the oath.'

Ezra repeated the oath and waited for the oversized tastevin to appear. There was a pause and some movement behind him and then a great roar of surprised laughter rose from the audience. He turned around and saw Inspector Chasselas holding a large silver urn into which another member of the order was pouring the entire contents of a bottle of Juliénas.

Everyone was laughing except Chasselas and Connie. Morand leaned towards him and whispered, 'You don't have to drink it all.' And then he winked.

Chasselas approached Ezra and handed him the silver urn. Their eyes met and the policeman allowed himself to smile. Ezra took the container and turned to the audience, raising it above his head, much as the bearer of St Vincent had done at the beginning of the ceremony. He looked over at Connie who sat tight-lipped in her chair. She had no intention of making herself part of this spectacle by standing up and recording the moment for posterity.

Ezra turned back to André Morand and lifted the urn to his lips. He could hold his wine but to drink a full bottle in a matter of seconds was not his idea of fun. Yet he knew it was something he had to do. It was a test devised by Chasselas to humiliate him. If he failed he would lose face in front of an audience who could probably effect such a feat with ease; if he succeeded he would have to remain on his feet and show no ill effects.

Ezra began to drink, shutting his eyes and opening his throat to allow the wine to flow down. The crowd, sensing that he was prepared to demolish the bottle, began to stamp their feet in unison, cheering him on.

Tears of shame burned in Connie's eyes. Why did he always play to the crowd like this?

Ezra could feel the heat of the wine in his throat and in his head. The sound of the cheering broke over him in waves. Beads of perspiration stood out on his forehead. The Compagnons on stage had begun to applaud in time with the stamping feet in the hall. The angle of the urn against Ezra's lips was getting steeper and steeper, then with a great flourish and an exhalation of breath he drew it away, empty. A great roar went up from the crowd.

Ezra walked over to Inspector Chasselas, looked him straight in the eye and handed him back the empty urn.

'Congratulations, Monsieur Brant,' said the policeman. 'I wonder what else you have a capacity for?'

Ezra made his way back to his seat, careful to maintain his balance as people reached out to shake his hand or slap

53

him on the back. He was glad to sit down and rest while the other inductees were taken through the ceremony. Connie said nothing but he could feel her anger and resentment emanating from every pore. She pointedly turned to talk to Madame Croix.

'Excuse me,' said Ezra. 'I'll be back in a moment.'

The night air was cold and damp. Veils of fog hung across the hills and the lights from farmhouse windows glowed orange in the darkness. He felt light-headed and realized how foolish he had been to accept Chasselas' challenge. He wondered if he should make himself sick before all the alcohol could work its way into his bloodstream. Instead, he found the men's room, a primitive shed attached to the barn when it had been converted into a meeting hall. He doused his face with cold water and studied it in the mirror. His complexion was heightened by the sudden intake of wine and his eyes seemed unnaturally bright.

As he was about to return to the hall, he heard the sound of horses' hooves and iron wagon wheels rolling over cobblestones. Out of the darkness and the low-lying fog loomed the silhouette of the distillery wagon. He heard the driver snapping the reins on the horse's back and make kissing noises through puckered lips. His passenger beat an enamel cup against a copper pot. The ghostly sound seemed to echo off the hills like a cry of pain. The man's legs dangled over the open tailgate. Between them, Ezra could see the embers of the fire on the steel pan below the still.

When he caught sight of Ezra he called to his brother and laughed. He extended the cup towards Ezra. He took a match from his pocket, struck it on the copper still and dropped it into the cup. A sheet of flame rose up illuminating the man's unshaven face. And suddenly it was gone and its absence made the night blacker than before. The two brothers burst out laughing as they were swallowed up by the darkness.

Ezra made his way back into the hall. He smiled at Connie who stiffened as he took his place somewhat heavily next to her.

'Here,' she said, 'I'm not lugging this around any more,' and handed him back the camera.

The last of the investitures was in progress – a French film star in a shiny black dress that looked as if it had been made from a plastic raincoat. André Morand kissed her on both cheeks and she raised one leg until the shin was parallel to the floor, her toe extended down to emphasize the line of her ankle as if she were filming a love scene.

'And now ladies and gentlemen, if you would kindly find your places at the table for dinner,' announced Morand.

Ezra found himself next to Dr Cyril Fournier who was already seated and had poured himself a generous glass of wine from the bottles placed at the centre. He had a big white moustache and instead of a bow tie he wore a large green silk scarf. He was almost bald but for a monk-like ring of yellowing white hair just above his ears.

As Ezra sat down the tastevin around his neck clattered noisily against the plate. Philippine and Philomena Croix giggled but their attention was soon turned from Ezra to

Paul de Blancourt who stood at the back of his designated chair smiling down at the assembled ladies. Madame Croix, a riot of flowers and bare shoulders, fanned herself with the menu card and even Connie, Ezra noticed, was not immune to the man's good looks.

'Good evening,' he said, nodding first to the men and then to the women. 'May I offer you my congratulations, Monsieur Brant. In a past life you must have been a son of Beaujolais.'

'And you, Monsieur, you are of the region?' asked Ezra.

'Recently, yes. I am from the South.'

He sat down between Connie and Madame Croix who began to fan herself even more vigorously. André Morand, his official duties discharged, joined the table and kissed each female on both cheeks before sitting down between Philomena Croix and her father. Valéry Croix was a ferret-faced man who reminded Ezra of Field Marshal Montgomery as he must have looked during the Battle of El Alamein.

Dr Fournier poured himself another glass of wine and one for Ezra then took a pair of ancient reading glasses from his breast pocket. He placed them on his beak of a nose and scrutinized the menu which he read out in a voice loud enough to be heard three tables away.

'*La terrine du chef, le gratin de fruits de mer, le rôti de porc aux pruneaux, des fromages, la tarte aux pommes, vin de Juliénas*. Not bad.'

The recital made Ezra salivate and, as was his custom, he tucked his napkin into the collar of his shirt to cover his chest. It gave him the look of a man who enjoyed his food and he had found that invariably he was served in restaurants with larger portions than anyone else. Connie had despaired at breaking him of this habit but as yet she was unaware of her husband's solecism. Her full attention was focused on Paul de Blancourt who was extolling the virtues of the Beaujolais region to her.

André Morand's conversation was directed at the female members of the Croix family while Ezra, his head beginning to spin, was left to listen to the increasingly inarticulate wanderings of Dr Fournier who had demolished three glasses of wine before the arrival of the terrine.

Ezra felt like the wedding guest cornered by the Ancient Mariner. Fournier's long, bony fingers gripped his forearm for emphasis as he spoke.

Ezra's question, 'Are you the only doctor in the village?' had prompted a monologue which Fournier delivered in a confidential whisper, his lips almost touching Ezra's ear. The smell of the old man's breath made him nauseous and he inclined his head away as if to offer him more of his ear.

He tried to concentrate but the wine was beginning to take its effect. If Fournier was the only doctor in the village he would have to have signed the death certificate for the woman in the morgue. He would know the cause of death. Or would they have brought in a coroner from Lyon? Was murder beyond the scope of the Haut St Antoine country doctor and the resident gendarmerie? Yet Inspector Chasselas seemed capable enough. He was no local hayseed. The way he dressed and his air of self-confidence suggested he had come through the ranks in Paris or Marseilles. French cops were tough, battle-hardened in Algeria during the troubles.

'You are a writer,' Fournier was saying in his conspiratorial tone, 'but do you like books? Old books? I have a collection of first editions of all the great French writers: Maupassant, Zola, Daudet, Paul Arène, Huysmans, the brothers Goncourt, the poets too. Verlaine, Laforgue, Mallarmé. You name them, I have them all. It is my hobby. Priceless volumes.'

'Really,' said Ezra, feeling trapped.

'Would you like to see them? I keep them in special glass cases in my home.'

'Aren't you afraid they may get stolen?'

'My house is above the morgue,' laughed Fournier. 'Nobody would break into a morgue.'

He emptied his glass and reached for the bottle.

'You know,' said Ezra, 'I have never seen a morgue.'

Dr Fournier shrugged. 'It is not very interesting.'

'Do you keep bodies there?' he asked, trying to appear less interested than he was in the old doctor's reply.

Fournier straightened up in his seat and pulled at his dress shirt. He mumbled something that Ezra could not hear and tapped the side of his nose with a forefinger, then shook his head before turning towards Philomena Croix.

He knows something, Ezra said to himself. They must all know. They are going through the motions, pretending that nothing has happened.

'Did you hear that, darling?' said Connie, leaning over to her husband. 'Monsieur de Blancourt owns that marvellous château we saw when we arrived this morning. The one on the hill just as we came into town.'

'To be perfectly honest, I don't own it, Madame. I am renting the property from the owner with the intention of purchasing it if I am happy here,' smiled de Blancourt.

'The view must be exquisite,' said Connie.

'You must see it for yourself. I would be charmed if you and your husband would be my guests. Why don't I call you at your hotel?'

He took a card from a gold case and presented it across the table to Ezra who replied in kind. Apart from his name and address there was no information on de Blancourt's card as to what he actually did.

'Are you in the wine business?' asked Ezra.

'Everybody in Beaujolais is in the wine business, Monsieur Brant,' said de Blancourt, and he flashed his winning smile at the table.

'We treat our wines as we treat our women,' enthused Morand. 'We love them dearly. *N'est-ce pas*, Monsieur Croix?'

The ferret-faced man who had said nothing all night nodded in agreement. Dr Fournier had slid down in his seat which made his dinner jacket ride up his scrawny neck. Ezra felt a presence moving behind him. A pair of hands gripped the old doctor by the shoulders and lifted him into an upright position. Fournier turned and blinked up at the man who stood behind him.

'I'm fine,' he said and patted one of Inspector Chasselas' hands that rested on his shoulders.

'I trust you are enjoying our Beaujolais hospitality, Monsieur Brant,' said Chasselas. 'We are renowned for it.'

He had changed out of his Compagnon's costume and

was now wearing a well-tailored and very stylish dinner jacket.

'Just fine,' said Ezra and he noticed with chagrin that he was slurring his words. Chasselas gave the slightest of bows towards Connie.

'We are taking good care of him, aren't we, ladies,' said Morand and the Croix sisters giggled into their table napkins.

As the meal progressed Dr Fournier became less and less animated. He appeared to have lost interest in the wine and his food lay untouched on his plate. Between them, Paul de Blancourt and André Morand kept the conversation flowing with talk of the harvest and the excitement building to the hour of release of the new wine while Ezra tried to keep his increasingly befuddled brain concentrating on the problems that preoccupied him. If the village had agreed on a conspiracy of silence then it could only have been orchestrated by Chasselas. Jacques Verrier's disappearance supported his guilt in the Inspector's mind. Nobody had mentioned his name during the evening; nobody had enquired why he was not present along with all the other members of the Compagnons de Beaujolais.

After the cheeses had been served Paul de Blancourt took out a leather cigar case and enquired of the ladies if they minded him lighting up. Even Connie gave her assent which annoyed Ezra so much that he refused the cigar de Blancourt offered him. He could see that they were Havanas and the smell of the smoke was even more tempting. Next to him Dr Fournier frowned and waved his hand in front of his face in a disgruntled gesture.

'I think I need some fresh air,' said Ezra, picking up on the old doctor's discomfiture. 'The wine is getting to me,' he said to the table at large. 'Perhaps you would like some air too, Dr Fournier?'

The old man looked up at him, distracted.

'I thought a little walk around the square might clear my head and I would be delighted with some company. You might like to show me your books.'

Fournier's eyes lit up and he nodded his head. Ezra pushed the camera into his dinner-jacket pocket and helped the old man to his feet.

'I won't be long, Connie, but perhaps Monsieur de Blancourt will see you back to the hotel.'

Connie gave him an icy glare and then turned and smiled at de Blancourt whose head was wreathed in blue smoke.

'The pleasure would be mine,' he said.

Madame Croix's jaw tightened and she chided her daughters for resting their elbows on the table.

Ezra supported Dr Fournier by his elbow as he led him through the tables towards the door.

'Do you have a coat?' he enquired.

'Yes, a black one with a lamb's wool collar. I hung it up on the rack.'

Ezra left Dr Fournier sitting on a chair at the entrance while he retrieved the coat. As he passed one of the tables his nostrils were assailed by a scent he had smelled before. He tried to place it but the effects of the bottle of wine hampered his memory. The fragrance was familiar to him and he wondered why. It was not a perfume Connie wore; it was more musky, a man's cologne. Then he realized it was the scent he had experienced that morning in Jacques Verrier's farmhouse. The man who had been arguing with Verrier was wearing it.

As he pretended to be looking through the coats he cast his eye over the diners at the table. There were four men seated around it. One wore the regalia of the Beaujolais order; the others were all in dinner jackets. Ezra could see that the man with his back to him had just been invested as he wore the tastevin with the green cord. He took Fournier's coat from the hanger and approached the table.

'Excuse me,' he said to the man with the tastevin. 'I'd just like to congratulate you as a fellow Compagnon. My card.'

The man took the card and frowned up at Ezra. The cologne he wore was more powerful at this range.

'My name is Ezra Brant,' he said extending a hand.

The man shook it without enthusiasm.

'Ah, you must be the fellow who guzzled the bottle. Is that par for the course in your country?'

Ezra smiled broadly as he studied the man. His accent was English. He was heavy-set, pale skinned and his left eyelid seemed to hang immobilized half-way over the pupil.

'I was on my best behaviour tonight. Usually it's a magnum. But you have me at a disadvantage. I don't know who you are.'

The man reached into his pocket and produced a card. It read: Derek Farmiloe, Owner, Beaujolais Bistro and Wine Bar, King's Road, Fulham, London.

'Great dinner. Everybody's here,' said Ezra in English. 'But I haven't seen our old friend Jacques.'

'Jacques? I'm sorry. I don't know whom you mean,' replied Derek Farmiloe.

Ezra's knees creaked as he lowered himself to whisper in Farmiloe's ear so that the rest of the table could not hear.

'Jacques Verrier.'

Farmiloe turned and his stationary left eyelid quivered for a moment.

'I know him only by reputation. Makes a good product. Now Mr Brant, if you'll excuse me.'

He turned away and began talking to the woman on his right. Ezra made his way back to the door. Dr Fournier sat where he had left him staring up into the rafters of the barn.

'If you'd like to slip on your coat, Doctor,' he said, holding it out. 'Your book collection sounds fascinating. Perhaps you could show it to me now.'

He guided the old man out into the cold night air. Inspector Chasselas watched them leave together.

Chapter Four

Ezra felt Dr Fournier's weight leaning heavily against him as they strolled through the village. The moonlight lit up the stark grey monument to the men who had died in the First World War. He could read the words chiselled deep into the stone: '*Pour les enfants de Haut St Antoine morts pour la France.*' And underneath, the names of battles and a list of those villagers who had made the ultimate sacrifice.

They passed the darkened windows of the *épicerie*, the Crédit Agricole, the tabac and a women's hair salon with the legend Colline Coiffeur picked out in gold letters above the door. The noise from the bistros and bars carried across the square on the razor-keen air. Moss sprouting through the cracks in the cobblestones was already covered with hoarfrost. Ezra marvelled at the blackness of the night undiluted by city street lights or advertising signs. The place seemed so tranquil and remote, too pastoral to be the scene of murder.

'That way,' said the old man, pointing to a narrow street running steeply up from the square. His breath was a ghostly vapour in the cold air.

The walls of the houses at the corners on both sides of the road had been scraped and gouged by truck drivers who had misjudged the turn. A signpost indicating the back route to Fleurie was bent and rusted.

Identical ivy-covered stone houses faced each other across the gentle parabola of cobblestones, each with its own tiny patch of vineyard. Intermittent shafts of moonlight piercing through ragged clouds illuminated the skeletal black frames of the hibernating vines.

Below the line of houses, on the edge of the village, they could see parked trucks and lorries of all sizes, their great metal flanks slick with dew.

'It's like this every year at Beaujolais Nouveau time,' grumbled Fournier. 'Lunacy for three days. Then it's over and the world forgets us for another year.'

'The producers are happy though,' said Ezra. 'They make their money out of six-week-old grape juice and don't have the expense of ageing their wine.'

'There is more to Beaujolais than *primeur*, Monsieur,' chided Fournier.

Ezra could feel the old man stiffen under his grasp. The French correctly referred to the new wine as *primeur*. The rest of the world called it *nouveau*.

'I couldn't agree more,' he said. 'Frankly, I have always found drinking Beaujolais Nouveau is rather like baby-sitting.'

'I have tasted Beaujolais that was forty years old,' said Fournier, gazing up to the heavens as if it was there he had consumed it. 'The 1947 Moulin-à-Vent of Mommessin.

The best they have ever made. Don't let anyone tell you Beaujolais cannot age, my friend.'

A man of Beaujolais would have associated himself with the vintage, thought Ezra. The best *we* have ever made, he would have said.

'You're not of the region then.'

'No, I am from Marseilles.'

Odd, thought Ezra. First de Blancourt and then Dr Fournier. And Chasselas too was not of the region. It was his experience that Burgundians were the proudest of French landowners and would only sell to other Burgundians. Yet three of the most important people in the village had no family connection with it.

Dr Fournier had begun speaking again, breaking into Ezra's train of thought.

'Look at me. A ship's doctor who spent too many years at sea. I have lived in Haut St Antoine on and off for eleven years and the good Lord willing I will die here. If He lets me. Ah, here we are.'

Dr Fournier occupied a small square house behind the fourteenth-century church off the main square. It was more modern than the ones they had passed but had less charm. The front garden was full of rose bushes that were obviously well cared for. Ezra sniffed one of the blooms.

'Fleurie!' he exclaimed.

'Yes,' said the doctor, taking a bunch of keys from his pocket and holding them up to his face, 'That's what they say. You can smell roses in the wines of Fleurie.'

* * *

67

Immediately the front door was opened Ezra caught the medicinal scent of formaldehyde. He wondered where the morgue was. The ground behind the house sloped steeply down into the valley. There must be a room in the basement.

Fournier switched on the light and Ezra found himself in a typical doctor's waiting room. There were drab chairs set around the walls and in the middle of the room was a table thick with the obligatory out-of-date magazines. The walls were covered with reproduction Daumier prints. It could have been a doctor's waiting room anywhere in the world: anonymous, depressing, worn down by the weight of aches and pains over the years. Ezra could just picture the coughing, groaning farmers waiting to complain about their livers and the old women looking for an elixir to make them forget.

'Come through, please. I keep my books in here.'

Fournier led the way through the surgery into a living-room. The walls were lined with glass-fronted bookcases from floor to ceiling. Judging by the dust that had accumulated on the ledges and surfaces Ezra assumed that his host was not married, and if he had a woman who came in to clean for him she was obviously forbidden to enter this inner sanctum. An odour of decaying paper, dust and dead flowers hung in the air suggesting that the windows had not been opened in months.

'Please feel free to look around,' said Fournier, throwing his coat over the back of a chair and placing his keys on the mantelpiece. 'But I must ask you not to touch the books. I handle them only with surgical gloves.'

Ezra nodded his acquiescence. Old books held no fascination for him. He wanted to see the morgue.

'I will fetch us some Marc de Beaujolais. Not that poison the Fréjac brothers peddle. I'll be back in a minute.'

Ezra could hear the old man pottering loudly about in the kitchen. He looked around for a door that might lead downstairs but there was none. The entrance to the morgue must be through the garden at the back. He crossed to the window and looked out.

Beyond the garden was a farmyard and on a slope of rising ground behind it was a small cemetery. A dog began barking which drew Ezra's attention back to the farmyard. Something moved by an old stone well not far from the back door of the house which was in darkness. He could see a shadow against the wall. A man stood up and moved hurriedly across the yard as if startled by the dog. At that moment the moon came out from behind a cloud bathing the scene in a phosphorescent silver light. Ezra could have sworn that the man who disappeared into the trees at the edge of the yard was Jacques Verrier.

As he strained his eyes for a clearer view, Dr Fournier came back into the room. He was carrying a tray with a bottle and two glasses which clinked together in his unsteady hands.

'Would you be good enough to pour the glasses? I don't trust myself any longer.'

He held up his quivering hands and studied them as though he had discovered them in a rummage sale and was debating whether to purchase them or not.

'A surgeon's hands,' he said, half to himself. 'Nobody could stitch as neatly as I, even at sea. Let me show you something.'

He crossed to a cupboard and opened it. The joints in his knees creaked audibly as he bent down. When he straightened himself up he held a wine bottle in his hands. Inside was a three-masted schooner under full sail, beautifully rigged, set in a plaster sea.

'Once I was able to do this,' he said, handing Ezra the bottle.

He held it up to the light. The intricacy of the work was astonishing.

'It's wonderful,' said Ezra.

'Yes,' replied Fournier, with unalloyed pride. 'I had surgeon's hands then. The hardest part was raising the sails. You will notice that the angle is not quite right. But perfection is boring, don't you think?'

Ezra put the bottle down on the tray and handed the old doctor a glass of the colourless liquid which he knocked back in a single gulp. The effect of the alcohol seemed to brace his body and he moved towards the bottle and poured himself another generous measure.

'There is not much else to do at sea,' the old man said, staring out of the window.

'Good health,' said Ezra, raising his glass but Dr Fournier was already swallowing his second drink. When he had drained it he dropped into an armchair and his eyelids began to droop. With one hand he pulled at the green silk scarf round his neck.

Ezra debated whether to question him about the murder.

While Dr Fournier might not have had the forensic knowledge to establish the time of death, at least he could have hazarded a guess as to the cause. Yet Ezra did not want to appear too curious in case Fournier reported their conversation back to Inspector Chasselas, so he took an oblique approach hoping the old man might let something slip.

'Excellent,' he said, holding up the glass. 'You mentioned the Fréjac brothers. Funnily enough, I saw them this morning. They offered me a taste. Ordinarily I would accept but you weren't the only person to warn me against it. Your chief of police did too. They must have quite a reputation.'

Fournier waved his hand in a dismissive gesture. 'Harmless fools. Interbreeding, you get a lot of that up here.'

'They don't actually sell that stuff to tourists, do they?'

'No,' said Fournier. 'They are tolerated because they are the last of the travelling distillers. Fifty years ago that was how they made marc here, going from farm to farm.'

His voice began to slow down.

'. . . They would give the farmer a few bottles and sell the rest. But the Fréjacs, they are so unsanitary . . .'

His chin dropped to his chest and his mouth fell open. He was breathing loudly through his nose and Ezra could see that he had fallen asleep in mid-sentence. He wondered whether it would be safe for him to steal down to the morgue now to look at the woman's body.

'Why don't you let me take your shoes off,' he said quietly, but the old man could no longer hear him.

With great deliberation he moved towards the mantel-piece and slid Dr Fournier's keys into the palm of his hand. He took another look at the sleeping figure and then retraced his steps back through the surgery and the waiting-room to the front door. Closing it quietly behind him, he moved around to the back of the house. A set of lichen-covered stone steps led down to the garden.

Ezra stood in the shadow of the house surveying the garden and the neighbouring farmyard beyond the low stone wall. He could see no movement there now and the dog who had disturbed the man he had seen (could it have been Verrier?) was curled up on a pile of hay at the entrance to the barn.

The ground closest to Dr Fournier's house was paved with interlocking bricks. This pathway led around the side of the house to a door with a small pane of clear glass at eye level covered with a wire grille. A narrower path led away from the door to a small gateway in the stone wall that opened onto a country lane.

He felt for the lock, running his fingers over the aperture to determine what style of key would fit it. He tried three before one opened the door.

As soon as he was inside he felt cold. The atmosphere was chillier than a wine cellar. Behind him a machine kicked in and made him start. It must be a thermostatically controlled cooling system, he said to himself. He waited until his eyes had grown accustomed to the darkness and then he moved slowly into the room.

There were no windows and the single pane of glass in the door admitted hardly any light. He took off his dinner jacket and hung it over the window and then felt along the wall for a light switch.

The sudden flash of neon bouncing off the white tiles dazzled him. An eerie blue light hummed on the ceiling illuminating a stainless-steel operating table in the centre of the room. Next to it stood an instrument cabinet and a plastic screen like a milk-coloured shower curtain. The only other visible object was a white coat hanging from a hook on the wall and next to it what looked like a fuse box.

Ezra opened the door to the box and inside was a row of six buttons. He pressed the first and a panel the size of an oven door opened on the far wall about three feet from the ground. He crossed to it and looked inside. It was empty. He closed the door, returned to the box and pressed the next button; but that compartment was empty too.

On his fourth attempt he found her.

Connie played with her wine glass, wishing desperately to be back at the hotel. The noise level in the hall, along with the heat, had risen as the evening progressed. The women's faces were flushed and their eyes sparkled in the candlelight. The conversation at the table bored her. André Morand was tipsy and well on the way to becoming offensively drunk. He annoyed Madame Croix by flirting with her two daughters, insisting the other members of the table toast their beauty. Their father, the thin-faced Monsieur Croix, was humming to himself, his eyes half closed, and Paul de Blancourt sat back, detached, watching events with an expression of amusement on his face. She saw him look at his watch. When he glanced over towards the door their eyes met. De Blancourt smiled at her.

'These things do go on, don't they,' he said. 'Perhaps you would like me to see you back to your hotel now. Unless you're waiting for your husband, of course.'

Connie hesitated. She knew Ezra would accept a drink from that old fool of a doctor and he would be there for an hour at least. The idea of having to witness Morand's lascivious attentions towards the simpering Croix sisters was more than her nerves could stand. Nor did she feel like allying herself to the indignation so patently expressed by their outraged and jealous mother.

'I think it is about time I left,' she said to the table at large. 'If you'll excuse me.'

Paul de Blancourt stood up too.

'Allow me to escort you then.'

He took the wrap from the back of her chair and placed it round her shoulders. He did it with such ease that Connie was not aware of his action until she felt his hand brush the back of her neck.

De Blancourt wished the company good-night and, taking her by the arm, he led her through the tables to the door.

Connie breathed in the cold night air. After the stuffiness of the hall it made her feel as if she had just dipped into a mountain stream.

'Do you mind if we sit down by the fountain? I don't feel like going back to the hotel just yet.'

She saw him steal a furtive look at his watch.

'Unless of course you have to be somewhere.'

'No, no,' said de Blancourt hurriedly. 'I am all yours, as they say.'

He led her across the square and they sat on the stone parapet. The fountain had been turned off for the night but there was water in the circular pond still.

'Are those fish in the pool?' she asked. 'I didn't see them there this morning.'

'That will be Gaston, the chef of Le Cheval Blanc. He always keeps his fish in the fountain. You really must eat there before you leave. His food is remarkable. The only reason he does not have a star is that he threw a customer out for reading his newspaper at the table while he ate. The problem was, the man was an inspector from the Michelin Guide.'

Connie laughed. She had forgotten how pleasant it was to be in the company of a man who made her laugh. Ezra had become so predictable and serious of late.

'Your wife didn't accompany you tonight, Monsieur de Blancourt,' she said. 'I wish I had the courage to say no to these things.'

'I am not married, Madame,' replied de Blancourt, smiling.

'But you wear a wedding ring.'

'I was married once. Several years ago.'

'And yet you still wear the ring.'

'It is not for sentimental reasons, I assure you. It is for my own protection.'

He said it so candidly and without conceit that Connie had to repress the urge to make a cutting remark. Instead she said, 'Do you have any children?'

'No,' he replied. 'And you?'

'A son. His name is Michael. He's fifteen and looks just like his father.'

'No, that is not possible. You are not old enough to have a teenaged son.'

It was the most transparent of flatteries but Connie enjoyed it. Perhaps she didn't look her age after all. Or maybe it was the darkness and the cold air that tightened the skin.

'What did you do that they felt moved to make you a Compagnon de Beaujolais?' she asked.

'I was instrumental in getting the local co-operative's wines served at an Elysée Palace function. They were very grateful.'

'You must have friends in high places, Monsieur de Blancourt.'

'When you do a man a favour he is eager to repay, otherwise he is in your debt, Madame.'

'But you still haven't told me what you do.'

'You Americans are so direct.'

'I'm not an American,' said Connie. 'I'm Canadian. Do I sound like an American?'

'Forgive me. I have the same trouble with the English and the Welsh. Of course you are Canadian. An American would not have asked to sit outside in the cold in the middle of November.'

'You have a wonderful way of evading my questions.'

De Blancourt sighed and looked up at the sky.

'I buy and I sell. Sometimes it's commodities. Sometimes land.'

'You must be very eligible then. A single man with his own château.'

'It is not as glamorous as it sounds, Connie. May I call you Connie? And you must call me Paul. The roof leaks. I have dry rot in one wing and the ground floor windows are so warped I cannot open them. But you will see it for yourself. I hope that you and your husband will accept my invitation to visit. I have business tomorrow but perhaps the next day. We can have lunch. It will have to be a late lunch because I have a funeral to attend.'

'Funeral?'

'Yes. A woman of the village. Now I don't have your Canadian blood so I must get my circulation going again by walking.'

He stood up and extended his hand to help her up.

'We'd love to come. What time would you like us?'

'Shall we say one o'clock?'

The hotel door was locked when they arrived. Connie pressed the bell.

'I want to thank you, Paul, for not asking me about my husband,' she said.

'But why would I speak of your husband when I am in the presence of such a charming woman?'

'It happens all the time, believe me. Ezra has that effect on people. He's public property and he loves it.'

'And you are a very private person,' said de Blancourt.

He took her hand and raised it to his lips. Just then the door opened and Madame Barrière appeared on the doorstep. Her eyes moved from Connie to de Blancourt and she gave a throaty laugh.

* * *

As soon as the door swung open Ezra saw her red hair flowing out from under the opaque plastic sheet. In a state of nervous excitement he approached the open door and grabbed the handle of the metal stretcher she was laid out on. A pair of metal legs fitted with wheels dropped to the floor as the apparatus slid out of the wall.

He pulled it out to its full extent and peeled the plastic sheet back from the woman's face.

The livid wound he had seen on her forehead when he had discovered her in Verrier's cellar that morning had been cleaned of blood. The skin of her shoulders and face was bluish. She had obviously been a beautiful woman. The breasts were rounded and full, the stomach and hips soft and fleshy. Ezra estimated her age to be about thirty-five.

He bent down to read the docket that was attached to her wrist. Written in black ink was the name Yvette Montreuil.

Where had he heard that name before? Then he remembered reading it on one of Jacques Verrier's barrels – Bernard Montreuil, *Tonnelier*.

He noticed that there was a white mark on the ring finger of the woman's left hand where she had worn a wedding band and a paleness around the wrist above it which must have escaped tanning in the sunshine. It could have been a watch although the shape was triangular.

Ezra stood over her, looking down into her face, wondering what had brought her to this fate. Why had Verrier fled before the police could question him and what had he been doing – if indeed it had been him – skulking around near the morgue in the moonlight?

He was about to slide the body back into the wall when he noticed a slight swelling at the base of the woman's neck, on the left side where it met the shoulder. He drew nearer and peered at the spot. In the centre of the swelling was a tiny puncture mark. The kind of hole a needle would have left.

Ezra lifted the woman's arm so that the docket bearing her name was close to the wound in her neck. Then he took the Polaroid camera from his pocket and framed a shot to include the woman's name and the suspicious needle mark in the back of her neck. He took three shots in succession, waiting between each for the camera to deliver the print. It seemed to take an eternity and he felt his heart pounding against his rib-cage, fearful that Dr Fournier would wake up and discover him with the body. In each of the shots the tell-tale swelling and the needle mark were clearly discernible.

Then he heard a creaking sound above his head. Someone was walking across the floor. A mental picture of Fournier's house flashed through his mind. The room above must be the living-room where the doctor kept his collection of books, where the old boy had fallen asleep.

Hastily, Ezra covered the woman's body, slid it back into the wall and closed the door as quietly as he could. He felt waves of nausea rising in his stomach. Beads of perspiration broke out on his forehead. He turned the lights off, thankful for the darkness and reached for his dinner jacket. He placed the photographs carefully in the inside pocket and slipped the jacket on.

The moon had broken out of the clouds by the time he

left the morgue. The air seemed sweet and perfumed after the cold, chemical odour of the white-tiled room. Ezra made his way up to the house.

The lights were still on as he moved along the path to the window. Flattening himself against the wall he leaned forward to look through the square glass panels. The tastevin he still wore around his neck swung out and clanged against the plaster. To Ezra's ears it rang like a fire bell in the stillness of the night. He pulled back and waited, listening to the pounding of his heart.

Holding the silver cup, he glanced into the room again. The winged chair in which he had left Dr Fournier was square to the window and its high back obscured any sight of the old man.

He moved around the house checking each window to make sure Fournier was alone inside. He had to return the keys. He could see nothing but if anyone wondered why he was there he could always say Fournier had dropped them on his way in.

He entered the house by the front door and walked quickly through the waiting-room and surgery to the living-room. Dr Fournier was there where he had left him. He looked down at the old man who appeared to be dead to the world. His chest rose and fell in the rhythm of sleep and his large white moustache quivered with every breath he took.

But his legs were covered with a crocheted blanket.

Had he risen to fetch it himself, Ezra wondered, or were the footsteps he had heard above him in the morgue someone else's? He had no intention of finding out. Placing the ring of keys on the mantelpiece he hurried out into the night once more.

The square was quiet when Ezra approached the front door of Le Sarment d'Or. The bistros were closed and the chairs had been placed upside down on the outdoor tables.

He tried the handle but the hotel door was locked. He looked at his watch. It was five minutes to two. He pressed the bell and heard an anaemic ring somewhere inside. A minute later a light went on in the hall and a dishevelled Madame Barrière wearing a fluffy pink robe appeared at the door, rubbing her eyes. She frowned at him through the glass before unlocking the door.

'I must apologize,' said Ezra, 'but I forgot my key.'

'Monsieur should be more careful,' said the woman, as Ezra squeezed past her.

'Could I have the spare key in case my wife has taken it up with her?'

It would be just like Connie to lock the door and then complain he had woken her up when he was forced to knock.

The woman lifted the flap on the desk and ducked inside. A man's voice called to her from behind the beaded curtain.

'It's all right,' she said. 'I can take care of it.'

She ran her finger along the row of pigeon holes until she reached Ezra's room number. He noticed that most of the boxes held passports which reminded him to reclaim his and Connie's. The woman handed him the spare key.

'You must return it in the morning, please.'

'Of course. May I have our passports.'

Madame Barrière shrugged.

'That is not possible.'

'Why is it not possible?' demanded Ezra, puzzled and annoyed.

'They are not here. The Chief of Police is holding them.'

'Are you telling me that Inspector Chasselas came here and took our passports?'

The woman flashed him an apologetic smile.

'Yes, Monsieur.'

'Let me get this straight. He asked you for our passports. Did he take anyone else's?'

The woman shook her head and stifled a yawn.

'What time was this?'

'The first time I was awakened tonight. About an hour ago.'

Chapter Five

Ezra was angry. What right had Chasselas to impound their passports? The first thing in the morning he would present himself at the police station and demand to have them back.

Unable to find the light switch in the corridor he felt his way along the wall to his room. He tried the handle and sure enough it was locked. He hoped Connie had not bolted it from the inside in which case he would be put in the undignified position of having to call out to her to let him in.

He slid the key into the lock and breathed a sigh of relief as it turned and opened the door. Connie was lying in the bed further from the door with her back to him; but he could tell by the set of her shoulders that she was not asleep. Her habitual sleeping position was on her stomach with the right arm raised and the left back, as if she were doing the side stroke.

He began to undress in the dark as quietly as he could, not wanting to give her the slightest excuse to start a conversation. He could tell she was angry as she always was when he came in late with more wine taken than was good for him. Once he had arrived home at five in the morning and as he was taking off his clothes she had stirred and sat up in bed. Immediately, he began to dress again and before she could admonish him, he had said, 'Sorry I disturbed you. I have to be out early this morning.'

He gazed down at her. The tension in her body under the duvet was almost visible and he waited for her to speak as he knew she would inevitably do so.

'You certainly made a spectacle of yourself tonight. If you're going to snore I'm going to sleep in the bathroom.'

'There's no need for that,' replied Ezra.

He knew he was in the wrong and this only made his wife's self-righteousness the more irritating.

'I thought you were seeing Dr Fournier home. What kept you?'

He did not feel like being cross-examined and so he went on the attack.

'To get proof that Verrier couldn't have killed that woman.'

'What are you talking about?'

'I saw the body. It's in the morgue under Dr Fournier's house.'

He sat on the bed and reached over for the lamp on the side table between them. Connie pressed her eyes shut as the light came on.

'Look. I took these photos. You'll see a swelling at the base of her neck. And a needle mark.'

'You mean you waltzed right in and took photos of a dead body!' exclaimed Connie.

'Nobody saw me. But it proves Verrier couldn't have done it.' Connie spread the photos out on the sheet in front of her and grimaced.

'That red hair's not natural.'

'Is that all you can say? She dyes her hair! Those photos will prove Verrier's innocence. He didn't have the time to inject her and then carry her to the cellar and drop her in. I was there all along. I heard him arguing with a guy upstairs after you left. And I ran into him tonight at the dinner. I'm sure it's him. An English restaurateur who denied he ever met Verrier. He's lying through his teeth.'

'Ezra, I know what you're thinking. But you are not to get involved in this.'

'I am involved,' he said. 'We both are. The police have confiscated our passports.'

'What does that mean?'

A look of fear crossed Connie's face. Her only dealings with police were when their son had got into minor scrapes with the law in Toronto – being caught drinking beer in the ravine with his grade nine friends; the starting pistol that went missing from the track coach's locker and was found in Michael's.

'It means we can't leave here until they are satisfied we're not implicated in the woman's death.'

'I want you to get a lawyer. I don't care what it costs. I am not going to be a prisoner here.'

'And where am I going to get a lawyer? The Yellow Pages?'

'Call the embassy in Paris first thing in the morning.'

'It's Sunday tomorrow.'

'I don't care. Somebody will be on duty. Don't be so cheap for once in your life. I've got to get back to Toronto even if you don't. I have a job, remember.'

'And I suppose I don't.'

Connie said nothing.

'I'll see Chasselas in the morning and I'll get our passports back,' offered Ezra. 'Trust me.'

Connie snapped the light out and rolled into her sleeping position.

'And how was your friend de Blancourt?' he asked.

'A perfect gentleman. Which is more than you were. He invited us to lunch on Wednesday. After the funeral.'

'Funeral?'

'For a woman of the village, he said. Do you think it's her,' said Connie, 'the woman you photographed?'

'She was the only one in the morgue.'

He sighed and continued undressing in the dark. He was too tired to hang up his dinner suit so he laid it carefully over the back of the chair. He lowered himself onto the bed and sank into its U-shape. He could feel the constriction in his nose because of the alcohol's swelling effect on his veins and arteries; it always happened when he drank wine. He hoped he would not snore.

Ezra lay awake staring at the ceiling, listening to a fly buzzing somewhere in the room. He considered getting up to swat it but he did not want to risk Connie's scorn if he appeared clumsy and ineffectual. Everything seemed to be a contest between them lately and neither wanted to lose face. If only she would share his enthusiasm for wine. Every year a new vintage, a new mystery to be unravelled.

It was not just booze as Connie saw it; it was man taking the perishable fruit of nature and transforming it through the witchcraft of fermentation into something permanent, breathing life into something that would otherwise die. Couldn't she as a woman understand that? Wine, he had come to realize, grows like a child and goes through as many phases. Even the life span of the great ones, the clarets, the red Burgundies, the Vouvrays and the sweet Rieslings from the Rhineland, approximated the human allotment of years. Each wine as individual as a thumb-print. Each with its own destiny.

Connie kept track of his consumption like an accountant; what she did not see was his great thirst. That's your thing, she had once said. You get on with it and give me my own space to find myself.

He fell into a shallow sleep troubled by dreams of a red-headed woman and leering, toothless men proffering enamel cups from a mobile distillery. Intruding into the dream was a loud, prolonged noise that seemed to rever-berate in the very marrow of his bones. It shook him into consciousness and when he opened his eyes he realized that the noise was coming from the street below. Connie was up at the window on tiptoe, looking left and right.

'What is it?' said Ezra.

'It's a car alarm. Why doesn't someone turn it off? It's not yours by any chance?'

'Ours doesn't have an alarm, Connie. It's a hired car,' said Ezra.

Somehow she had managed to make him feel responsible for awakening the village because lights were now going on in the houses across the street. She had a habit of doing that. Whenever anyone sounded their horn in the street within her hearing, she immediately assumed that his driving was at fault.

Angry neighbours began to lean out of windows shouting at the offending vehicle.

'I see it,' said Connie.

It was a white Mercedes parked illegally at the edge of the square. The plates were English.

The insistent noise continued and seemed to gather intensity. Ezra raised himself out of bed and joined Connie at the window.

'I'll go down and see if I can stop it,' he said.

Before he could turn to reach for his robe, he heard purposeful footsteps ringing on the cobblestones. He saw a man approach the Mercedes which continued to bellow like a dinosaur in heat. The man walked once round the car trying each of the door handles. They were all locked. Ezra saw him take an object from inside his jacket and swing it with both hands at the driver's window. There was a loud crash as the glass shattered, yet still the alarm persisted. Villagers and guests at their windows cheered heartily.

Calmly, the man put his hand through the hole and reached inside for the handle. Once he had opened the door he slid inside and was lost to Ezra's view.

The noise continued for another thirty seconds and then the car hood popped up. The man appeared again and opened the hood to its full extent. He began rooting about inside, pulling at the wiring, throwing it aside like so many fistfuls of hair. The noise stopped as suddenly as it had begun. The man turned to the façade of the hotel, yelled up, 'Now it has something to scream about,' gave a little bow and melted back into the night. A burst of spontaneous applause echoed across the square from those standing at the windows.

'The village locksmith, I suppose,' said Connie, returning to her bed and when Ezra tried to join her there, 'Just because I'm laughing doesn't mean I'm in the mood.'

The mood had become increasingly less frequent over the past two years, mused Ezra. Why was it that a woman's desire for love-making diminished in a direct ratio to a man's need for it? It must be nature's way of population control. He lay back in his bed, hands behind his head, using the cracks in the ceiling as a Rorschach test.

The Mercedes was nowhere to be seen next morning when Ezra made his way across the square to the police station. The only evidence of the late-night drama was a few fragments of glass in the gutter where the car had been parked.

The sky was overcast and the swollen clouds reminded Ezra of March snowbanks in Toronto. The last bulwark of winter. He smelled rain on the air. The weather matched his mood. He had a quick breakfast of croissants and coffee in the hotel's dining-room served by Monsieur Barrière whose lavender-ringed eyes showed he too had had little sleep the night before. Connie preferred to remain in bed so he had eaten alone. He hid behind the latest issue of *The*

Wine Spectator which he had remembered to pack at the last moment. He rarely got enough time to catch up on the trade journals at home.

When he stepped into the street he could see that the cafés around the square were already crowded. Men in blue overalls and caps smoked cigarettes and drank tiny cups of espresso standing at the bar. Several of them had small measures of brandy to fortify them for the day's work in the cellars to come. The younger ones were playing the pin-ball machines, their bodies twitching and contorting in an effort to control the little steel balls.

Inspector Chasselas was at his desk when Ezra brushed past the duty officer and walked straight into his office.

'Ah, Monsieur Brant, I thought you might call,' greeted Chasselas.

'You know why I'm here,' said Ezra.

He stood close to the desk, towering over the Inspector, the anger in his voice calculated to show he meant business.

'You have come to shed light on last night's disturbance outside your hotel,' offered Chasselas, tapping his fingertips together. 'An Englishman's car was vandalized.'

Chasselas did not seem to be disturbed by the incident, in fact the faint smile at the corner of his lips suggested that his sympathies lay with the perpetrator.

'That's your problem, Inspector. I want to know why you are holding our passports.'

'Sit down, Monsieur Brant. Please.'

'I would like them back. Now. You have no right to hold them.'

'A murder has been committed in my jurisdiction. You

were at the scene. You discovered the body and yet you did not report it immediately. Several hours passed before you came to me. I think a judge would say that I have every right to ensure that you do not leave France before the matter of your innocence has been cleared up.'

Ezra sat down. He realized he could not intimidate Chasselas by blustering.

'I imagine that an autopsy was performed on the woman.'

'Of course.'

'And how did she die?'

Chasselas opened a buff-coloured file on the desk in front of him.

'According to the report,' he said, scanning the document on the top, 'the lady in question died from a blow to the left temple delivered by an unknown assailant.'

'Who did the autopsy? Dr Fournier?'

'Monsieur Brant, it is I who asks the questions.'

'Well, that's all bullshit.'

'Oh,' said Chasselas, raising an eyebrow to emphasize the irony of his remark. 'You are a forensic pathologist as well as a wine expert?'

Ezra took his wallet from the inside pocket of his jacket and withdrew from it the three Polaroid photos of Yvette Montreuil's body. He handed them across the desk.

'Now tell me she died from a blow to the left temple.'

Inspector Chasselas' relaxed and playful mood changed as soon as he took in the photos. Ezra could see his face harden as he sat up purposefully in his chair.

'Where did you get these?'

'I took them myself last night. When I escorted Dr Fournier home.'

'He showed you the body?'

'Not exactly. I borrowed his keys.'

'I must ask you why, Monsieur Brant? What possible reason could you have for breaking into a morgue to photograph a corpse?'

'I didn't break in.'

'How you got inside is not the issue. You were trespassing. I could have you locked up for this.'

Ezra ignored the threat and continued his attack.

'Yvette Montreuil died because she was injected in the neck. Does your report say anything about what was found in her bloodstream?'

'This is police business, Monsieur Brant. It is not your affair.'

'Since you want to lock me up as the possible murderer I'd say it is my affair. Yvette Montreuil was dead or at best disabled before her body was thrown into Verrier's cellar. The wound you say killed her resulted from hitting her head on the edge of a barrel. That rules me out for a start because I heard her body being dropped.'

The anger and indignation he felt came pouring out of him. Chasselas regarded him with a sidelong glance as if he was deciding between several courses of action. Ezra sensed that he had an advantage since Chasselas had not corrected him or taken refuge behind an authoritarian display of his own power.

'Furthermore, if you don't give me those passports I shall call our embassy in Paris and explain this whole sorry business because from where I sit it smells awfully like a cover-up to me. There's a conspiracy of silence in the village. Everybody must know but nobody's talking. And I think it's you who's orchestrating it.'

Ezra waited, glaring at Chasselas, challenging him to speak. The Inspector closed the file and opened the top drawer of his desk. He took out a passport and riffled through the pages.

'You do a lot of travelling, Monsieur Brant. Travel they say broadens the mind. Here in Haut St Antoine people do not travel. There are farmers within a kilometre of here who have never been to Lyon, let alone Paris. Some of them have never been farther than the next village. They make their living from vineyards their families have owned for generations. This is a very sensitive time, Monsieur Brant. The eyes of the world are on Beaujolais. We have merchants and restaurateurs coming here from four continents to buy our *primeur* wines. The release of the new wine has become an event of international importance. It is eagerly awaited all over the world. Beaujolais Nouveau is a symbol of joy and hope. And also of thanks, a harvest festival. Can you blame us for not wanting to tarnish its image?'

'What are you saying?'

Ezra had been caught off guard by the Inspector's sudden candour.

'A scandal at this time might, how shall I say, put prospective buyers off. They may not want to deal with our co-operative. They may choose to go elsewhere. We have recently been honoured by having the wines of our village served at the Elysée Palace. Any hint of scandal and naturally that will be the end of that.'

So that was it. The murder was being hushed up until after the release of Beaujolais Nouveau in case it hurt sales for the local co-operative. When the great Beaujolais race was over and the world had gone home then they would deal with it. But the wild card was Jacques Verrier. Where was he?

'Are you telling me you're going to keep the lid on this thing until after the release date?'

'Haut St Antoine cannot afford negative publicity at this crucial time, Monsieur Brant. The people of this village depend on Beaujolais Primeur. If news of this unfortunate incident leaks out it could ruin a year's work. For someone who cares so much about wine, I'm sure you would not want to be the cause of suffering to those who make it. All for the sake of three days of silence.'

'And in the meantime, what happens?'

'We proceed with our enquiries, discreetly.'

A shaft of sun broke through the clouds and flashed on the policeman's glasses. For a moment Ezra could not see his eyes.

'I am a journalist, Inspector, and this is news. I could be on the phone to our Paris office as soon as I leave here.'

'I am aware of that, Monsieur. Perhaps if I were to return your passports you might give me the three days I am asking for.'

He took Connie's passport from the drawer, placed it on top of Ezra's and held them both up like a conjurer showing a pack of cards to his audience.

'Does this mean I am no longer a suspect?' asked Ezra.

'It means you have your passports back,' said Chasselas, sliding them across the desk, 'in return for your discretion. And I will keep these photographs.'

He tucked the shots of Yvette Montreuil into the file and closed it.

'If you should learn the whereabouts of your friend Jacques Verrier,' said Chasselas, 'I trust you will tell me. Leave the detection to the professionals.'

Ezra felt a sense of triumph as he climbed the stairs to the hotel room. He had the passports back but he had not had the opportunity to prove Verrier's innocence. Nor did he get the sense that Chasselas had dismissed him as a suspect. Yet something about the interview troubled him. Chasselas had not shown any interest in the photos other than the fact that he had been able to gain access to the morgue in order to take them.

Even the most cursory inspection of the body would have revealed the existence of a needle mark at the base of the neck. This would have prompted an investigation into what might have been injected into the woman. Blood samples would be taken; her stomach would be pumped. A pathologist might even have to cut into her to see what effect the substance had on her liver, veins and arteries. But there had been no other marks on the body. 'The lady in question died from a blow to the left temple delivered by an unknown assailant,' were the Inspector's words.

There had not been time for Dr Fournier to conduct a thorough post-mortem yet Chasselas had referred to a report in the file. He had said that an autopsy had been performed. Was that why he needed another three days? There had been no autopsy. Perhaps the Inspector did not consider Dr Fournier capable of conducting one and was waiting until after the Beaujolais release when the village would be quiet again to bring in a competent medical expert to do the job. Why was he protecting the old doctor?

Connie was seated in front of the mirror combing her hair when he opened the door to their room. A breakfast tray was set on the writing desk. Connie enjoyed having breakfast in bed when they travelled. It meant she did not have to dress and make up for the dining-room.

He waved the passports at her and smiled.

'Taaddaa!'

'Good man,' she said. 'What do you intend doing this morning?'

Ezra had decided to take a look at the co-operative whose wines had been served at the French President's table. The winery was located just outside the village. Chasselas had implied that a sudden revelation of the woman's murder would ruin its prospects for sales to visiting tourists. On the contrary, he thought, human nature being what it is, the scandalmongers would descend upon Haut St Antoine like flies to carrion. Whether they would purchase wine was another matter. Serious buyers, such as hotels and prestigious restaurants, might well not want the name Haut St Antoine on their wine lists if the story broke in the press.

'There's a couple of wineries I have to see,' he said. 'You're welcome to come with me.'

'I think I'll just take a leisurely bath and wander round the village and shop. I don't know what to buy Michael.'

'Don't you buy me anything, Dad,' Michael had said to him before the limousine took them to the airport. 'It'll only end up at the back of my desk drawer.'

Ezra had delegated the responsibility of Michael's present to Connie. He would take charge of the gift for the family dog, a beagle named Steppenwolf. For Enoch the cat who had perfect pitch, and whose meow in A could tune up an orchestra, there would be fish purchased at St Lawrence Market.

'Let's meet for a glass of wine in the bar on the corner at noon then.'

Before she could answer there was a knock at the bedroom door.

'Maid service already?' she said.

Ezra opened the door on a short man with a beak-like nose wearing a tight-fitting black suit.

'Monsieur Brant,' he said, glancing up and down the corridor. 'My name is Mirze.'

He handed Ezra a card. Ezra had enough time to read the word *avocat* before it was snatched back and returned to the man's breast pocket.

'May I come in?'

'My wife is not in a fit state to receive visitors,' said Ezra, realizing immediately how stilted his French was.

Connie howled with laughter behind him.

'For goodness sake, Ezra, let the poor man in.'

Mirze slid into the room and bowed at the waist to Connie.

'Théophile Mirze, Madame. *Enchanté*,' he said.

Connie's hand moved involuntarily to close her light robe at her throat. He looked like the kind of man who carried a Swiss Army knife on a key chain and kept his loose change in a small leather pouch.

'Perhaps we could meet outside,' said Ezra.

'It's all right,' said Connie. 'He's here now.'

Mirze bowed again.

'I am the lawyer representing Jacques Verrier. There is a warrant out for his arrest.'

'If you're looking for him I'm afraid I don't know where he is.'

The lawyer appeared uncomfortable, glancing nervously from Connie to the door.

'You don't understand, Monsieur. It was Jacques who sent me to you.'

'Ezra,' said Connie. 'I am not letting you get involved in this.'

'Just a minute, dear. Let him speak. Why did he send you to me?'

'Jacques wants to see you, Monsieur.'

Connie, who had been studying Théophile Mirze's reflection in the mirror, turned in her chair to address him.

'My husband has already had enough trouble because of Verrier, thank you.'

'Connie, please. Let him finish.'

Mirze looked gratefully at Ezra. He rocked on the balls of his feet as he spoke.

'My client is in hiding. He will give himself up to the police when he has spoken to you. He believes you are the only person who can prove his innocence.'

'What does the warrant say?'

'He is accused of murdering a woman of the village named Yvette Montreuil.'

'What is her connection to Jacques?' asked Ezra.

The image of Verrier cradling the dead woman's body in his arms was still fresh in his mind. Mirze shifted his weight from one foot to the other; his eyes flicked to Connie, who had turned her back scornfully on him, and then to Ezra.

'She was his mistress. It was well known in the village.'

Connie gave a snort of derision which seemed to implicate the entire male sex. She picked up her brush and began pulling it forcefully through her hair.

'Everything seems to be well known in the village,' said Ezra, half to himself. 'But she was a married woman, wasn't she?'

It was Mirze's turn to be surprised, a sentiment registered by the sudden upward movement of his pencil-thin eyebrows.

'Yes. To the barrel-maker, Montreuil.'

A cooper's tool had been used to open the trapdoor above Verrier's cellar. He had forgotten to mention this to Inspector Chasselas.

'Surely the police would have interviewed the husband in a case like this?' said Ezra.

'I am not a friend of the police, Monsieur. They don't take me into their confidence.'

'Where is Verrier now?'

'I cannot tell you but I will take you to him.'

'No!' said Connie, rising to her feet. 'Can't you see what you're doing? The man is a fugitive. What good can you do? If you see him you become an accessory. Let him get arrested and talk to him then if you must.'

'Connie, a man has been wrongly accused of murder. I can't just turn my back on him. He's asked for my help. That's the least I can do.'

'Well, go, damn you,' shouted Connie, as she stormed towards the bathroom. 'But don't expect me to bail you out.'

She slammed the door behind her.

The two men faced each other in silence. Mirze gave a little shrug and Ezra shook his head sadly.

'We must not be seen together,' said Mirze. 'I will leave by the back door and meet you in five minutes behind the hotel. My car is parked there. A white Peugeot. Thank you, Monsieur.'

As their voices trailed away down the corridor Connie emerged from the bathroom and sat down in front of the mirror, staring angrily at her reflection. She grasped a hank of hair and held it out.

'Where does Medusa get her hair done in a hole like this?'

Ezra clutched the dashboard with both hands as the little lawyer sped through the Beaujolais countryside. Mirze threw the car around the paved roads as if he were an accomplished rally driver. Ezra was torn between keeping his eyes on the onrushing tarmac and looking about for familiar landmarks or signposts to determine in which direction they were travelling. The tyres screeched as they negotiated a particularly sharp bend.

'Do we need to drive so fast?' asked Ezra.

'Time is of the essence, Monsieur.'

'Where are we heading for?'

'We will be there shortly,' was all the lawyer would tell him.

He's enjoying this, Ezra said to himself. It must be the only excitement he's had all year.

Vineyard and farm flashed by his window; the signposts were a blur. The land was becoming less hilly. We must be heading south, thought Ezra. On a distant hilltop he saw a château whose shape and spires were familiar to him. Corcelles-en-Beaujolais. It was a wine estate. The building itself dated back to the fifteenth century. Ezra recalled that Maurice Utrillo had stayed there many times and had painted it.

They crossed a small bridge. A man was fishing in the river and behind him cows grazed on the lush green grass.

Mirze turned left and began to drive up into the hills. He skirted the town of Villié-Morgon and took a dirt road that divided two large expanses of vineyard. The car bumped and slithered over the muddy track and as it breasted a rise Ezra was treated to a vista of undulating vine plants below him as far as the eye could see. The odd copse of trees and red-tiled farmhouse punctuated the vineyard landscape. Smudges of smoke rose from various parts of the valley.

Ezra could see men working along the rows of vines just to the right of him. They were pruning the canes with secateurs and throwing the dry wood onto a fire that burned in what looked like a wheelbarrow. It was an old oil drum cut lengthwise with two struts of wood bolted on the sides as handles and a wheel fixed to the front.

He imagined how this scene would look at harvest time. The vines a sea of green with clusters of purple grapes the size of large pine cones awaiting the pickers. They were gypsies mainly and families from eastern Europe who came every year to earn money and have a vacation at the same time.

Ezra was seized with the sudden urge to buy a plot of land here with a broken-down old farmhouse and do it up for his retirement. He could grow grapes and make a little wine. But Connie would never leave Toronto. The dream faded as spontaneously as it had arrived.

'I was born in this parish,' said Mirze, bringing the car to a halt so that Ezra could admire the view. 'That is my village over there. Les Versaud.'

'Is that where Jacques Verrier is hiding?'

Mirze shook his head and pressed his foot to the floor once more. He passed a point where two tracks met at right angles and braked sharply. The Peugeot slid across the road and came to rest against a low bank. Mirze threw the gear shift into reverse, backed up to the turning and took a winding route up to the top of a hill.

They passed a walled-in cemetery set on the crest of a low hill, surrounded by vines. Beyond a ring of trees Ezra could see a small hut in the top corner of a vineyard. It was the kind of shelter where the workers might congregate to eat their lunch in bad weather.

Mirze brought the car to a halt and pressed the horn twice. The door, its planks painted alternately red, yellow and green, opened and Jacques Verrier appeared.

Even at this distance Ezra could see he had not slept. The vintner's eyes seemed to have sunk into his head. But his face lit up in a smile when he saw Ezra.

'Thank you for coming, *mon ami*,' said Verrier, embracing him. He was wearing the same clothes he had on the day before when he had greeted Ezra in the cellar.

'Inside, hurry,' said Mirze, scanning the horizon.

There was a bed in one corner of the hut and a long wooden table set with a loaf of bread and some sausage on a thick white plate. A few bottles of unlabelled wine stood in one corner. Ezra imagined Verrier snatching them from his cellar before he fled into hiding. Yet if he was running for his life would he have thought about burdening himself with wine bottles? Perhaps this hut was a refuge he had used before, where he kept a small supply of wine for his meals. Perhaps this was where he took Yvette Montreuil to be alone, away from prying eyes in Haut St Antoine.

The vintner took a corkscrew from his pocket and fetched a bottle from the corner.

'I am sorry to compromise you like this, Monsieur Brant,' he said, pouring the wine into three glasses already on the table. 'But I need your help. I am accused of murder but I am innocent.'

'I know that.'

'Will you help me?'

'I will do what I can,' said Ezra. 'But you must be honest with me. I have to know what happened.'

Verrier slid a glass of wine over to him and raised his own.

'*Á votre santé*,' he said, and the three men sipped their wine. 'What do you want to know?' asked the vintner.

'How long have you been hiding here?'

'I came yesterday soon after you left my house. Only Mirze and my sister know I am here.'

'Did you come back to the village last night?'

'No. I told you. I have been here.'

Ezra searched his eyes for any movement to suggest he was lying but Verrier returned his glance with calm assurance. If it hadn't been the vintner skulking around the morgue in the early hours of the morning who was it?

'Tell me about Yvette Montreuil,' said Ezra.

Verrier stood up and walked to the window. He began speaking with his back to Ezra.

'Yvette and I were in love. She was going to leave her husband and come to me.'

'How long had it been going on for?'

'Two years. It was difficult for us to meet. Her husband was suspicious of her. He is very jealous. He used to beat her and she would come to me in tears and show me the bruises.'

'Did she drink? I mean was she in the habit of drinking in the morning?' asked Ezra.

'She would drink wine with me as we are now,' said Verrier. 'Why do you ask?'

'Because yesterday morning when I arrived in Haut St Antoine I nearly hit a woman who looked as if she was drunk in the street. The next time I saw her she was lying dead in your cellar.'

Verrier and his lawyer exchanged glances. He wondered if he should reveal to them that he had seen the body in the morgue and had his own suspicions about how Yvette Montreuil had met her death. And should he repeat his conversation with Inspector Chasselas and why the village wanted the murder hushed up at this time? He decided he would wait until he had heard what Verrier and Mirze had to say.

'Who would profit by having you convicted of murder?' he asked.

Again Verrier and Mirze exchanged glances as if deciding silently between them who would answer Ezra's question.

'In a village like Haut St Antoine,' said Mirze, 'you make good friends and bad enemies. Monsieur Verrier has refused to sell his wine to the co-operative.'

'They are sugaring their wines,' shouted Verrier.

Mirze gestured with his hand to keep the noise down.

'And there is an unknown buyer who wants to purchase his estate through a lawyer in Paris, but Jacques does not want to sell.'

'The health inspectors keep coming round but they can find nothing wrong with my operation,' said Verrier. 'Whoever it is is trying to pressure me to sell but I will fight with every drop of blood I have in my body.'

'And then there is Yvette's husband, Bernard Montreuil.

Jacques purchased fifteen new barrels from him in April and he is pressing for his money.'

'I told him I would pay him when I have sold my wines. He knew that,' cried Verrier.

'That may well be,' said Mirze, 'but he only wants his money.'

'What about the Englishman who came to see you? Derek Farmiloe. You left me in the cellar to meet him.'

Verrier's anger turned to surprise.

'He is a customer of mine. He buys my wine for his restaurant.'

'But you were arguing,' said Ezra.

Before the vintner could reply, the door of the hut flew open as if kicked off its hinges. A uniformed gendarme carrying a sub-machine-gun burst into the room. Behind him came Inspector Chasselas who took in the tableau of surprised faces at a glance.

'Monsieur Brant, I am disappointed in you,' he said. 'I thought we had an understanding.'

Chapter Six

Connie sat on the end of the bed, tears of exasperation welling up in her eyes. In her hand she held a broken gold bracelet.

She had snagged it on the edge of the dresser as she had risen in anger to flounce out of the room. After Ezra and Mirze had left she had crawled around the dusty carpet on her hands and knees looking for the missing link, but to no avail.

She was angry with Ezra for having upset her. She had promised herself that she would let him do what he wanted. It was an emotional trade-off – part of the distancing process she was working on. It was her way of emerging from his suffocating shadow. Becoming her own person instead of the wife of Ezra Brant.

She tried to analyse whether she was more angry with her husband than herself for reacting in the way that she had. The broken bracelet was a punishment for falling back on her old responses. Life did that to you. If you break faith with yourself, something bad always happens.

She loved that bracelet more than any other piece of

jewellery she owned. Ezra had given it to her when Michael was born. She valued it more than the diamond he had handed to her at La Scala the night he had asked her to marry him. The waiter had smiled and suddenly two glasses of champagne materialized – on the house – which made Ezra positively beam.

The ring had been his mother's. Connie hated the Victorian setting but she had not wanted to offend him by suggesting that she have it remodelled. And now after all these years she saw little point in having it changed. Curiously, the outmoded style was coming back into fashion again, according to *Vogue* magazine. Besides, if they separated she would probably not wear it any more.

But the bracelet was the one gift from Ezra that she would not have exchanged. For a man who prided himself on his sensory acuity he had no imagination when it came to understanding what her tastes were. The blouse he had bought in Brussels with its fussy lace collar was two sizes too large. The leather handbag from Barcelona looked like something the Queen Mother might carry. The tiny bonsai tree from Japan which needed more care than Steppenwolf, the beagle; the trick drinking glass from Thessalonika and the turtle with the painted shell from Miami that died five days after he brought it home were among the other disasters.

She had finally despaired last autumn when he had bought her a pair of leather gloves from a street market in Florence. They were electric blue and matched nothing she had. When he asked why she wasn't wearing them Connie had replied, 'I'll have to buy an entire new outfit to match.' He had looked so crestfallen that she tactfully suggested that buying presents, like being met at airports, was so fraught with problems that it was better not to waste the time or the money. She could see his sigh of relief. The burden of shopping abroad had been lifted from him for ever.

But the bracelet was perfect – links of white, yellow and pink gold tastefully plaited together. He had presented it to her in her hospital bed with Michael in her arms. His hair had been jet black then like the down on her son's head. Fifteen years of marriage and he had gone completely white – 'Like a red wine that loses its colour with age,' he used to joke. He was always joking then. He had said he was going to christen their son, Botrytis, and they had both laughed. But he joked very little of late. He had become preoccupied and obstinate. And now because of his obstinacy she had broken her beautiful bracelet. Just like a Taurus. Stubborn and wilful, not thinking of her needs at all.

Connie picked up the telephone and dialled the front desk. 'Could you tell me if there is a jewellery store in the village, please?' she asked, when Madame Barrière answered.

'What is it you are looking for, Madame?'

It irritated Connie to give information to strangers. She would share with her women friends the most intimate moments of her life but hoarded inconsequential details from those she did not know.

'I just need someone who is familiar with jewellery.'

'Monsieur Moreau, the watchmaker, also sells rings and brooches. He has a shop just off the main square, Madame. On rue de Cherche-Midi. There's a big clock over the door. You can't miss it.'

Remembering the cobblestones she chose a pair of flat shoes and descended the stairs. She deposited the key in the slot on the desk and left the hotel. The brisk morning air made her hunch her shoulders and she hurried across the square, her knees locked as if she were wearing a hobble skirt.

Down the street she saw the large gold-painted pocket watch above the door of Monsieur Moreau's shop. As she opened the door a bell rang and the two occupants leaning over a glass-topped counter turned their heads in her direction. They stared at her in silence as if the presence of a stranger was an unwelcome intrusion.

The man, in his sixties, with bushy black eyebrows and a closely cropped white moustache, had a jeweller's glass suspended from a leather thong around his neck. In his hand he held a small pair of pliers with elongated jaws like a baby alligator. The woman was thin and pale. Wisps of her greying hair hung from a knitted cap pulled down over her ears. Her left eye turned disfiguringly into her nose giving her a look of madness and alarm.

In her hand she held a watch by a shiny black strap which still bore its price tag. On the counter were the two halves of a black velvet strap the man had obviously replaced. The watch itself was black with a gold rim but the shape of its face was unusual. Connie had never seen a triangular watch before.

* * *

Inspector Chasselas enjoyed the moment of shocked surprise. His head nodded as his eyes wandered around the room. He let his gaze linger on Théophile Mirze and Ezra could see by his expression the contempt he felt for the lawyer.

'So this was the love nest,' said Chasselas, the ghost of a smile playing about his lips.

The shame of discovery momentarily froze Ezra to silence but the anger he felt at the injustice of the situation caused him to rise to his feet and position himself between Chasselas and Verrier.

'Why did you follow me?'

'Because I knew you would lead me to Jacques Verrier, Monsieur Brant.'

'Unless you have a warrant you have no right to be here,' he blustered, not knowing if this were true under French law or not.

He hoped Mirze would pick up the ball.

The gendarme took a step forward and Ezra could hear the click of his machine-gun as he released the safety catch. A gesture from Chasselas checked him.

'You won't be giving us any trouble, Monsieur Brant. You are now an accessory. Harbouring a suspected murderer.'

Ezra looked across at Mirze but the lawyer stood white-faced behind his chair, gripping the wooden back with all his might.

'You don't have a warrant,' Ezra repeated.

'I do not need a warrant to hold a suspect for question-ing, Monsieur Brant.'

He motioned to the gendarme who pushed his way past Ezra. Verrier sighed and levered himself to his feet.

'I'm sorry,' he said to Ezra. 'You will have to get the papers for your wine from my sister. I hope we will meet again before you leave.'

The gendarme pulled his hands behind his back and cuffed his wrists together.

'Where are you taking him?' demanded Ezra.

'He will be held at the police station in Villefranche. We have no detention facilities in Haut St Antoine,' said Chasselas affably.

'On what evidence are you holding him?'

'I was not aware that you were a lawyer too, Monsieur Brant. I thought Jacques Verrier already had the benefit of a great legal mind,' he said, smiling at Mirze.

'But you can't just march him off in handcuffs for no reason.'

'He is a suspect. My, you Canadians are so fastidious.'

'What about the woman's husband? Have you arrested him too?'

'Bernard Montreuil's whereabouts all of yesterday morning have been accounted for, Monsieur Brant. He was mending his sister's sewing machine at my house. He is my brother-in-law.'

Ezra stood in the doorway watching as the gendarme put his hand on Verrier's head and pressed it down to allow him to slide into the back seat of the car. He got in beside the vintner. Inspector Chasselas waved as he took the driver's seat. The car had been parked some fifty metres from the hut so they would not have heard its arrival.

'What are you going to do now?' said Ezra, turning back to Mirze who was sitting in the chair Verrier had occupied and was drinking from his glass of wine.

'I will demand his release unless there is a formal charge, of course.'

'What I don't understand is why he would have run if he was innocent.'

'There was an argument the night before Yvette was killed. Her husband threw her out and she went to find Jacques. He was not there and Marie-Claire sent her away. She is very religious, Marie-Claire, you know, the sanctity of marriage vows and all that. When Jacques returned home she told him what she had done and he was furious. He went looking for her and found her drinking in a bar. Jacques told me she accused him of being there in the house all the time and using his sister to end the affair. Everybody heard the argument. For Chasselas that would be motive enough.'

'Did she return to her own home after the argument?'

Mirze shrugged.

'Would she have come here? If she needed a place to sleep and couldn't go home this would be the obvious place.'

As soon as he had spoken the words he wished he had kept the thought to himself because he saw a look of alarm cross the lawyer's face. Mirze, too, knew more than he was telling.

If Jacques Verrier was in any way implicated in his

lover's death he would need to know there was no
incriminating evidence left lying around the hut where they
had met for their assignations. If Jacques were innocent
what would compel him to run and hide here? This could
only be the most temporary of refuges. Perhaps he had
panicked and could not face the police. In his grief
he had returned to the place where the two of them had
found happiness in each other's arms. But what if he were
coming to destroy evidence that might have proved his
guilt?

Was that why he had tried to keep me from going to the
police? To give him time to drive up here and clean the
place of fingerprints or any other tell-tale sign of Yvette
Montreuil's presence?

And whom had Verrier spoken to before he had gone
into hiding? He was the only one other than me to have
seen the body, thought Ezra. A woman had phoned
Chasselas to tell him of the murder but the Inspector had
not recognized her voice.

'Come,' said Mirze. 'We will go back to the village.'

Ezra was silent during the drive back to Haut St Antoine.
The more he thought about it, the more puzzled he
became. There was no telephone in the hut so how had
Verrier communicated his whereabouts to Mirze unless the
lawyer knew beforehand? If Verrier had lied and it was
the vintner he had seen in the barnyard behind the morgue
the previous night then perhaps he was on his way to visit
Mirze. Did the lawyer live in the village or have an office
there?

'If I'm going to help Jacques I'll need your phone number so I can keep in touch with you,' he said.

'You can reach me at my office.'

Mirze withdrew the well-thumbed card from the breast pocket of his jacket. The address was in Fleurie, several kilometres away from Haut St Antoine.

'What about your home number?'

'That is my home number,' said the lawyer. 'I work out of my home.'

'You mean, your wife lets you?'

'But I am not married, Monsieur,' replied the lawyer. His tone suggested indignation and sorrow at the same time.

'Never mind,' said Ezra.

They drove along in silence again until they reached the outskirts of the village. As they approached the square Ezra said: 'Do you know a man named Derek Farmiloe, an English restaurateur?'

Mirze geared down noisily.

'We get many Englishmen in Beaujolais at this time of year.'

'You haven't answered my question.'

Why was everyone so reluctant to answer the simplest of questions? He either knew the man or did not.

'He has done business with Jacques, I believe. Wine business.'

'Does he want to buy the estate?'

'Jacques has not mentioned that to me.'

'But someone wants to buy him out. You mentioned a lawyer in Paris acting for an unknown buyer. Who is the lawyer?'

Mirze shifted uncomfortably in his seat.

'That is information Monsieur Verrier should tell you.'

'Monsieur Verrier is on his way to jail. And if your local constabulary have their way he could be guillotined for murder. So if you want me to help just tell me. Christ, this is like dragging teeth.'

'His name is Bouffard. He has offices on the rue de Rivoli. I have never met him but he has written several times to Jacques.'

Ezra looked at his watch. It was 12.10. He had said he would meet Connie for a glass of wine at noon.

'What is it you intend to do, Monsieur Brant?' asked Mirze, as he brought the car to a halt in front of the hotel.

'Jacques didn't kill Yvette Montreuil and I don't like being played for a fool. I'm going to find out who did kill her.'

'Be careful. This is a small community. If you ask too many questions people get upset.'

'What are you saying?'

'Let the police handle it.'

'But they've already convicted him!'

'I'm just telling you to be careful. For your own safety and for your wife, please.'

'Look, I'm late already,' said Ezra. 'I want you to phone me at the hotel as soon as you've seen Jacques in Villefranche. First, you have to get him out of jail. Leave a message if I'm not there. If I find out anything I'll call you.'

116

* * *

Connie sat in the bar, facing the door, nursing a small glass of Beaujolais. The newly mended bracelet hung from her wrist. All it required was a new link at the clasp. The watchmaker had repaired it in silence and when she had paid him and left his shop she could have sworn she had seen the woman with the astigmatism watching her from a doorway across the street.

The village made her uncomfortable. There was a sense of doom in the air. She couldn't put it into words but she felt the same premonition of impending disaster she had experienced when her parents had been killed in a train crash ten years ago. The accident had happened on her thirty-eighth birthday. She had to will herself to get on a train ever since and her subsequent birthdays had become painful memories rather than wistful celebrations.

She hoped that Paul de Blancourt might come by. She had no intention of contacting him but if he were to pass the window she would have waved and invited him in to join her for a glass of wine. He was the only person who might have lifted the cloud of despair that seemed to hover over her ever since she and Ezra had arrived in France. Why? She loved France. It must be Ezra.

She smiled at the adolescent thought that Paul might happen by and went back to the local newspaper she had bought. She reread the tiny item tucked away at the bottom of the third page about Yvette Montreuil's death. The printed facts were barely enough to make a story. It seemed that the editor had felt compelled to report the death with the fewest details he could include to justify the item.

'The body of Yvette Montreuil, wife of the barrel-maker Bernard Montreuil, was found yesterday morning in the cellars of *négociant-éleveur* Jacques Verrier & Cie. The dead woman had a wound to her temple consistent with a fall. The local gendarmerie in Haut St Antoine under Inspector Gabriel Chasselas is investigating the case. The funeral will be held on Wednesday at 10 a.m.'

So that was the funeral Paul de Blancourt had mentioned.

She thought about the photographs Ezra had taken of the red-haired woman. How undignified and degrading. She would hate to think of her own naked body being violated like that even if she were dead. But maybe Ezra was right. Perhaps there had been a cover-up. Even in the photographs she could see the swelling at the base of the woman's neck and the tiny puncture mark. But it should be none of his concern. There were people whose job it was to deal with unpleasantness like that.

She consulted her watch and clucked her tongue in annoyance that Ezra was late. Then she saw a car draw up outside the hotel and she recognized her husband's broad frame and mop of white hair. She felt a sudden urge to run across the square and hold him but she restrained herself. The impulse would have confused him and signalled feelings that were there only spasmodically. It astonished her that he could still evoke that response in her and when she analysed it, as she did whenever her emotions took her by surprise, she understood that it was his vulnerability that prompted her to react the way she had. For such a large man he seemed so unprotected from the wickedness of the world.

Ezra had the childlike belief that the natural response of strangers to his approach would be benign and welcoming. For Connie, suspicion and cynicism were protective armour to be worn against the world until it proved itself harmless or at least neutral. And now she had good cause to feel that way. This place, for all its forced sense of occasion, was gloomy and claustrophobic. The murder, which no one mentioned yet everyone knew about, had taken possession of the village.

Walking through its streets was rather like strolling through a graveyard. She found Haut St Antoine oppressive and desperately wanted to be far away from it.

Ezra waved to her as he entered the bar. He sat down at the table and motioned to the barman to bring him the same order as Connie's, only in a larger glass.

'Sorry I'm late, darling,' he said, as if he had forgotten her anger at his departure earlier that morning. 'But Chasselas followed us and he's arrested Verrier. They're holding him in Villefranche. That creepy lawyer has gone there to try and get him out.'

'What an eventful life you lead, Ezra,' she said, determined not to let her anger at his lack of further apology show. 'Did you see this?'

She slid the newspaper across the table and pointed to the story. Ezra read it.

'What does *fidèle* mean? Faithful?'

'Consistent with.'

'According to this they're treating it as an accidental death. Or maybe Chasselas has told them not to say anything while he's investigating.'

Ezra dropped his voice as though he were talking to himself. 'Maybe by arresting Verrier he's trying to give the real killer a false sense of security.'

'Ezra, look at me. I'm frightened. Something's awfully wrong here. I've got a bad feeling about it.'

He knew what was coming. It was another of her premonitions. She wanted them both to leave Haut St Antoine. To get back to Toronto and familiar surroundings as soon as they could. That was her reaction to the least sign of discomfort when she was away from home. He put it down to mild xenophobia. Whenever she travelled to another city or country she was inevitably sick for a day and had visions of appalling disasters.

'Just till Thursday, Connie. I've got to do my story and then we'll go.'

'I don't like the way people look at me here. I'm not wanted. I can feel it. And nor are you.'

Mirze's warning came back to him. If you ask too many questions it could upset people . . . for your own safety and for your wife. He could see that Connie was genuinely upset. Perhaps it would be better if she went to Paris and joined him *en route* when he had the Beaujolais Nouveau and was racing up to London. Yet if he proposed the idea she would say 'no' on principle. It had to be her idea, as if she were in control of her own destiny.

'Look, I'm going to be tied up for the next couple of days visiting wineries, Connie. You know how you hate that.

120

The shopping doesn't look so good here anyway. Why don't you go to a city? I can meet you on my way back to Paris.'

Connie gave him a sideways glance.

'Why are you trying to get me to go shopping? That's not like you. Do you know how expensive France is?'

'You don't have to go crazy.'

'I suppose I could go to Paris and meet you,' she said, staring out at the fountain.

She was thinking of the fish she had seen not twelve hours ago. She wondered if they were still swimming about.

'Sure. There's a hotel in the sixteenth *arrondissement* I know,' said Ezra. 'It's clean and cheap and there's a great bakery downstairs.'

'I'll find my own hotel, thank you very much. But I can't go.'

'Why not?'

'Paul de Blancourt invited us to lunch, remember. It would look rude if I wasn't there.'

She had no idea why she had used that excuse not to leave the village. She had no compunction about breaking social engagements on other occasions if the mood took her.

Ezra frowned. Connie was unhappy about staying in Haut St Antoine yet she would delay her departure just to have lunch with a man they hardly knew. She sensed what he was thinking and said quickly, 'Don't you want to see the inside of that château?'

'He said Wednesday. If you are that keen on studying his

curtains why don't you just trot up there and knock on his portcullis while I visit the co-operative.'

Ezra tried to keep his voice light and ironic but the twinge of jealousy he felt gave a cutting edge to his tone. Connie stiffened.

'Well, perhaps I will. There's no point sitting bored in the hotel room while you go off boozing. And the idea of Paris is beginning to look better and better.'

How easy it was to start the whole battle all over again. Like exhausted warriors they leaned on each other until they had enough strength to swing another blow. There were some couples he knew who used arguments as a way of heightening the feelings between them, to inject an element of danger into their marriages. But Ezra needed serenity and a sense of peace. He detested arguments and all the more because he could never remember what he had said in the heat of the moment. Connie recalled his every word six months later and delighted in throwing them back at him.

But there were no winners; they were both diminished by their fights and he often thought what life would be like for him alone if they decided to separate. He enjoyed his own company and did not need the comfort of belonging to a group. Even as a boy, at his boarding school in Port Hope, he was not part of a clique. He refused to join in the ritual ragging of his younger peers. It seemed so unfair that a gang of them would descend on one unfortunate student and victimize him for being different. As a result they had turned on him. His bedclothes would be thrown over the rafters in the dormitory or he would be forced into a garbage can in the changing room and doused with Heinz ketchup. Boarding-school had made him hate cruelty above all and although he was large for his age he refused to use his size to his own advantage.

He wondered why these memories came flooding back to him as he drove out of the village towards the co-operative. Connie had walked up the hill to de Blancourt's château, refusing his lift. More and more often they were going their separate ways. How long, he wondered, before that became a permanent arrangement?

The co-operative of Haut St Antoine stood at the base of a low hill a mile outside the village. From a distance its white walls and flat wooden roofs looked like a series of interconnected aircraft hangars. The enterprise seemed to have grown with the prosperity of the region. The court-yard was filled with trucks. Pallets of green bottles wrapped in plastic stood ten feet high next to outdoor storage tanks. Not the kind of image the Beaujolais chose for their posters and brochures but a necessary means of ensuring a livelihood for the less ambitious growers in the region who were content to sell their grapes and let others get on with the business of making the wine, bottling, promoting, marketing and exporting it.

Growers who made wine from their grapes could sell the greater portion to the co-operative and keep some back to market under their own label for passing tourists. A *vente directe* sign outside their houses advertised the fact that they had wine for sale.

But Jacques Verrier had not been one of them. He had refused to sell any of his wines to the co-op because he accused them of adding sugar beyond the legal limit to bring up the alcoholic strength. Nor did he sell directly to the public. Verrier relied on lesser yields in the vineyard to ensure the wines that bore his *négociant* label had more concentration and flavour. They were wines for the *cognoscenti* who were willing to pay a premium for them.

There was so much activity in the courtyard of the co-operative that Ezra decided it would be more prudent to park the Citroën outside its walls. He pulled the car off the road onto a patch of grass and walked through the wrought-iron gates. He asked directions to the director's office from a man in a white coat who sat on a stool by the entrance holding a clipboard, logging the trucks in and out.

Through an open door to his left Ezra could see the bottles chattering along the bottling line. *Embouteillage*, the French called it, the same word they used for traffic jams. The noise always reminded him of those long-gone days when milkmen delivered bottles to each household doorstep in the early morning. How often had he been awakened as a boy by the chink of milk bottles in their metal crates.

Dusty travel posters of Beaujolais decorated the walls of the waiting-room outside the director's office which also housed the secretary's cubicle. A roll of flypaper hung suspended from the ceiling by a thumb tack above her head. The tubular furniture was worn and uncomfortable. The woman who sat behind the desk was more interested in trying to remove a ballpoint mark from her cream-coloured blouse than she was in the arrival of a visitor.

Ezra smiled at her and held out his card.

'Ezra Brant, from Toronto,' he said.

It was a useful opening since most people around the world had relatives in Toronto.

'I'm a wine writer.' The woman studied the card for a moment. 'I would like to see the director.'

She took the card and opened a door behind her. Ezra watched her until she disappeared out of sight. He occupied his time by studying the sprawl of papers on the desk. There were computer printouts and a stack of telephone messages, an artist's rough for a series of labels and a stack of invoices with a cheque clipped to the top of each. He tried to read the name upside down but was interrupted by the return of the secretary who told him that Monsieur Beaupré, the director, was busy for the moment but he would be happy to have Ezra shown around the winery and he would join him later.

Ezra politely declined the tour but asked if he could use the men's room. The secretary pointed to an adjacent building. Ezra thanked her and walked across the court-yard but when he was out of her sightline he turned and moved quickly towards the receiving area where the trucks deliver the grapes at harvest time. The stainless steel fermenting tanks were what he was interested in seeing.

A workman in rubber boots and blue overalls was sluicing down the cement corridors between the rows of tanks with a plastic hose. He whistled tunelessly and made no effort to redirect the jet of water away from Ezra's feet.

125

Ezra stepped back and allowed the man to pass. He tapped gently on the nearest tank. He could tell by the sound that it was full. A small chalk board suspended by a wire from the nozzle proclaimed its contents as Beaujolais-Villages. It would be bottled in the spring.

If he could taste the wine from the tank he could tell if it had been sugared during fermentation. The wine would have a candied nose and the alcohol would be higher than the fruit would suggest. There was no way that he could turn on the tap without arousing the suspicion of the cellar worker. But if the co-operative was sugaring their wines they would have to maintain a supply of beet sugar somewhere.

He approached the workman and hailed him from a safe distance. 'Excuse me, my friend,' he said in French. 'I've got a truckload of sugar out there. Where am I supposed to put it?'

The man turned off the water and took the stub of a cigarette from behind his ear.

'You from Villefranche?'

'Yes.'

'You don't sound like it. And besides, we don't use that word around here.'

He tapped the side of his nose with a bony index finger and winked. Ezra played along with the charade.

'Just a joke. Where do you want me to stack it?'

The man jerked his head towards a door at the end of the cellar.

'You must be new. Bring your truck around to the back entrance. The boss doesn't like you to park out in front.'

'I want to see if the load's going to fit first,' said Ezra, striding purposefully towards the door.

He tried the handle but it was locked.

'Can you open this?'

The man shrugged and reached into his overall pockets. He drew out a large bunch of keys and began to sort them, holding them up to the light of the window.

'We had a delivery two weeks ago. Don't know why they'd want more. Crop's not that big.'

He inserted the key in the lock and opened the door, holding it ajar for Ezra to peer in. Fifty kilo bags marked 'Bentonite' were stacked shoulder high around the room. It reminded Ezra of a bunker created by sandbags. Where had he seen that image before? And then he remembered. In the attic of the family home in Rosedale there was a trunk full of letters and photographs his father had sent to his mother during the desert war in Egypt. Monty's war, his father had called it. As a young boy Ezra loved to shut himself away in the attic, dress up in his father's uniform and imagine himself fighting Rommel.

There was one photo in particular that stood out in his mind. Major Harry Brant in khaki shorts and a Sam Browne belt leaning against such a bunker, smoking a pipe. He missed his father during the war. He would sit at his desk in his study and suck on the empty pipes in the oak and ivory rack. The acrid taste of stale tobacco conjured up images of his father and to this day he could not smell pipe tobacco without seeing his father in his mind's eye dressed in his officer's uniform.

Bentonite, Ezra knew, was the trade name for a

diatomaceous earth used by wine makers to fine their wines before the final filtration. A pale brown, powdery substance, it swells to many times its original size when wet and as it falls through the wine it absorbs solid particles left behind after fermentation. The better red wines of Bordeaux and Burgundy are fined with whisked-up egg whites, five or more to a barrel depending on the quality of the vintage. In the olden days, they used to use ox blood.

Ezra could see that the amount of Bentonite in the room was out of all proportion to the annual needs of the co-operative, large as it was.

'That's a lot of Bentonite,' he said, and the man grinned, exposing nicotine-stained gums.

Ezra ran his fingers over the heavy paper of the nearest bag. There was no dust on it which he would have expected from the powdery clay inside. The surface of the bag felt sticky. He squeezed the bag and he could feel the granules of sugar inside. He looked for the company name printed on the outside and as he bent down to read the small print he became aware of someone else standing behind him.

Ezra straightened up and turned round to face a large man in a tight-fitting blue suit. His black hair seemed lacquered to his skull. A silk handkerchief wilted from his breast pocket and his shoes were two-toned, blue and white. His face was plum-coloured with rage.

'What are you doing here? Who let you in?'

Ezra looked around but the obliging workman had vanished. In his place stood two burly cellarmen, arms folded over their leather aprons. They too eyed Ezra with less than friendly interest.

* * *

The road up to Paul de Blancourt's château was steeper than Connie had imagined. She was wearing the wrong shoes and the exertion had made her thigh muscles tighten painfully.

The air was still and warm and smelled of the earth. The sky was robin's-egg blue. She felt damp with perspiration, a sensation she hated. She plucked at the silk of her blouse with both hands and shook it to keep the material from sticking to her skin.

She rested against a low stone wall placing her handbag next to her. The château loomed large above her, set off against the blackness of hills. Behind her a vineyard sloped steeply down to a gully and rose again. The contours were defined by the parallel rows of wooden stakes supporting the black vine-stocks. They had been pruned back to pitifully twisted arms that ended in a fist. Ezra would have said it wasn't prime vineyard land. The best were south-facing to catch the first rays of morning sunshine. Sunlight built up grape sugar; the more sugar, the more potential alcohol. It was one of the few pieces of information she had absorbed. Usually, she allowed Ezra's wine babble to wash over her and recede like waves on the shore leaving no trace of their passage. Her women friends always handed her the wine list when they dined together on their 'girls' night out' and were amused when she confessed she had no idea what to order. That was Ezra's department. Let him get on with it. It was like being a passenger in a car. There's no need to remember directions or signposts.

An old man came in sight, pushing a black bicycle up the hill. He raised his cap as he passed and blew out his cheeks in rebuke at the steepness of the incline. Lashed to the pannier behind his saddle by a length of elasticized rope were two thin bread-sticks. Connie smiled at him. She liked the idea of buying freshly baked bread every day. It was her ambition to retire to France when the ministry pensioned her off. A small farm in the Dordogne or Périgord where Ezra could have a vineyard and make wine if he must and she could read and learn the potter's art. She fancied the idea of a small studio where she could throw pots and plates and sell them to the tourists.

It was curious that Ezra still figured in that mental picture she had of her old age. But even if they separated she would come to live in France. Another twelve years unless they gave her early retirement. She wondered what she would look like in twelve years. She was getting round-shouldered already from hunching over that microscope each day, analysing endless slides of food samples sent over by ministry inspectors. If people could only see what scurried about on the food they bought in supermarkets they would give up eating.

She levered herself up and dusted off the back of her skirt. The effect of the sun and the wine made her feel giddy. She dabbed her forehead with a tissue and began to climb the hill again. Her throat was dry and she thirsted for a glass of water. Yet the nearer she got to the château the more reluctant she became to enter it.

Was it the thought of Paul de Blancourt? He wasn't expecting her and her spontaneous decision to pay him a visit was motivated solely by her exasperation with Ezra. Or was it? And what if her unexpected arrival was an inconvenience? Or his invitation had been one of those casual politenesses uttered for form's sake and not expected to be taken up?

As she approached the château Connie could see that it was not the fairy-tale castle it appeared to be from the town below. It was badly in need of repair. The honey-coloured stones of the outer wall were covered with moss and leathery caper plants sprouted from cracks where the masonry had crumbled. Tiles were missing from the steeply raked roofs and the shutters and window frames were rotting. The massive oak door with its rusty iron hinges was studded with bolt heads. Over the lintel was a carving of grapes and vine leaves worn smooth with age and barely discernible.

To the left of the door was a bell-pull. The pitted iron handle had been recently attached to the chain by a piece of wire. She reached for it and then pulled her hand back.

Would he think her brazen dropping in on him like this? She could say she had been out walking and just happened by. No, he would never believe that. She could say Canadians did that sort of thing. A friendly gesture. Just popping in to say hello. She could pretend she was doing some research for Ezra. An article he was writing. On what? Menopausal women having a sudden urge for a little romance in their lives? Not what men mean by romance. Just being in the presence of someone who makes you feel attractive, desirable. Who makes you feel good about yourself. But nothing more.

And besides. She needed a glass of water.

Connie could hear the bell echo across the courtyard behind the high stone wall. It sounded extraordinarily loud, shattering the afternoon calm and setting off a flight of panic-stricken rooks from the turrets overhead. Her first instinct was to turn round and flee, but the idea of him looking down from a window and witnessing her tottering off in her high heels kept her rooted to the spot.

She waited a couple of minutes and pulled the bell a second time. She was about to give up with a sense of relief that no one was at home when she heard the sound of a bolt being drawn back. The door inched open and a short, square woman in a faded blue floral dress stood barring the entrance. Her greying hair was twisted into a loose bun and her face was weathered from too long in the wind. Her eyes were opened wide as if she expected to recognize the woman who stood before her.

'Good afternoon,' said Connie. 'Is Monsieur de Blancourt in, please?'

'Eh?' said the woman, looking beyond Connie to the horizon.

'Monsieur de Blancourt. Is he here?'

The woman continued to stand at the door alternating her gaze from Connie's mouth to the dusty road behind her. Connie wondered whether her lipstick had smeared.

'I've come to see Monsieur Paul de Blancourt,' she repeated slowly, as if to a child. 'He invited me to visit him.'

The woman gave a little shrug and began to close the door. Connie uttered a small cry of exasperation.

'At least let me have a glass of water.'

The door opened suddenly and behind the woman stood a beaming Paul de Blancourt.

'Connie! But this is wonderful. Please come in.'

He advanced towards her and guiding her by the elbow he led her through the door and across the cobbled courtyard.

'You must forgive Marthe. She is deaf. She only lets in those people she knows. She is, however, a wonderful cook.'

'If she's deaf,' said Connie, unmollified, 'how did she hear the bell?'

'Through her feet. The bell is loud and it makes the stones vibrate,' laughed Paul. 'Come, this is a pleasant surprise. I will show you around. But first may I offer you a drink? A Scotch perhaps.'

'Water would be fine.'

'But where is your husband?'

'He's visiting the co-operative.'

'A dedicated man, Monsieur Brant, always working,' he laughed.

The water from the well tasted of granite. Connie sat with her knees pressed together on the edge of a leather sofa in de Blancourt's study. It was the only comfortable room in the château as far as she could see. The main rooms he had ushered her through were as sparsely furnished as a museum. The chairs appeared to have been placed so that the occupants were forced to look outside the room rather than facing each other.

As they walked around the château Connie mentally redecorated it. A plant here, a flower arrangement there.

A ruffle for the curtain to soften the rigorous straight lines. A floor-length tablecloth to cover ugly legs. And instead of the burnt-amber and moss-green colour scheme, sun yellow with white for the skirting boards and the plaster ceilings painted white to allow them their feeling of height and airiness.

Only the study gave Connie the impression that someone lived there. Three walls were covered with bookshelves, the fourth was lined with prints of birds. Two leather chesterfields faced each other across the wide expanse of a glass coffee table supported by four stone gargoyles which looked as if they had once graced a cathedral façade. At the centre of the table was the largest brandy glass Connie had ever seen. It was filled with book matches from restaurants all over the world.

The room was too relentlessly masculine to be comfortable and Connie could read nothing of its owner in the antique oak chairs, the old sea chest, Toby jugs and pewter mugs that appeared to have been placed with great deliberation. The only object which seemed out of place was a large telescope that stood on a tripod by the double floor-to-ceiling window in the centre of the outside wall.

'That is my passion,' said de Blancourt, with a nod towards the telescope. 'Looking at the stars.'

'I read mine,' said Connie. 'It saves a crick in the neck.'

He laughed.

'I must compliment you on your French, Connie. To have a sense of humour in another language is a gift.'

He sat on the chesterfield next to her. He had removed his jacket and Connie could see the dark impression of the hair on his chest through the light material of his shirt.

'Ezra and I plan to retire in France,' she said quickly.

She felt her breath catch in her throat and she reached for the glass of water.

'That's a good idea. The air of France is good for you, Connie. It makes you look radiant.'

'Ezra would like to own a small vineyard. Maybe make a little wine. You know how it is. The critic thinks he knows better than the artist.'

De Blancourt's arm slid along the top of the couch and rested lightly behind her back. She leaned forward and reached into the brandy balloon filled with matches. She took out a handful and began to read them.

'The Plume, Regent Hotel, Hong Kong. Mustards, St Helena, Napa Valley. Felidia, New York. Beaujolais Bistro, London. Have you eaten in all these places?'

'Yes. It's what you might call a hobby. But this one, no,' he said, dipping long fingers into the glass and extracting a black matchbook with the name 'Chow Chow' written on it in large gold letters. It was in the shape of a dog's bone.

'This one is from Hollywood. It's a restaurant for dogs.'

'Three star?' asked Connie, smiling.

'Worth a diversion, at least,' replied Paul.

'Ezra and I have a dog,' said Connie. 'A beagle called Steppenwolf.'

Her fingers were playing with a blouse button.

135

'Do I make you nervous, Connie?'

He was smiling.

'Why do you say that?'

'Because you have done nothing but talk about your husband ever since you sat down.'

'I'm sorry. I shouldn't have come.'

'Why did you come?'

'A little exercise. There's not much to do in the village if you're not interested in wine. And you did invite me. We Canadians can be very forward.'

Paul laughed.

'Well, I'm delighted you did. You have given me an ideal excuse for not doing the things I ought to be doing.'

Connie sighed and leaned back in the chesterfield. She wished that Ezra could have said something like that. She could not remember when he had last interrupted his work to concentrate on her.

She became aware that Paul was studying her face. His head was cocked a little to one side and the sunlight glanced off the side of his face. He had half turned towards her. The movement caused his knees to touch her thigh. Connie only became aware of it when she glanced down to avoid his eyes but she did not draw herself away.

Ezra's first instinct was to present his business card to the man in the two-toned shoes. But from the look on his face he seemed in no frame of mind for formal introductions. Probably the director of the co-operative.

'Are you from the INAO?' demanded the man.

Ezra knew he was referring to the Paris-based Institute

of Appellations of Origin. This body which made the wine laws also policed them, employing fraud inspectors whose job it was to make spot checks on wineries to ensure that they respected the local regulations.

'No, my name is Brant. I'm merely a wine writer,' he replied as calmly as he could.

'Worse,' grimaced one of the cellarmen and the director smiled. He had a gold tooth.

'I am Jean-Marie Jobert, deputy director of the Caves Co-operative de Haut St Antoine,' he said, making the title sound like a Bourbon prince. 'Forgive me, but I don't like civil servants snooping around my winery. A simple mistake you understand. Here as you see we keep our Bentonite for fining. Come, I will show you the bottling line and then you will taste our wine.'

'Thank you, but if you don't mind my wife is waiting for me back at the hotel.'

'Then you will take some bottles back with you. Our wines are served at the Elysée Palace. You can write that. Étienne, get Monsieur a three-pack. And the brochure.'

He turned back to Ezra.

'Where are you from, Monsieur?'

'Toronto.'

Jobert looked disappointed.

'I have friends in Montreal. The chairman of the Quebec Liquor Board. You know him?'

'By name only,' said Ezra.

Jobert took him by the arm and began to propel him away from the open room, down a corridor of tall stainless steel tanks with a capacity of 20,000 hectolitres each. From each of their faucets hung a small blackboard chalked with the name of the wine inside.

'Be careful of the pipes,' said Jobert stepping over the plastic tubing that ran from one of the tanks into a wheel-mounted electric pump. A glass window at the coupling point showed the flow of the purple wine. The pipe extended to the wall. Through the window Ezra could see a tanker truck parked outside, the tube fixed to its belly like an umbilical cord. They must be shipping in bulk, Ezra thought. But something seemed wrong.

'What's that?' he asked the deputy director.

'We sell wine *en vrac*. How do you say in English? Bulk wine.'

'But what is it?'

Jobert frowned.

'Beaujolais. What else?'

A quote of Talleyrand's rose from the swamp of Ezra's memory, 'The power of speech was given to man so that he could disguise his thoughts.'

Jobert took his arm again and moved him purposefully towards a doorway large enough to accommodate the passage of a tractor. He held the heavy overlapping slats of plastic apart to allow Ezra access to a lofty storage room the size of an aircraft hangar. Cases of wine on skids were piled to the ceiling. Two yellow forklifts buzzed around like bumper cars, carrying the skids holding sixty cases across the cement floor to a loading dock. Outside was a flatbed truck waiting to receive the wine.

'Exportation,' said Jobert with a sweep of his hand. 'You see those boxes. They are for Alberta. Be careful.'

Jobert pulled him by the elbow as a forklift glanced by him. Ezra glowered at the driver who lifted his chin in a mute expression of scorn and attribution of blame for the near accident.

Ezra was about to remonstrate with the deputy director when the burly cellarman arrived back carrying a cardboard box and a file folder. He handed them to Jobert who began to rock on the balls of his feet.

'Thank you for visiting the Caves Co-operative de Haut St Antoine. I hope you will return to your country as an ambassador for our wines. On behalf of our two hundred and fifty-three members I would like to present to you some bottles of Beaujolais to enjoy in your own home and also some documentation about our co-operative. Please visit us again when you are in Beaujolais.'

It sounded like his standard speech of dismissal for tourist groups who arrived in buses for the obligatory tour of a winery. Ezra thanked him for the wine and shook hands with the two cellarmen.

'If you will excuse me, Monsieur Brant, it is a busy time for us.'

'Of course.'

'It will be quicker for you to leave by that door,' said Jobert, indicating the open space that gave out onto the loading dock.

'Thank you,' said Ezra.

Jobert and the cellarmen moved off through the pile of cases and Ezra began to walk towards the loading bay. When he no longer heard their footsteps he turned and looked back. The forklift drivers were busy in another part

139

of the stock room. He had one more thing to do before he left the cellars. To check on the tank that was being pumped out. He had never heard of Beaujolais Nouveau being sold in bulk and something about the pumping operation had disturbed him.

He walked quickly to the plastic-covered doorway and slid through the slats. The automatic pump was still vibrating on its rubber wheels. He stood over it and studied the circular glass at the point window where the tubing coupled with the machine.

Then he realized what had troubled him. The direction of the flow of the wine was not *into* the tanker that stood outside but *from* the tanker into the cellar.

Ezra checked the glass column that ran like a giant thermometer on the outside of the tank. The vein of wine it contained was purple and densely opaque, not like young Beaujolais at all. He put his index finger at the meniscus of the wine and waited. A minute later the level had risen an inch above his nail. Perhaps they were transferring wine from another of their facilities, he thought.

He opened the brochure to see if it gave any information on the number of cellars or crushing plants the co-operative owned. 'With the inauguration of the new bottling line in September 1989,' he read, 'all the operations of Caves Co-operative de Haut St Antoine were finally consolidated under one roof in the newly constructed winery just south of the village. The three-hectare site was purchased in 1976 by the founding members of the co-operative from the family of Eric Mirze, its first director. We are proud to be the first winery in Beaujolais that is totally computerized to ensure that all phases of winemaking are governed by the strictest quality controls...'

Eric Mirze. Could he be the father of Théophile Mirze, Verrier's lawyer? Or an uncle? If so, the family obviously had money.

Ezra followed the line of the pipe to the wall and stood on tiptoe to study the tanker outside. The licence plate was Italian and painted on the door of the cab was the company name, Fratelli Strappini, Puliga. He pulled out his notebook and jotted down the licence number and the name.

So that's what they didn't want me to see, he said to himself. The sugar is just a blind. Virtually everyone in Burgundy chaptalises their wine to give it an extra degree or two of alcohol. The law permits it up to two per cent but what Jobert and his cronies were doing was downright fraud. They were trucking in cheap but powerful wine from southern Italy to beef up their Beaujolais. No wonder the Elysée Palace enjoyed it. He smiled to himself as he left the tank room. It would make a good story if he could get the driver to confirm his theory: the co-op's wine had been adulterated with the powerful wine from the heel of Italy, just enough to give it body and colour but not enough to alter the characteristic taste of Beaujolais.

And the delivery time was significant. Just prior to the release of Beaujolais Nouveau there would be trucks from all over Europe descending on the region. No one would raise an eyebrow when they saw Italian plates.

Then another thought struck him.

Perhaps the wine that was bound for the Alberta Liquor Control Board had been similarly treated. Now that would be a story! He stopped and turned to the area where Jobert had indicated the Alberta consignment was awaiting shipment.

His sudden change of direction saved his life.

A skid of wine boxes fell from the top of a pile and crashed to the cement floor on the spot where his next step would have taken him. Some of the boxes, mummified to immobility with heavy plastic wrapping tape, split open sending bottles skittling across the cement floor. Several smashed on impact showering his shoes and trouser legs with wine and broken glass.

Ezra dropped the carton he had been carrying and leaned against a wall of boxes for support. Blood coursed through his body and every pulse throbbed in unison like an army of drummers. The sound of the sea rang in his ears and he thought he was going to pass out. His body was cold and hot at the same time and beads of sweat broke out on his forehead and upper lip.

Almost immediately a forklift slithered around the corner and stopped in front of him. The twin steel blades, like the horns of a bull, were extended to their full height.

'What the hell are you doing! You could have killed me,' shouted Ezra.

But the man did not speak English. He gave a high-pitched nervous laugh and put the machine into reverse. Within seconds he had disappeared into the shadows and Ezra was alone. The only sound he could hear was the beating of his heart.

'You don't mind driving me, do you?' asked Connie,

staring into her whisky glass to avoid looking into Paul de Blancourt's eyes.

'No, not at all.'

'It's just that Ezra will be there all day if I don't drag him out. Once he starts discussing wine time means nothing to him. You'd think it was the only subject in the world.'

She knew she was talking too much, justifying herself, filling the silences between them but she could not stop herself. A foolish middle-aged woman prattling on. He can't be interested, she said to herself. In her confusion she had a sudden need to be with her husband. It wasn't guilt, just a feeling of being adrift, floating perilously close to the lip of the falls, unable to control her direction. Ezra had always been her anchor when she felt this way and although it angered her to admit it, she had absorbed his values while she dismissed them to his face. Constantly arguing with him, challenging his every statement in an effort to assert her independence of him. And now she needed to be with him to re-establish contact with old realities.

'We will go.'

He stood up and offered her his hand.

'It's all right,' she said, easing herself out of the sofa without his assistance. Once on her feet, she smoothed the wrinkles in her skirt and patted her hair. She noticed that she had a run in her stocking but she no longer cared.

'You're not sorry you came?' asked de Blancourt.

'Are you?' she replied.

The afternoon sunshine bathed the study in a buttery

light. Connie felt indolent and heavy, as though her body would no longer respond to her will. The effort of moving across the room was like walking under water.

'If you don't mind, I'd like to freshen up before we leave.'

'Of course. Across the hall, the second door on your left.'

Connie felt safe in small places. As soon as she locked the bathroom door her breathing became less laboured. The cold sensation of the porcelain bowl under her hands and the stippled, water-stained mirror comforted her.

She studied her face as she allowed the flow of cold water to heat up. The hazel-grey eyes flecked with green, her best feature, set wide apart. The small head, slightly flat which forever frustrated her desire to wear hats. The thin, long face was the twin of her father's with its prominent nose, a feature Ezra continually teased her about. It had become a running joke between them – which of them had the bigger nose. Hers was long and aquiline; his was broad and flat. Michael had inherited his father's, more was the pity.

'You don't mind driving with the top down?' said de Blancourt as they stepped into the courtyard.

Parked in a stable was a red Maserati. She would have expected it of him.

'Ezra always says that once in his life a man must own a sports car and a woman must go blonde.'

'Have you ever been blonde?' asked de Blancourt, as he opened the passenger door for her.

'Only in my mind.'

They drove in silence. De Blancourt switched on the radio. A man was singing about love and disillusionment. His voice was guttural. There was no melody and he half-spoke, half-sang the words. Why are French songs so suicidal, she thought to herself.

In the vineyard to her right a man in blue overalls was pushing a wheelbarrow. The contents were smoking. With a hand shovel he was scooping up ash and scattering it on the base of the vines.

'What's that man doing over there?' asked Connie.

'He's using the ash from the pruned canes as fertilizer. The Beaujolais are very frugal. They waste nothing,' laughed de Blancourt.

'May I ask you a personal question? What makes you live here?'

'Look around you, Connie. Is it not beautiful? The vineyards, the old farmhouses. In the summer you should see the fields full of poppies.'

'But you don't strike me as a man of Beaujolais. I picture you in Paris, racing your Maserati through the Bois de Boulogne.'

He laughed again, the muscles in his throat contracting.

'I like Paris, but in cities people have little time for each other. And when people have little time they take short cuts and there are bound to be victims.'

'I'm not sure I understand,' said Connie. 'There are victims everywhere. Even here. Like Yvette Montreuil.'

She was not sure why she had mentioned the dead woman's name but the effect was immediate and dramatic. Paul de Blancourt braked sharply. Connie, without her seat belt, was thrown forward and her head almost hit the windscreen.

'Forgive me,' he said. 'There was a rabbit in the road. Are you all right?'

'It's nothing,' said Connie, who had seen no rabbit.

She never occupied a passenger seat without driving every inch of the way with the driver, a habit that infuriated her husband.

'Here, let me see.'

'I said it's nothing.'

De Blancourt put the car in gear and accelerated away. Below them, set in a valley a mile down a steep hill, Connie could see the white corrugated roofs of what appeared to be a factory complex.

'What's that?'

'That's the co-operative.'

'It looks like a tractor factory.'

'You might say it's the only industry there is around here. Apart from the individual growers who sell their own wine.'

'Oh my God!' said Connie.

She stared at a bulky figure in a heavy blue overcoat struggling up the hill towards them.

'It's Ezra.' She had a sudden premonition of disaster. 'Quickly, something must have happened.'

De Blancourt accelerated down the hill and drew up beside the panting Ezra. Connie stood in her seat holding onto the top of the windscreen.

'Whatever happened to you? Where's the car?'

Ezra, purse-lipped, looked first at her and then at de

Blancourt. The sight of them together exacerbated the conviction he had that since his arrival in Haut St Antoine he had become a quarry. Things happened around him and to him over which he had no control. The knowledge had generated in him a vague sense of directionless anger.

'My dear fellow, you look as white as a ghost.'

'Someone slashed the tyres of my car,' he said.

'Then it's a good thing we came along,' smiled de Blancourt. 'I'll send a man over to have it towed to the garage.'

'Why would anyone slash your tyres?' said Connie.

'It's that time of year,' said de Blancourt, shaking his head. 'Here, squeeze in the back.'

He opened his door, got out and pulled back the driver's seat. Ezra contemplated the narrow space and grunted. When he had settled in sideways, his knees almost touching his chin, de Blancourt put the car in gear.

'Where did you park?'

'Just outside the entrance to the co-op. On the grass verge.'

'We get some crazy people here now,' said de Blancourt. 'Some of those truck drivers are like soccer hooligans. It's the Beaujolais race. It brings out the worst in them. You should see what they do to get an advantage. Letting down tyres, stealing distributor caps, putting sugar in gas tanks. Anything to stop a competitor getting away before them.'

Ezra stared sourly at the back of de Blancourt's head. He had found an immediate target for his frustration. De Blancourt's smoothness irritated him.

Connie, sensing her husband's mood, half turned towards

him and rested her hand on his shoulder in a gesture of sympathy. She knew it wasn't the vandalism that had upset Ezra. He would have been angry at the time but it would have passed. Something else had happened. The apprehension, temporarily forgotten, returned.

'Are you all right?' she asked.

'I'm fine,' said Ezra through his teeth. 'Just dandy.'

She knew that tone of voice. It was his pit-bull mood. A cold resolve to see the matter through. Nothing she could say now would convince him to leave Haut St Antoine.

Chapter Seven

There were no cars for hire in the village and the local taxi driver had taken the day off to visit his mother in a Villefranche hospital. So Ezra was reduced to asking Madame Barrière to loan him her bicycle. He had not cycled since he was at McGill but, he told himself as he cocked a leg over the saddle, riding a bike was like making love – once you learned how to do it you never forgot.

The bike had no gears and the brakes required a grip of steel to have any effect. He could feel the muscles in his thighs complaining after the first kilometre; the saddle rasped against his groin with every movement of his legs.

And people do this for pleasure, he mused.

To take his mind off the pain he thought about his meeting with Verrier's sister. Connie had told him about the watch. She had also mentioned Paul de Blancourt's reaction to the name of the dead woman. In return he had told her about the fraud he had uncovered at the co-operative, making light of the 'accident' that nearly befell him. They had argued about his determination to stay,

Connie pleading with him to let the matter drop. They had become involved in a deadly game and there was no one to protect them.

'You have to tell the police,' said Connie. 'That's what they're there for.'

'But I can't prove anything. It could have just been an accident.'

'But your tyres.'

'Chasselas isn't going to give me my own personal gendarme for that. He wants me to leave as much as anyone.'

'Then why don't you take the hint? We could be ready in an hour for Paris. Let the rental company worry about the car.'

But Ezra was adamant.

'I want you to go,' he said. 'I have to stay and finish this.'

'I'm not going without you,' she replied.

'You're just going to be bored out of your mind sitting in the hotel. You can help me by going to Paris. You can speak to the lawyer who's trying to buy Verrier's property.'

They had compromised. Connie would go to Paris and wait for him there. But she would leave after Yvette Montreuil's funeral the next morning. Her curiosity about the woman had been aroused and she had a morbid desire to see the dead woman's husband as well as the public display of grief by the village.

Before setting out Ezra had telephoned Théophile Mirze to find out if Verrier had been released. The lawyer was not there and his secretary would not divulge any information. He had hung up on her in exasperation.

* * *

He stopped pedalling and coasted down the gentle incline to Verrier's farmhouse. He propped the bicycle against the wall and negotiated his way across the muddy forecourt. The house looked abandoned. All the shutters had been drawn across the windows giving the façade a look of blindness. It was as if the house and its occupants no longer wanted contact with the outside world.

The brass door-knocker gave a muffled thud as it embedded itself into a deep indentation in the wooden door. Ezra waited but there was no sound from within. Perhaps Marie-Claire had gone to Villefranche to visit her brother in jail. He knocked a second time and when he was sure there would be no response he turned to go.

But something drew him back – a feeling that there was someone in the house. Someone who had heard him knocking and was waiting for him to leave.

He walked around to the back of the house. The windows were not shuttered here and he had a clear view into the living-room where he had seen Verrier the morning of the murder. With no one to occupy the overstuffed furniture the room looked like a museum. On the wall were tinted photographs of a girl's first communion and oil paintings of local beauty spots by an amateur artist whose signature took up an inordinate amount of space in the right-hand corner.

Pressing up against the rose bushes to get a better angle of vision, Ezra caught some movement through a door which led to the kitchen. He edged his way along the wall and peered through the next window.

What he saw made him pull back and flatten himself against the stones.

Seated at the kitchen table, her face in profile to him, was Marie-Claire Verrier. She wore the same clothes he had seen her in when he had first met her. She was sitting motionless, staring at her hands.

They were covered with blood.

His first instinct was to escape. He had seen enough of death and violence since his arrival in Haut St Antoine. Maybe Connie was right. This was not his business. He had stumbled upon a murder and because of his own stubbornness and pride he had put himself and Connie in danger. Yet who was there to see justice done? Verrier stood accused of Yvette Montreuil's death. The police were more interested in hushing the matter up and even Verrier's own lawyer could be conspiring against him.

He edged back to the side of the window and glanced furtively into the kitchen. Marie-Claire was standing now with her back to him. He could hear the sound of running water. She reached for a dish towel and began to dry something. As she turned Ezra could see it was a large kitchen knife.

When she saw him her hands fluttered to her mouth in alarm. The knife clattered on the stone floor at her feet.

And then she smiled in recognition and beckoned him inside.

'Excuse me, Monsieur,' she said, her voice trembling. 'You gave me such a fright standing there. But I am so glad to see you.'

She moved towards him and clutched him by the arm,

talking quickly as she led him to the kitchen table. There was blood on it but what drew Ezra's attention was a large circle about three feet in diameter chalked on the wooden boards. Around the circumference were letters of the alphabet in random order and below each were grains of wheat.

'Look. The circle of knowledge,' the woman kept repeating. 'The cock has told me what I wanted to know.'

In the stone sink lay the carcass of a headless rooster, its black feathers slick with blood.

Alectryomancy, Ezra said to himself. He had read about this ancient form of divination practised by peasants. A male bird is placed in the circle and whichever grains of wheat he eats will spell out the answer to your question. Then the medium must be dispatched to preserve the occult's secret.

'What question did you ask?' said Ezra.

'Did my brother kill Yvette Montreuil?'

'And what did it say?'

'No. He did not. The cock ate N and O and then back to the N. But first it ate P.'

'Did you ask who did kill her?'

'You are only allowed one question, Monsieur.'

Ezra tried to hold back a smile.

'Well, if you had asked the bird who had killed her it would have answered both questions, wouldn't it.'

Marie-Claire considered the notion and then dismissed it with a shrug of the shoulders.

'But I don't care. I was so happy that Jacques did not do it that I kissed the rooster before I cut his throat.'

153

Ezra shuddered and immediately he regretted his remark. He didn't need to show her that she lacked intelligence. She had little enough to be proud of. The face and figure old before their time. The shoulders hunched and bent from years of hard work in the vineyard. The disfiguring cast in her eye. He sensed that she lived for her brother and without him she had no purpose in life.

A large black Labrador, attracted by the scent of the blood, lumbered into the kitchen wagging its tail. Marie-Claire caught him by the collar and pushed his rump until he sat down. His long, pink tongue hung slackly over brown teeth. His eyes were cloudy and his large head bobbed up and down with his heavy breathing. Marie-Claire patted his ears.

Ezra noticed the triangular watch she was wearing, the same shape as the sunburn mark on Yvette Montreuil's wrist.

'That's a beautiful watch,' he said.

'Yes,' she smiled. 'It was my mother's. She wanted me to have it.'

'But didn't your brother give it to Yvette?'

It was a stab in the dark but the woman's reaction showed he was right in his conjecture. Her colour suddenly heightened and she closed her cast-eye, glaring at him with her good one.

'How did you know that?'

'Because there was a sunburn mark on her wrist exactly like it.'

Marie-Claire covered the watch protectively with her right hand. Then she rose and took a rag draped over the tap and began to mop up the blood on the table.

'Jacques should not have given it to her. Mamma meant me to have it.'

'You took it from her body, didn't you? Before the police arrived,' he said gently.

The woman sat in silence staring at the flagstone floor.

'Look, you did nothing wrong. It's our secret, I promise. You must understand that I want to help Jacques. So please tell me the truth.'

He was speaking to her as he had done to Michael when he had been accused of stealing the gym teacher's starting pistol.

'That bird has told you your brother is innocent. I know he is too. If you tell me the truth I might be able to help him get out of jail.'

'You must get Jacques free, Monsieur. Who will look after the wines if he is not here?'

There were questions Ezra wanted to ask but he knew that he had to get the woman talking freely first.

'Tell me about Yvette. What was she like?'

'We did not get on. She was a whore. She bewitched my brother. Why would he have given her Mamma's watch?'

'Did your brother want to marry her?'

'No!'

The vehemence of the response startled Ezra. If Yvette had left her husband and was free to marry Jacques that would have put Marie-Claire in a precarious situation. She would no longer be mistress of the house and Jacques' wife would hardly have tolerated her presence under her roof in the light of their feelings for one another.

'Why do you say that?'

'Because Jacques knew there was another man.'

'Her husband?'

Marie-Claire gave a guttural laugh. 'I told you she was a whore.'

'Who was this other man?'

'I don't know. I heard my brother and her arguing several times about it.'

'But you didn't hear any names.'

'I told you.'

'Did you see her around the village with another man?'

'I didn't go looking for her.'

Ezra could see that he had exhausted that line of enquiry.

'How long has Théophile Mirze acted as Jacques' lawyer?'

'The Mirzes have been our lawyers for as long as I can remember. My father used them. I remember them sitting in the next room drawing up his will together when I was a girl.'

'I thought Théophile's father was the director of the co-operative.'

'No, that was his uncle, old Monsieur Eric Mirze. He's dead now. They say that old quack Fournier prescribed the wrong medicine.'

'Dr Fournier?'

'Yes.'

'Was there a – oh, what's the word in French – an enquiry, a post-mortem?'

'No. He died of you know what.'

Ezra looked blank.

'I don't know what.'

Marie-Claire clucked her tongue and pointed to the chalked letters on the table, spelling out the word too feared to be spoken, C-A-N-C-E-R.

'Cancer,' said Ezra.

Marie-Claire pressed her index finger to his lips. It smelled of blood and onions. Then she took a box of salt and poured some into his palm.

'Quickly,' she said, agitated. 'Throw it over your shoulder.'

Ezra did as he was told. He could see the woman visibly relax. She gave a nervous laugh and pulled the dead rooster from the sink. Then she sat down at the table opposite him and began to pluck the feathers.

'An Englishman named Derek Farmiloe came to see your brother the morning I found Yvette's body. I heard them shouting at each other. What were they arguing about?'

Marie-Claire pursed her lips and exhaled in a gesture that expressed disgust and irritation at the same time.

'He comes every year, that English. I don't know why Jacques does business with him. He is always trying to break the rules.'

'In what way?'

'He tries to get Jacques to release the new Beaujolais before midnight. And he always wants to push the price down.'

'What does he buy?'

'Always a twenty-litre barrel.'

'And then he races it back to London for his restaurant?'

She shrugged her shoulders.

'I don't know and I don't care.'

'So you think they were arguing about money or the release time?'

'Yes.'

'What about Yvette's husband, the barrel-maker? Jacques owed him money.'

'But he will pay. He always pays his debts. He gave me an envelope the morning they came to arrest him. It's still locked in his desk. But I can't face Bernard,' she said with a sob.

'Would you like me to deliver it for you?' asked Ezra.

There was more to his offer than relieving a lonely, frightened woman of the chore of handing over an envelope. It would be an ideal way to meet Bernard Montreuil.

'That is very kind of you, Monsieur.'

She rose and crossed to an adjoining room. Through the open door Ezra watched her approach a roll-top desk and reach inside her dress for a key on a piece of string. Without removing it from around her neck she bent double and inserted it in the lock. She slid the top up, reached inside and with a quick movement like a conjurer producing a rabbit from a hat she withdrew an envelope. Carefully, she closed the desk again and locked it. She turned and Ezra looked away at the cock's head in the sink. One baleful eye was staring up at him.

Marie-Claire held the envelope to her chest. On the front

was printed in a round childish hand, 'Monsieur Bernard Montreuil (*Père*).'

'It's payment for the barrels,' she said. 'It must be given to Bernard personally and he will write me a receipt. I trust you, Monsieur. You have kind eyes.'

Ezra nodded.

She handed the envelope to him. He was expecting something the size of a letter, slim enough to contain an invoice and a cheque. But what he got was bulkier, almost an inch thick. Verrier was paying the cooper in cash. And it felt like a substantial amount of money. He knew that French farmers had a deep-rooted suspicion of banks and were given to keeping large sums of money under the floorboards or in a sock, but if the wine maker was paying in full for his new barrels he could be holding franc notes worth $10,000 or more. Why would Verrier make the transaction in cash? Was he evading tax or was it dirty money? It did not seem strange to his sister. Was all his business done in cash?

'I'll take it straight over now,' he said, suddenly aware of the responsibility he had accepted.

The woman nodded. Ezra rose from the table and stole one last look at the balding cock on the table. How could something so repulsive end up tasting so good, he said to himself. At the door he hesitated and turned as a thought occurred to him.

'One thing before I go. A woman called the police station to report the murder. Inspector Chasselas didn't recognize her voice.'

Marie-Claire smiled without showing her teeth.

'That's because I wrapped a handkerchief around the phone and put a pebble in my mouth,' she said.

Bernard Montreuil's cooperage was situated on the other side of Haut St Antoine. Ezra had no desire to be seen cycling through the village; the less Inspector Chasselas knew of his movements the better. So his only recourse was to take a circuitous route around the base of Mont Brouilly and double back to the village from the north. It didn't look that far on the map but each thrust of the pedals was torture to his knees. A wind had risen and was blowing directly at him, making his progress even slower. The road was narrow and winding. In the distance he could hear the high-pitched whine of a motor cycle.

To take his mind off the strain on his thighs and his sore behind he thought about the dead woman's husband. He had beaten her, Verrier had said. A jealous man capable of violence. Verrier had owed him money, a great deal it seems because new barrels cost nearly $600 each and in his mind's eye Ezra conjured up the neatly stacked rows of new casks in the vintner's cellar.

The sound of the motor cycle was louder now and Ezra looked over his shoulder to see where it was. The rider was approaching at high speed. He wore a helmet with a black visor. The road in front of Ezra began to dip sharply and he applied the brakes to allow the man to pass. The whine of the machine rang painfully in his ears. He felt a rush of air and a sudden jolt as the rider swerved into him, catching him a glancing blow on the shoulder. As he fell he saw the man career off the tarmac onto the grass verge and right himself with his foot before accelerating away up the hill out of sight.

'You son of a bitch!' shouted Ezra.

The long grass had broken his fall. He lay in the ditch with the bike on top of him, its back wheel still spinning. He patted his breast pocket to ensure that the envelope was still there and then eased the frame off of him. He stood up, gingerly feeling himself for any injury. His whole body was shaking and he wondered if his legs would obey him when he tried to mount the bike again.

If the falling skid of wine cases had been an accident there was no mistaking the intention of the man on the motor bike. He deliberately swerved in order to hit me, Ezra said to himself. And knowing he had, he didn't stop. I need a gun, something to protect myself with. If I report this to Chasselas what can I say? I was nearly hit by cases of wine and then I was knocked down by a motor-cyclist I couldn't identify. He'd probably just shrug his shoulders and say, 'You should take more care, Monsieur Brant.'

A comment Michael had made came back to him. 'It's a jungle out there, Dad. It's not like when you were a kid. There's violence on the streets.' He had made the statement after two boys with shaved heads had cornered him behind the Eaton Centre and demanded his Doc Marten boots. They were the colour of ox blood, his pride and joy with their fourteen holes and fat, black laces. Michael refused to hand them over and the pair had beaten him until he had complied. He returned home with bruised ribs, a cut lip and a black eye, angry and sullen, but he had

161

refused to go to the police. 'It happens all the time,' he said. 'Let's just forget about it.'

But Ezra could not forget about it. Over Michael's objections he had marched him over to 51 Division, seething with indignation and self-righteousness. The police constable who took the report nodded sympathetically, shook his head at the right moments and said that they would be in touch if the boots were found. Of course, they never were.

Connie had said it was the money lost that had upset him but it was more than that – it was the injustice of it all that made him angry. The sense that people could take what they liked and inflict pain on others to gratify their wants. He had tried to instil his values into his son but he had come to recognize that what Michael said was true. There was violence on the streets and there were no more sanctuaries. Even in such a pastoral landscape as Beaujolais.

Painfully, he lifted his leg over the saddle and began to pedal.

The cooperage was set back behind a two-storey farmhouse in a cobbled courtyard. Piles of newly cut staves were piled up to head height, drying in the air outside a large barn. Above the door hung a sign which read '*Tonnellerie Bernard Montreuil*'. In fresher paint the words '*et Fils*' had been recently added. He looked around to see if there was a motor bike parked but there was none.

Ezra felt for the envelope in his pocket once more and entered the barn. His nostrils were immediately assailed by the sweet, clove-like scent of new oak. He stood in the doorway and glanced around him. The walls were hung with a plethora of tools that looked like medieval instruments of torture. Two-handed knives of all shapes, jiggers, chives, crozes and windlasses that resembled giant thumbscrews. The wall had been painted with the silhouette of each tool so that it could be put back in its proper place. Ezra noticed that one was missing. The naked white shape was the exact outline of the gimlet he had seen driven into the trapdoor that opened onto Verrier's cellar.

The work benches were stacked with planes and cutting implements all neatly aligned. There was no sign of the bung-boring tool there. Rows of finished barrels of different sizes were piled around the walls. In the centre was a 'horse', the low bench with its foot-activated vice the cooper uses to hold the staves while he shaves them to shape. A brazier with hot coals smoked nearby and next to it stood a half-finished barrel, its staves still straight, splayed like the petals of a wooden flower, held in position by a single iron hoop. Montreuil would place it over the fire and allow the heat to bend the wood held under pressure from steel cables drawn tight by a winch.

'Hello,' called Ezra, but there was no response.

He wandered over to the workbench. Above it, perched on a small wooden shelf that looked as if it had been designed specially for it, was a ship in a bottle, virtually obscured by a thick layer of dust. It looked like Dr Fournier's handiwork.

As he turned to move away he felt a rasping under the soles of his shoes. On the cement floor he saw heaps of metal filings, as fine as wire wool, glinting in the sunshine that streamed in through the high windows.

Odd, thought Ezra. He bent down, licked his thumb and pressed it against the glittering debris. He studied the shavings closely. They looked like aluminium. Yet the barrel hoops were made of steel. Then his eye was drawn to the workbench.

It was strewn with templates, at least a couple of dozen. Ezra cocked his head to read the names: Weinhof, Piggy's, The Diner, Coq au Feu. They appeared to be the names of restaurants or wine bars. Then he saw the name, 'Beaujolais Bistro'.

He picked up the thin strip of metal and studied it. The edges of the letters were covered with various colours of spray paint which suggested that it had been used several times. If the barrel-maker had gone to the trouble of having a template made up then Beaujolais Bistro must have been a regular customer. Marie-Claire Verrier told him that Derek Farmiloe had done business with her brother for several years. What was the connection between the three men?

Ezra was about to put the template back where he had found it when he heard the crunch of footsteps behind him. He turned and was confronted by a boy of about his son's age. He was carrying a large barrel. He held it in front of him in such a way that it accentuated the size of his shoulders and forearms. He was not very tall but the muscles in his arms and shoulders bulged like a body-builder's. His mouth was open and his head leaned to one side under the effort. The muscles in his neck stood out like

164

ropes. The dull eyes regarded Ezra without curiosity as if his presence in the cooperage was expected though the reason for it temporarily forgotten.

'Can you do this?' enquired the boy in a nasal voice.

With a sudden movement and a grunt he swung the barrel out in front of him and lifted it above his head. He held it there, turning a full three hundred and sixty degrees as if to show there was nothing behind his back to assist him in this feat.

'That's amazing,' said Ezra, genuinely impressed by the boy's strength.

'My name is Ezra. What's yours?'

He slid the template back onto the workbench. The boy looked up at a point in the rafters. Then he lowered the barrel and placed it with infinite care on the floor.

'You come for a barrel?'

'No, no. I'm delivering a payment to Monsieur Montreuil.'

'Bernard. My name's Bernard.'

'You were named after your father?'

Ezra was fishing but the boy ignored the bait.

'A payment?'

'Yes.'

He was about to add that it was from Jacques Verrier but he could not tell what effect this information might have on the boy. After all, Verrier was in jail, accused of murdering his mother.

'Of course I was named *after* my father. He was born before I was.'

The boy's face slowly ignited into a beaming grin. Ezra smiled and nodded his head.

'How silly of me.'

'You're not from around here,' said Bernard.

Ezra could see the emotion in the boy's face change from good-natured humour to suspicion.

'I come from Canada. Here, I have something for you.' He slipped his hand behind the lapel of his jacket and unclipped a maple-leaf pin he habitually wore when he travelled abroad. His accent might be taken for American but the symbol would correct that misapprehension.

'Let me pin it on your shirt and then you'll be an honorary Canadian.'

Bernard smelled of sweat and axle grease. His plaid woollen shirt, unbuttoned to the navel, revealed the well-defined musculature of his stomach. Michael would have called it 'a six pack'. The boy nodded when Ezra stepped back and held his shirt out to inspect the welcome gift.

'Canada,' he said. 'Mounties.'

'Yes, Mounties,' replied Ezra. 'Is your father around?'

Bernard shook his head.

'Do you know where he is?'

'At the funeral parlour. My mother's dead.'

He's probably making final arrangements for the burial tomorrow, thought Ezra.

'I'm sorry. May I offer my condolences.'

The formality of the phrase sounded foolish and trite as soon as he had uttered it; but he knew of no way to communicate a sense of sorrow to a stranger except in priggish clichés. Connie would have put her arm around the boy and said something such as, 'You poor love, how you must miss your mother.' She was good at situations like these. She knew exactly what to say.

The boy gave a sob which he stifled in his throat and then looked up at the rafters once more. Tears glistened in his eyes.

'Would it help you to talk about her?'

'She's dead, that's all.'

'Yes. You must have loved her very much.' Again his words rang falsely in his ears. 'What was she like, your mother?'

Bernard pondered the question. He pursed his lips and made a humming sound in his throat. Ezra waited but it was not the boy's voice he heard next. The words, sharp and demanding, came from the shadows between two rows of barrels. And they were spoken in English.

'Why are you badgering the boy?'

Ezra turned and squinted in the direction of the voice. He heard the sound of footsteps before he could see a form emerging from the darkness.

It was Derek Farmiloe. He was dressed in a military style camel-colour overcoat with leather buttons, his hands deep in his pockets.

Ezra wondered how long he had been standing there listening. He glanced quickly at Bernard to gauge the boy's reaction to Farmiloe's sudden appearance. As soon as he recognized him Bernard hopped from one foot to the other like a puppy.

'It's ready, it's ready, Monsieur!' he called out.

'Do you mind leaving us alone, Bernard,' said Farmiloe in French. 'I will see you back at the house.'

The boy slapped his hands against his thighs and then adopted a body-builder's pose.

'That's very good, Bernard. Keep it up. Now wait in the house for me.'

The boy smiled and without looking at Ezra he turned and ran out of the cooperage.

'He's not all there,' said Farmiloe, reverting to English, 'but harmless enough if you handle him right.'

'You seem to know him very well,' said Ezra.

'I come to Beaujolais quite a lot. I count them as friends, the Montreuil family. Now, Mr Brant, may I ask why you are asking all these questions? Everywhere I go people are talking about an inquisitive Canadian journalist.'

'I'm hardly a journalist,' replied Ezra. 'I write about wine.'

'Then I would stick to your last if I were you.'

'If I want to remain healthy, is that what you mean?'

'The Beaujolais are very outgoing, very hospitable people. They'd do anything to make you feel welcome but they don't like you enquiring into their private affairs.'

'So I've noticed. But you're English, Mr Farmiloe. You don't mind if I ask about yours?'

'Fire away, old boy.'

'Jacques Verrier is in jail for a murder he didn't commit. I can prove that he couldn't have done it. And so can you.'

'What makes you say that?'

'Because I was in his cellar when the body was dropped

through the trapdoor. And I heard you arguing with him upstairs.'

Farmiloe took the hands from his pockets and began twisting a large ring on the little finger of his left hand.

'Perhaps.'

'There's no perhaps about it. Yet you denied knowing him when I asked you at the dinner.'

'I thought you might be a competitor. Every year I buy Verrier Beaujolais-Villages Nouveau. His, as you probably know, is consistently one of the best. Not cheap, mind. But always first rate, even in poor vintages. Naturally, as a businessman I want to get as good a price as I can. Jacques wanted to put his up twenty per cent over last year. Of course, I would argue with him.'

'But you also wanted to get the papers early so you could get a head start on the competition.'

Farmiloe laughed.

'My dear fellow, you have been busy. Well, there's nothing wrong with a little corner cutting in a good cause. In the beginning it was easy enough to be first back to London but so many nutters have got into the act now. It's damn good publicity for my restaurant to be first, you know. By the way, are you in the race?'

'I intend to be.'

'A word to the wise then. Avoid the autoroute. Packed with lorries. The back roads are faster in the end.'

'I see you do business here too,' said Ezra, picking up the template and holding it up in front of him.

'Yes,' said Farmiloe. 'I have my barrel made here every year. The customers like it. They think the wine tastes

169

better if they see it being drawn from a cask. Of course, you and I know that's a crock of shit as you Americans so colourfully put it.'

Ezra let the remark pass without comment.

'But perception is all in this business. Yours too I imagine,' continued Farmiloe.

'So you serve the wine directly from the barrel.'

'Yes, I just bung in a little spigot and Bob's your uncle. The barrel stands on the bar and the stuff's gone in two days. So it's worth all the effort.'

'And what do you do with the empty barrel if you get a new one every year?'

'I auction it off, old boy. Amateur wine makers. And I give the proceeds to the juvenile diabetes foundation. Now if you'll excuse me, I think that's enough interrogation for one day. Good day to you.'

He watched as Derek Farmiloe walked towards the farmhouse. The windows, he noticed, were hung with black cloth. In one he saw Bernard's face peering out at him. He smiled and waved but the boy let the drape fall back into place.

Ezra mounted his bike again and pedalled slowly out of the cobbled courtyard. He listened carefully for the sound of engines and at the approach of a car he pulled over and stood on a stone wall until it had passed.

It was only when he reached the bottom of the hill that he realized he still had Jacques Verrier's envelope.

'How are you going to get me to the station tomorrow if we don't have the car?' asked Connie.

She was packing her suitcase when he arrived back at the hotel. She had ordered him a brandy which was waiting on his bedside table. Monsieur Barrière, *le propriétaire*, had a collection of vintage-dated Armagnacs going back to 1895. Connie knew he liked old Armagnac and as a gesture of contrition and genuine concern she had bought him one.

'If your friend is as good as his word then we should have the car back today. If not, you can always ask him.'

Connie accepted the remark, not willing to have to justify herself further. Her calculated lightness of mood was a strategy she had always used to deflect him from criticism of her.

'I thought you might need something to warm you up after your Tour de France,' she said, brightly. 'Our friend with the industrial strength BO swears it's 1895 Bas Armagnac. Can you tell? At thirty dollars a shot I sure hope it is.'

Ezra glared at the glass of amber liquid. It was covered with a paper doily.

'Thirty dollars!' he exploded.

'It's all right. It's my treat. So don't go getting your knickers in a twist. I just thought it might cheer you up, that's all.'

Ezra lifted the glass and sniffed it. The odour of prunes and violets filled his head.

'Thank you,' he mumbled and took a sip.

'There's a couple of things I'd like you to do for me in Paris,' he said. 'Someone is trying to buy Jacques Verrier's estate anonymously. Mirze gave me the name of a Paris law firm acting for them. I have to find out who it is.'

'And they're going to tell me, just like that?'

'You'll find a way.'

'Anything else, sahib?'

Ezra took a card from his wallet.

'Can you phone this restaurant in London. Speak to the manager and ask him if they're going to have Beaujolais Nouveau this year. And will they be serving it from the barrel again. You can pretend you're a customer.'

'From the barrel again. Anything else?'

'Yes. Get the number of the juvenile diabetes foundation in London and say you're Derek Farmiloe's accountant and you can't find last year's receipt for a donation he made either personally or on behalf of his restaurant. It would probably have been in late November or early December.'

Connie looked at the card.

'Beaujolais Bistro. Why do I know that name?'

And then she remembered the giant brandy glass with the book matches from restaurants around the world in Paul de Blancourt's study. She was about to remark on the fact and then she stopped herself. There was little to be gained by mentioning Paul's name to Ezra in his present frame of mind.

'What's that?' asked Connie, curious about the envelope he was absent-mindedly tapping against the palm of his hand.

'It's money Verrier was going to give to his barrel-maker. His sister asked me to deliver it.'

'In cash?' exclaimed Connie. 'Why would she ask you?'

'Actually, I offered. She doesn't want to have to face him

under the circumstances, I guess. Bernard Montreuil is the dead woman's husband.'

'Your good deed for the day. You're all heart, Ezra, that's your trouble.'

He grunted and took another sip of Armagnac.

'But why would he pay up now, Ezra? When he's in jail. Surely he'd need all the money he could get for lawyers if he's up for murder.'

To Ezra, it would be natural for a man to settle his debts and tie up loose ends in case he faced a jail term, innocent though he was. It took Connie's cynical mind to find a sinister motivation.

'And furthermore, what is the sister doing, handing over large sums of cash to a complete stranger?'

'I'm not a complete stranger, for God's sake. I'm doing them a favour.'

'But are you doing yourself a favour, Ezra? The trouble with you is you're too trusting.'

He did not sleep well that night. The envelope seemed to throb menacingly under his pillow, keeping him awake all night. He had thought of asking the Barrières to lock the money away safely somewhere but Connie's suspicions had sparked his imagination. What if he had been set up? If Chasselas suddenly burst in with a search warrant and discovered the wad of bills he could be implicated in the whole sorry business. But what had Verrier or his sister to gain by involving him? Connie was right. The vintner would need every penny he had to prove his innocence. Why would he settle a debt with the husband of a woman he stood accused of murdering? The barrels he had bought were still there in his cellar and the wine they contained would be collateral enough to cover the unpaid invoice.

Did Verrier even know that his sister was settling his debt? If not, why was she doing it now? Surely it could wait. Was she, in fact, the loving, concerned sister she presented herself to be? She had been jealous of her brother's infatuation with Yvette. Afraid perhaps that she would be displaced in the household. Verrier had given away the watch that her mother had promised her. Was she afraid that he would cut her out of her share of the estate as well?

For his own peace of mind the sooner he delivered the envelope to Montreuil the better. Tomorrow was the funeral. He couldn't just go up to Bernard Montreuil, hand it to him and ask for a receipt. But he could return it to Marie-Claire Verrier.

The entire population of Haut St Antoine, it seemed to Ezra, had turned out for Yvette Montreuil's funeral. The procession of cars was parked along a country lane. The mourners and the curious had to pick their way up a track through the vineyard to a walled graveyard set on a knoll two hundred metres from the road.

The wind blew the priest's cassock which billowed out like a phantom spinnaker. His hands, the colour of tallow, held a prayer-book to his stomach as he waited for the flower-decked coffin to arrive at the grave side.

'That's Montreuil's son,' he whispered to Connie. 'The short kid in front. And that must be Montreuil on the other side.'

Father and son held the front end of the coffin. Four other men whom Ezra did not recognize completed the pall-bearing party. They had to stoop at the knees to keep the coffin horizontal.

From his vantage point at the edge of the crowd he could study the faces of the villagers who had come to pay their last respects. Whatever they had thought of Yvette Montreuil in life they appeared determined to do the right thing by her in death. Dressed in black, the women veiled, their expressions were solemn, their demeanour showing nothing of the sensational manner in which the woman had met her death.

Ezra caught sight of Inspector Chasselas. He was dressed in a well-tailored blue serge overcoat. When their glances met the policeman cocked a quizzical eyebrow as if puzzled by his presence. Then he nodded solemnly, looked away and continued talking in a low voice to a man who wore a chain of office round his neck. The mayor, most probably, Ezra thought. Next to him stood Dr Fournier staring into the open grave, no doubt contemplating his own mortality. Ezra recognized the deputy director of the co-operative standing beside Fournier and behind him, craning his neck for a better view, was Théophile Mirze. He saw Valéry Croix, his wife and two daughters and there were other faces he recognized from the Compagnons de Beaujolais dinner. Faces that he recalled as flushed with wine, animated and jovial, were now fixed with sombre, grey expressions.

He looked around for Derek Farmiloe and then he spotted him, down by the road, smoking a cigarette.

'Why is everyone looking at us, Ezra?' whispered Connie.

Sidelong glances and quickly averted eyes signalled to her that they were strangers, not welcome to participate in such rites.

'Do you think we should leave?'

Before he could reply Paul de Blancourt suddenly materialized at his side. At the same moment he could feel Connie's hand slip under his arm. So, they were all here, all the players in the drama, thought Ezra. Except for Marie-Claire Verrier.

'I hope you got your car back,' whispered de Blancourt.

'Yes,' said Ezra. 'Thank you for attending to it. How much do I owe you?'

'Nothing. It is the least the village can do in the face of such hooliganism.'

He smiled at Connie who smiled weakly back.

The priest began to chant the prayers for the dead. His voice was thin and reedy.

The mourning party stood to one side of the open grave. Ezra was facing Bernard Montreuil. He was a short man, stockily built with a square, truculent face that seemed to express anger rather than grief. The predominant feature was a pair of bushy, undisciplined eyebrows that capped hooded and fleshy blue eyes. In his black suit and white shirt buttoned at the neck he appeared to be much older than Yvette.

Next to him stood his son who shifted his weight from foot to foot, his head moving from side to side like a metronome. As the priest droned on the boy's movement became more violent, accompanied by a growling sound in his throat. His father placed a hand on his shoulder but the young Bernard shook it off. All eyes were on him and even the priest hesitated momentarily in his automatic recitation of the prayers.

Suddenly, the boy sprang forward and grabbed the ropes that supported the coffin from the two men who held them. Planting his feet in the mud, he bent his knees and took the strain. The assembled mourners watched in stunned silence as he began to lower the coffin single-handedly into the grave.

He bared his teeth and the veins in his neck stood out with the effort. The lacquered coffin jolted downwards into the earth and came to rest with a thud. A murmur ran through the congregation like the rustling of leaves in the wind and suddenly, as if in tribute to the boy's feat, the mournful blast of a steam whistle rose from the direction of the village and echoed off the surrounding hills. Heads turned and the mobile distillery came clattering up the incline at a greater speed than Ezra had ever seen it travel. The brothers Fréjac were gesticulating wildly and pointing in the direction of Montreuil's cooperage.

A billowing column of black smoke rose from the red-tiled roof of the barn.

The funeral broke up in pandemonium as Bernard Montreuil and his son raced from the grave side, shouting and cursing, followed by several of the men.

'So much excitement,' said Paul de Blancourt. 'Why don't the three of us go back to my château for a warming drink?'

Connie looked at Ezra.

'My train, remember.'

Her uneasiness registered with him but for some reason he wanted to see how she reacted to de Blancourt in his presence. She had been tense and nervous ever since she had visited the man yesterday.

'There are other trains,' he said. 'Why don't you drive my wife and I'll follow in my car.'

Connie grimaced at him and turned away.

'You can't miss it,' said de Blancourt, 'just follow the road out of the village and up the hill.'

He took Connie by the arm and led her down the track to where his red Maserati was parked.

Ezra had left his rented Citroën under a tree on a side road, well away from the funeral procession. As an outsider, and one who had been made to feel unwelcome in the village, he had determined to keep a low profile. As he approached the car he made a mental note to check the tyres and look for any other signs of vandalism.

'Monsieur Brant.'

The voice startled him.

Marie-Claire Verrier stepped out from behind the car. She was pale and her whole body was trembling.

'Madame Verrier, are you all right?'

'Don't let them see me. I don't trust any of them.'

'What happened?'

'The money. Did you give it to Bernard?'

'No. I passed by but he wasn't there. I still have the envelope.'

'Is it safe?'

He withdrew the envelope from his inside pocket just far enough for her to identify it.

'Thank God. It might have burned in the fire.'

'How did you know there was a fire?'

'Look for yourself. It can only be Bernard's property.'

The smoke continued to balloon out over the cooperage and now Ezra could smell it on the wind.

'To be frank, Madame, I was going to return the money to you. It's not a good time for me to give it to Monsieur Montreuil. And I shall be leaving the day after tomorrow.'

'But you must!'

'Why don't you do it through your lawyer if you don't want to see him?'

'No. This is between Bernard and me. No one else must know.'

'Well, I suggest you do it yourself then.'

He was tired of all the intrigues and mysterious alliances among the villagers.

'I cannot keep the money in my house, Monsieur Brant. I was robbed last night.'

'Robbed?'

'Yes. I went to pick up my egg order from Madame Pierrevert as I do every Monday after dinner and when I came back Jacques' desk was open.'

'Did they break in?'

'The back door was unlocked.'

'You left it open?'

'This is Haut St Antoine, Monsieur. Not Paris.'

'What was taken?'

'Thank God the money was not there. All they got were the papers.'

'Papers?'

'The documents for the sale of Verrier Beaujolais-Villages Nouveau. The *acquit vert* for your barrel, Monsieur. It was stupid of me. I forgot to lock the desk. With Jacques in jail . . .'

She broke off in mid-sentence, staring fixedly over his shoulder. Ezra turned to face Inspector Chasselas.

'Good morning, Monsieur Brant,' he said affably. 'Still among us, I see.'

'Yes, Inspector, very much so. Madame Verrier was just telling me that she was burgled last night.'

'Oh? I am surprised she did not tell me first.'

Ezra turned back but Marie-Claire Verrier was nowhere to be seen.

'A strange woman,' said Chasselas, tapping his forehead with his index finger.

The policeman seemed less than interested in the robbery. Ezra was detetemined to make sure that he knew all the circumstances.

'Apparently, the only things that were taken were the documents relating to the sale of Beaujolais-Villages Nouveau. Including mine.'

'The *acquits verts*. Yes,' nodded Chasselas. 'A pity. Without them you cannot take the wine out of the country.'

'I shall just have to get another set from Jacques Verrier.'

'But that is not possible, Monsieur Brant. Jacques Verrier has been charged with murder. He cannot sign any contracts while he is in jail awaiting trial.'

180

'Then his sister can sign them.'

'She has no signing authority, I'm afraid. Unless he had the foresight to give her power of attorney, but I very much doubt if he had the time to do that.'

Ezra felt the blood rising in his face. Anger against the injustices he had witnessed coupled with the physical threats to his own life finally erupted.

'Well isn't that just dandy. Ever since I arrived in this town I have been lied to and threatened. I have had my tyres slashed and somebody has tried to kill me. Not once but twice. And documents that belong to me have been stolen. Now I'm angry, Inspector. Not frightened, angry. Something is rotten here and I intend to find out why you and the rest of the village are trying to railroad an innocent man. I'm going to do what I came to do – take part in the Beaujolais race. And then I promise you I'll be back. That you can count on.'

Inspector Chasselas pursed his lips.

'While you remain here, Monsieur Brant, you must respect the law of France. As chief of police I represent that law. If you have any complaints you will come to me and I will take the necessary steps.'

'Then you can bloody well find out who tried to crush me under a stack of wine cases at your co-operative. And who tried to run me off the road on a motor bike,' he flared.

'Those are serious allegations, Monsieur. If you are prepared to swear an official complaint I shall look into it.'

'Oh, forget it,' said Ezra and he climbed into his car. Inspector Chasselas watched him as he accelerated up the hill towards Paul de Blancourt's château.

* * *

Ezra laughed at his own bravado. How was he going to make good on his vow to enter the Beaujolais race when he didn't have any wine? He could buy a barrel from another vintner but somehow he felt that that would be disloyal and Verrier needed the money now. He had twenty-four hours to come up with an answer.

He pulled into the courtyard of the château and parked next to the red Maserati. The cobblestones were slick with dew. Spongy green moss squelched under his feet. The door to the château was open. He scraped his leather soles on the iron grid and stepped inside.

He found himself in a large hallway hung with tapestries so faded with age that he could not tell what they were meant to depict. There was a fetid smell in the air of damp clothes and old leaves. To his left was a large staircase, its stone steps worn to a curve that reminded him of the free-flowing concrete lines of Gaudi's Barcelona apartment houses.

Above him he heard de Blancourt's explosive laughter. He climbed the stairs and headed in the direction of the irritating sound. Through the open door of what appeared to be a study he could see Connie, sitting on a leather sofa. De Blancourt, standing, was about to place a glass on the coffee table in front of her. As he leaned down he glanced at the door and drew himself upright. Immediately, Connie sprang to her feet. Her shoulder came into contact with de Blancourt's arm and made him spill the drink.

'Ezra! What took you so long? Oh, I'm so sorry, Monsieur de Blancourt. How clumsy of me,' said Connie.

Her voice was high and shrill.

De Blancourt took a handkerchief from his breast pocket and began to mop his hand. Had he been about to kiss her? That's all I need, thought Ezra.

'I ran into Inspector Chasselas,' he said.

'Ah, the good Inspector,' said de Blancourt. 'May I get you a whisky?'

'Yes, I think I could do with one.'

'Soda?'

'Straight up.'

'Straight up,' repeated de Blancourt. 'I like that expression. It's so . . .'

He was reaching for a word.

'How about, refreshingly North American, naïvely colonial, ingenuously Canadian.'

'Ezra,' remonstrated Connie, 'what's the matter with you?'

'Nothing that a whisky won't cure.'

He took the glass de Blancourt proffered and wandered over to the window.

'And what did you think of this morning's theatricals, Monsieur de Blancourt?'

'I have learned that nothing is as it seems in Haut St Antoine. Grief makes people do strange things. You must not be too hard on us, Monsieur Brant. We are no better and no worse than anyone else.'

'You sound like a true son of the soil,' Ezra said. 'I should tell you if you haven't already heard. Marie-Claire Verrier's house was robbed last night. They stole the *acquit vert* for my Beaujolais-Villages Nouveau. Now why would

183

anyone do that?' He glanced back at de Blancourt. 'Strange, wouldn't you say?'

'Maybe they were looking for something else.'

Ezra was standing by the telescope.

'Nice,' he said running a finger along its shining brass case.

'The stars are a hobby of mine,' said de Blancourt.

'You should get a good view of Orion these nights,' said Ezra.

'Yes, it's very clear,' agreed the Frenchman.

Ezra looked at him for a moment and then at Connie. Even the most amateur astronomer knew that in November Orion would not be visible by telescope in this part of the heavens. And the telescope was not angled up at the sky. It was locked into a position that pointed into the valley.

'Mind if I take a look?'

Before de Blancourt could reply he squinted into the eyepiece. The telescope was trained on Bernard Montreuil's cooperage. With the merest change of focus he had a clear view of the entrance. He could see the local firetruck and the volunteer firemen rolling up their hoses. The fire had obviously been put out. Montreuil himself, in his shirt-sleeves, his face smudged with soot, stood by the door gesticulating wildly at Derek Farmiloe. He was being restrained by two other men.

'I think we'd better make tracks, Connie,' he said. 'You've got a train to catch.'

They drove in silence back to the hotel, both wrapped in their own thoughts. As he drew up at the kerb, Connie said, 'Do you mind telling me what that was all about?'

'What was what all about?'

'You know perfectly well.'

'Your friend Paul de Blancourt is a little too smooth for my liking,' he said.

'First, he's not my friend,' she countered, 'and second, you were very rude. We were his guests.'

'Well, Miss Manners, perhaps it's a good thing you're going to Paris.'

'And what does that mean?'

'Anything you like.'

'Then perhaps you're right,' she replied. 'A little distance isn't such a bad idea after all. I don't think you deserve this but at least it shows I was thinking about you. I found it in the glass bowl on the coffee table.'

She handed him a book of matches. The black cover was printed in gold lettering with the legend, 'Beaujolais Bistro'.

Chapter Eight

Connie was booked first class on the TGV, the bullet train from Lyon to Paris. She would telephone on her arrival and let Ezra know where she was staying. They would arrange a meeting place outside Paris so he could pick her up on the race to London without losing any time.

They drove to Belleville in silence and then headed south on the Autoroute du Soleil. As they passed the first signpost for Villefranche, Ezra said, 'I wonder if they'll let me talk to Jacques Verrier?'

'I wish you'd give it up, hon.'

Hon was short for honey, a term of endearment Connie used when she was neither pleased nor angry with him. The diminutive, Ezra had always felt, made him sound like a barbarian.

'We've been all through that. In a couple of days we'll be on our way to London and that'll be an end of it.'

But he recognized that it would not be over until Yvette Montreuil's murderer had been found. Connie knew him well enough to understand this too.

Ezra felt more at ease now that she was leaving. The attempts on his life proved to him how dangerous the situation had become. At least Connie would not be a target and her absence would allow him to move about more freely.

There was another reason why her departure from Haut St Antoine gratified him. Though he would not admit it to himself, the idea of separating her from Paul de Blancourt had much to commend it. His pride could not bring him to ask her directly if anything had happened between them, and if he accused her she would have been outwardly affronted, while secretly delighted at his show of jealousy. He would not give her that satisfaction. Had she known what was in his mind she would have accused him of being dishonest with himself.

'The trouble with you,' Connie had once said, 'is that you don't take marriage seriously enough.'

'The trouble with you,' he had retorted, 'is that you take it too seriously. You analyse it to death. You don't just let it happen.'

If she had let it happen this time was it his fault as much as hers?

'Why do you keep looking in the rearview mirror all the time?'

'Motorway drivers,' he replied. 'They all think they're at Le Mans.'

Ezra carried Connie's suitcases to her reserved seat in the first class compartment. Why, he wondered, did she need two when she would only be in Paris for a couple of days? It would be much more convenient for him to drive up with the rest of her clothes. But it was so like her not wanting to be separated from her belongings.

'Don't do anything silly, will you, Ezra,' she said as they kissed peremptorily on the platform.

'Silly?'

'You know what I mean.'

He watched the train slide out of the station before returning to the car. He drove the twenty-eight kilometres to Villefranche in a state of mounting excitement. He felt unencumbered, as if he had temporarily shelved all responsibilities and was a young man again, prepared to take on the world. Connie was safely on her way to Paris. He could come and go without having to justify himself to her.

Yet one part of him began to miss her already. She could be infuriating at times but there was a certain comfort in being able to predict how another human being would respond to most situations even if that response would probably irritate you.

At Villefranche he asked directions to police headquarters, reasoning that a man charged with murder would be held in the city's most secure holding cells. His guess proved correct. He had less trouble than he thought in gaining access to Jacques Verrier. He spoke to the sergeant on the desk and told him he was a friend of the vintner's from Canada. The gendarme had a sister in Trois Rivières and was very accommodating. Ezra could talk to Verrier for ten minutes as long as there was an armed guard present in the room.

He was shocked by the vintner's appearance. Verrier

had aged ten years in jail. His ruddy glow had turned to putty. His shoulders sagged and his eyes were dull but he managed a smile as he sat down across the table from Ezra. They were seated in a box-like interrogation room with a single window. A guard stood by the door facing Verrier, arms folded across an Uzi sub-machine-gun.

'How long do I have?' Ezra asked the guard in English.

'Monsieur?'

'You don't speak English?'

The man shook his head. Ezra turned back to Verrier.

'How are you, Jacques?'

He shrugged. 'As you see me. Do you have a cigarette?'

'I'm afraid I don't smoke,' he said in French and then switched to English.

'The guard doesn't speak English so let's do it that way.'

Verrier nodded. He seemed uninterested in the proceedings.

'What does your lawyer say?'

'Monsieur Mirze is working to get me out on bail but it takes time. You know I am innocent.'

Ezra looked back at the guard whose expression remained blank and anonymous.

'Tell me. What do you know about Paul de Blancourt?'

Verrier shrugged again and locked his fingers together.

'He is a wealthy man.'

'How did he make his money?'

'They say by importing cheap wine from Algeria but that's finished now.'

'Did he know Yvette Montreuil?'

The vintner's eyes clouded with anger. 'You mean was he her lover?'

'Your sister told me that there was another man.'

'Marie-Claire talks too much.'

'Do you know who that other man was?'

'No. She would not talk about him. We argued about it. All she would say is that he gave her money but she said there were no strings attached.'

'Did she say what the money was for?'

'To help her son. He needed special medical attention. Brain damage.'

'Did she say how much money?'

'No.'

'Could it have been de Blancourt?'

'You'll have to ask him yourself.'

'Goddamn it, Jacques. I'm trying to help you. Just give me a straight answer. I'm sick and tired of hearing riddles all the time.'

Verrier's head dropped and he covered his face with his hands. When he removed them his eyes glistened with tears. He shook his head. 'It could be, I don't know. I don't care now. She's dead.'

'Listen Jacques, you've got to help yourself. Tell me about her son. Was he born that way or did something happen to him?'

'It happened during the birth. She talked about it a lot. The doctor said the – how do you call it? – the cord was wrapped around the baby's neck. Ever since then she was terrified about getting pregnant.'

'Who delivered the baby? Was it Fournier?'

'Yes.'

Verrier looked up and for the first time there was animation in his eyes. 'How did you know that?'

'He's the only doctor in Haut St Antoine.'

If Fournier had been responsible for the mental condition of Yvette Montreuil's son maybe it was he who was giving her money. Guilt at his own negligence perhaps, or a way to avert a malpractice suit. Ezra decided to change his approach.

'I went to the co-op yesterday, Jacques. I saw them dumping a truckload of Italian wine into one of their tanks. You know what that means.'

Verrier nodded.

'Right after that someone tried to kill me. In the shipping room a pallet of wine fell from the top of the pile. It just missed me. It was no accident. Then a guy on a motor bike tried to ride me off the road on my way to see Bernard Montreuil.'

Verrier blinked as if he had been struck across the face. 'You saw Bernard?'

'No, he wasn't there. Your sister gave me an envelope to deliver to him. She said it was to pay for the barrels.'

Ezra studied him carefully to judge the effect of this information on him. Verrier half turned and raised his face to the silver beam of light that angled through the window. Obviously, she had done it without his knowledge.

'How much?'

'I don't know. The envelope was sealed. But I never got to give it to him.'

'Where is it now?'

'Back at the hotel, locked in a safe place,' he lied.

He could feel the envelope in his inside breast pocket.

'Don't give it to him. Give it to Mirze.'

'Why would your sister ask me to give it to Montreuil?'

'She cannot stand to be in debt to anyone. If you owe someone money she thinks God will punish you if you don't pay. But a man like Bernard, it doesn't matter. God can wait.'

Ezra felt that he was getting nowhere. The petty feuds and jealousies of Haut St Antoine seemed to take precedence over everything, rendering Yvette Montreuil's murder just another banal incident in the day-to-day vendettas of its inhabitants.

'Your lawyer, Mirze, do you have faith in him?'

'Théo? He's as smart as he has to be. He has good connections in the bureaucracy. Why do you ask?'

'Because you're still here. You should be out on bail.'

'Bail costs money, Monsieur.'

Ezra was about to say something but he checked himself. Jacques Verrier did not seem overly anxious to be out of jail. There had been no urgency in his request that Ezra hand over the money to his lawyer. Perhaps he felt safer in custody. Behind bars he was immune from the vengeance of Bernard Montreuil, *père et fils*.

'At the funeral your sister told me that someone had broken into your house and stolen all the *acquits verts* for your Beaujolais Nouveau.'

The information did not seem to upset Verrier who merely sighed and shook his head.

'Your sister was all right. She was out on an errand when it happened.'

'I don't know what the world is coming to, Monsieur. There was a time when you could leave your doors wide open and no one would think of entering your home uninvited.'

'I'm told I can't ship your wine out of the country without papers,' said Ezra, underwhelmed by Verrier's vacuous flight of nostalgia.

'When you go through customs maybe you could use those papers with Marianne printed on them. Preferably in large denominations.'

Ezra smiled. Marianne, he recalled from his reading, was the bare-breasted symbol of the French Revolution featured on the country's banknotes. Her bust was modelled on those of prominent actresses such as Brigitte Bardot and Catherine Deneuve. The shape changed every ten years according to the current sex goddess. How very French. There would be a revolt of a very different kind if a Canadian bill featured a naked woman. Nor could he imagine Canadian actresses lining up for the distinction of having their mammary glands immortalized by the Mint.

But bribing an official could be dangerous. He could just see the headline in his own newspaper: 'Wine Writer Arrested For Beaujolais Bribe.'

'Interesting thought but I can't risk it. How can I get the right papers?'

'Go to my neighbour, Jean-Michel Parent. Tell him what happened. He is my friend. He will try to help you.'

'Why would anyone want to steal those documents, anyway?'

Verrier shrugged.

'If they had them, they could make any early start, couldn't they,' said Ezra. 'What about that Englishman, Derek Farmiloe?' The vintner said nothing.

'He seems to be well known in the village. He comes to see you every year and every year he buys a barrel from Bernard Montreuil.'

'For his restaurant,' said Verrier, raising his palms upwards in a dismissive gesture.

'Your wine and Montreuil's barrel,' mused Ezra.

'*Non*, Monsieur,' said Verrier, straightening up in his chair. 'My wine, my barrel. He buys my wine in my barrel.'

A buzzer sounded in the room startling Ezra. The guard stepped forward and placed a hand on his shoulder indicating to him that it was time to end the visit.

Ezra rose and shook Verrier's proffered hand.

'Thank you,' he said. 'I know whom to talk to now.'

It was early afternoon when Ezra left the police station in Villefranche. He realized he had eaten nothing since his breakfast croissant before the funeral but his mounting excitement outweighed his hunger. The one piece of information he had gleaned from the vintner promised a new avenue of enquiry. Farmiloe bought Jacques Verrier's Beaujolais-Villages Nouveau in a barrel, yet each year he purchased another barrel from Bernard Montreuil. Why would he go to the added expense?

He had seen Farmiloe emerging from the shadows of the cooperage. The restaurateur seemed to know his way around very well and Ezra recalled his drawling voice, saying, 'I come to Beaujolais quite a lot. I count them as friends, the Montreuil family.' Perhaps Yvette Montreuil had been a better friend than the two male members of the family. The way Farmiloe had treated the young Bernard suggested an intimacy that could only have grown over a long association. Was he the other man who gave money to help with the boy's medical bills?

Farmiloe had come to the winery that morning and argued with Verrier. Moments later Yvette Montreuil's body had been dropped through the trapdoor into the cellar. A tool from Bernard Montreuil's cooperage had been driven into the wood to act as a handle – and left there. Montreuil would have hardly incriminated himself and no artisan would willingly give up one of his tools. It had to be someone who had access to the cooperage without arousing suspicion.

Should he alert Inspector Chasselas? No, he decided. He needed more proof. He could not connect the Englishman with the attempts on his own life. Unless Farmiloe was part of a much larger conspiracy that involved the entire village.

But was he just being paranoid? The falling wine pallet could have been accidental and the man on the motor bike a bizarre happening. Yet both incidents had occurred within minutes of each other.

These thoughts crowded through his head as he drove at speed along the autoroute. Where would Farmiloe be now?

Since he had already chosen his Nouveau it was unlikely he would be tasting in other cellars. Most probably he was still with Bernard Montreuil. Ezra shifted gears as the turn-off sign to Belleville flashed by. He would head straight for the cooperage. But should he drop off the envelope at Mirze's office first? He did not enjoy the idea of carrying around a large sum of someone else's money since the robbery.

Something in Marie-Claire's account of the incident came back to him. Why had he not caught the inconsistency immediately? She had said that Jacques' desk was open and yet he had seen how carefully she had locked it after taking out the envelope of money.

And she had left the back door unlocked at night when she went to fetch her weekly order of eggs. It just wasn't in character. She was a frightened, suspicious woman all by herself in the house. Surely she would have locked the door. And she wore the key to the desk round her neck. The thief would have had to break the lock to get in. Nothing else was missing which suggested whoever stole the papers knew exactly what they were looking for.

At Belleville he took the northern route that swung around north of the city avoiding its centre. On the N6 he turned north to the village of St-Jean d'Ardières and west towards Pizay. The sun was shining and on both sides of the road the sleeping vineyards stretched into the distance. To his right was a long, straight avenue of trees that defined the driveway to the Château de Pizay, a fourteenth-century castle set in formal gardens whose hedges were trimmed like show poodles.

The road to Morgon was straight and unobstructed so

197

Ezra put his foot to the floor, enjoying the speed and the rush of wind through the open windows. But he was forced to slow down after a few kilometres as he approached Morgon at which point the road began to bend and climb into the foothills.

In the distance, to his left, he could see a car parked under a tree at the side of the road. As he approached he noticed the driver's door was open. There was steam rising from the bonnet and the front end was a twisted mass of metal buried in the trunk of an oak tree.

Ezra brought the Citroën to a halt, reversed onto the grass verge and stepped out into the road. The countryside was deserted. It was almost as if the car had been placed there at the base of the tree. There were no skid marks on the tarmac. Nothing to indicate the driver had tried to avoid a collision at full speed with the tree.

He moved towards the wrecked car. It was a dark green Jaguar with British licence plates. The windscreen was smashed on the driver's side and as Ezra approached, he saw a foot protruding through the open door. The sole of the shoe was pathetically white and the leather hardly scratched as if the wearer had just purchased them. With a sickening sense of foreboding he leant forward and peered into the car.

Lying across the front seat, his head bleeding profusely onto the tan leather, was Derek Farmiloe.

Ezra felt his stomach churn. He wanted to be sick. He placed a hand on the car roof to support himself. The sun was shining white in the sky. A crow flapped its wings on a bough above his head. Smoke rose from the chimney of a farmhouse half-way up the hill to his left. The world went about its business oblivious to the body and the mangled car.

The engine was still idling and Ezra feared that there might be an explosion so he reached across the body and turned off the ignition. As he did so he brushed against the glove compartment door which, weakened by the impact of the collision, sprung open. The sensation of the walnut door hitting his elbow made him start. Inside, resting under a can of leather polish, was a map. Ezra took it out. It had been folded open to a prescribed route. A network of roads from Haut St Antoine going north had been marked in a red felt pen. The thick red line avoided the motorway and major highways, sticking to back roads, skirting the villages of Fleurie, Moulin-à-Vent, Chénas, Juliénas and St Amour. The line stopped at Calais.

It must be the fast route for the Beaujolais race Farmiloe had talked about, thought Ezra.

He stuffed the map into his coat pocket and tried to avoid looking at the bloody face of Derek Farmiloe.

The man had obviously not attempted to stop. Otherwise there would have been rubber marks on the road. The surface was dry; visibility was perfect. Why had he crashed? Was it suicide?

He forced himself to take another look inside the car. The Jaguar was a right-hand drive. Farmiloe was lying in a distended position across the seat, his left leg on the floor wedged between the accelerator and the brake and his right projected out of the door on the driver's side. Either he had had his foot hard on the accelerator, in which case it would have been suicide, or he had been trying to stop but the brakes would not respond.

He bent down, careful to avoid the blood, and tried to depress the brake pedal with his hand. It was wedged against Farmiloe's ankle. He pushed the foot forward to free it and tried the brake again. It went straight to the floor without any resistance.

Derek Farmiloe had been driving a car with no brakes.

Ezra looked for the seat belt. It had broken away on impact. Or had the attachment been tampered with?

He slid the clip into the slot and heard a faint click. With a sharp movement he tugged on the buckle and it came away from its clasp.

There was no doubt in his mind that Derek Farmiloe's car had been fixed to kill him.

Ezra carefully opened the door to the back seat and looked inside. There was a faint lemony odour which emanated from the leather seat. It was immaculately clean as if it had been freshly polished. He noticed a faint discoloration on the armrest by the door behind the driver's seat. Then his eye caught sight of a long hair held between the tan leather and the chrome door handle plate.

It was a red hair, the colour of Yvette Montreuil's.

In the distance Ezra could hear the pam-pon, pam-pon of an oncoming siren. It sounded grotesquely comic to his ears, like a cartoon donkey. But it made him feel guilty, as if its braying implicated him in Farmiloe's death, accusing him of murder.

He stood by the side of the crash watching a black Citroën approach. The car drew up twenty feet away and

Inspector Chasselas stepped out of the back seat. His driver remained at the wheel. Chasselas was followed by a uniformed gendarme with a camera. A machine-gun dangled from a leather strap across his shoulder.

'Monsieur Brant,' said the Inspector, as he approached the Jaguar. 'Wherever my job takes me I find you. Now do you mind stepping aside and letting me do my work.'

Ezra stood speechless as the policeman walked briskly to the car. Before he looked inside he turned to Ezra and said, 'Wait here. I have some questions for you.'

Ezra watched him as he bent down to examine the interior of the car. Chasselas shook his head and ordered the uniformed officer to photograph the body. Ezra could not hear the low conversation between them because the sound of a second siren battered the still afternoon air. A cream-coloured ambulance came to a shuddering halt near the Jaguar and two uniformed men alighted from the back carrying a collapsible stretcher. Behind them, easing himself gently to the ground, came Dr Fournier holding a worn black leather bag.

The old man bowed to Ezra when he recognized him. He shook his hand and then proceeded to the car without a word.

'Is he dead?' Chasselas demanded.

Fournier placed his leather bag on the roof of the Jaguar, opened it and took out his stethoscope. He fixed it around his neck like a chain of office and knelt down. Ezra could see him press his fingers against the pulse of Farmiloe's left wrist and then behind his ear. Chasselas shuffled his feet impatiently as if he already knew the answer to his question

201

and was merely awaiting corroboration from the medical expert.

Fournier straightened up and nodded.

'Body bag,' said Chasselas to the stretcher bearers who disappeared into the ambulance in search of one.

'Dr Fournier, will you issue the certificate? You can drop it by my office at your earliest convenience.'

Dismissed, Fournier nodded, shook hands with the Inspector and walked slowly back to the ambulance.

'Now, Monsieur.' Chasselas turned to face him. 'Death seems to follow you about like a pet dog.'

'So it would seem.'

'If I were a superstitious man I'd say that you are bad luck or perhaps even dangerous. May I ask how you came to be here?'

'I was driving back from Villefranche and there it was.'

'Ah yes, you went to visit your friend, Jacques Verrier.'

'You are very well informed, Inspector.'

Chasselas smiled. 'I would find a more secure hiding place for his money than the hotel safe, Monsieur.'

Ezra cursed himself silently. The guard who witnessed his conversation with Verrier had not spoken English but the interrogation room must have been bugged. Why had he not anticipated that? He tried to recall his conversation.

Chasselas relished his victory for a moment as he watched Ezra's discomfort. And then he continued, 'Did you witness the accident?'

'No.'

'How long have you been here?'

'I arrived two minutes before you did. I tried to see if

there was anything I could do and then I was going to call for help.'

'We will continue this conversation in my office,' said Chasselas. 'You will follow me, please.'

The paramedics had removed Farmiloe's body from the Jaguar and zipped it into a body bag. They placed it on the stretcher and hoisted it into the back of the ambulance.

Chasselas watched the operation, then returned to his car and sat in the back seat. The driver started the engine and Ezra could see his eyes in his rearview mirror waiting for him to pull out onto the roadway.

Ezra was sandwiched between the ambulance and the police car as the procession moved up the incline towards the village. He felt as if he were under arrest.

At least the five-minute drive gave him a chance to think. Chasselas could not presume that he had anything to do with Farmiloe's death. The Inspector knew his movements. He had been driving back from the jail when the accident occurred. Farmiloe had been coming from the opposite direction to him. Yet the last thing he had said to Verrier in the interrogation room was that he knew whom to talk to now. From that exchange Chasselas could have guessed that it was Derek Farmiloe he was going to see.

He wondered if they had sufficient grounds to detain him. The evidence against Jacques Verrier had been flimsy enough yet he was still languishing in jail.

Ezra took the Englishman's route map out of his pocket and slid it under his seat. He did not want to give Chasselas any reason to make him more suspicious than he already was. He thought of locking Marie-Claire's envelope in the glove compartment but decided against it.

The black Citroën pulled into the compound behind the police station. Ezra followed, glancing in his mirror to see if the ambulance was still there. But it had continued on, probably going directly to the morgue, he thought.

The village square was full of activity. Banners had been strung from the trees announcing the arrival of the new Beaujolais. The cafés were crowded with tourists and truck drivers. Young blond men wearing World War One flying helmets and jodhpurs, their faces painted purple, competed with each other as to who could swallow their wine the fastest. Others dressed as clowns rollerskated in the roadway to the amusement of the old men in berets who sat in their habitual seats near the fountain. Sports cars, bearing plates from all over Europe, nudged their way through the narrow streets, the drivers honking their horns at the women on the pavements. A carnival atmosphere had gripped the village. By midnight the revellers would be hellbent for the French coast or the Swiss and German borders with their booty of Beaujolais Nouveau.

Seated in Chasselas' office, Ezra felt as though he had been summoned before the headmaster. His circumstances reminded him of Trinity College. He was fifteen. He had been caught with a bottle of Sauternes in his room. Henry, as the boys used to call the stern, taciturn principal, had beaten him with a cane for this transgression, although he seemed more interested in finding out who the shipper was and the vintage of the wine. Ezra had left the book-lined study, cluttered with overstuffed leather furniture, holding back tears of pain. At the door Henry had said, 'Next time, chill the wine before you drink it. Sauternes should be served cold.'

Chasselas looked nothing like Henry who was bald and had the solemn expression of a Methodist preacher but the way the policeman stood at the window, gazing out through the slats of the venetian blind at the activity in the square, reminded Ezra of his old nemesis.

'Tell me again exactly how you found Monsieur Farmiloe.'

'I've told you three times, Inspector.'

'Once more, if you please.'

'I dropped my wife off at the station in Mâcon, then I drove to Villefranche to see Jacques Verrier.'

'And the time of the train you said was 1335 hours.'

'That's right.'

'And which platform did the train leave from?'

'Platform eight.'

'Go on.'

'I drove to Villefranche and asked directions to the police station.'

'What time was that?'

'It must have been a little after two. I saw Jacques Verrier and we must have talked for about twenty minutes before a buzzer sounded and I was told to leave.'

'And you did.'

'Yes.'

'Where did you intend going?'

There was no point in avoiding the truth. Chasselas had already been informed of the conversation in the interrogation room.

'I was going to see Derek Farmiloe.'

'For what purpose?'

'I thought he could help clear Jacques.'

'And what made you believe that?'

'He was at the winery when the body of Yvette Montreuil was dropped into the cellar. I heard them arguing.'

'You heard them arguing. But you did not see Monsieur Farmiloe.'

'No.'

'Then how do you know it was him?'

'There was a smell of a very distinctive aftershave in the hallway where they had been standing. I smelled it again that night at the Compagnons de Beaujolais dinner. On Derek Farmiloe.'

The sun glinted on the policeman's moon-shaped glasses and Ezra could not see his eyes but his lips were smiling. He knew what was coming. Connie always joked that in the next life he would come back as a bloodhound.

'Maybe your Canadian legal system is different, Monsieur, but French courts would not accept such evidence as conclusive proof that Derek Farmiloe was the man you say you heard arguing with Jacques Verrier. I have been in the police force for over thirty years but never have I seen one of our tracker dogs take the witness stand.'

Chasselas sat down at his desk, pleased with himself. Ezra shifted uncomfortably in his chair.

'And now, of course, we cannot corroborate your story because Derek Farmiloe is dead,' continued Chasselas.

'I'd say murdered,' countered Ezra.

'I am talking about murder, Monsieur. But I'm curious to know why you are too.'

Ezra could see the trap. If he told Chasselas that he had tried the brakes then he could be accused of tampering with evidence. Chasselas might find grounds to jail him for that alone.

'Because there were no tyre marks on the road. If it had been an accident there would have been skid marks.'

'Exactly. And do you know why there were no skid marks?'

'I imagine the brakes failed.'

'They didn't fail, Monsieur. They were cut.'

'Then it is murder.'

'Yes. And there is another small detail.'

Chasselas rose and crossed to the window. He faced Ezra so that the light was behind him and his eyes were in shadow.

'Your fingerprints were found on the car.'

'I might have touched it, yes.'

'Let me put it another way, there were only two sets of prints found on the car. Derek Farmiloe's and yours.'

'What possible reason would I have for wanting Farmiloe dead?'

'Maybe you did not smell his aftershave. Maybe you saw him and he saw you. With the body of Yvette Montreuil.'

Ezra rose from his chair.

'I don't have to take this crap from you, Inspector. You

can't intimidate me. If you had the slightest proof of what you're saying you'd have me arrested. So don't come near me again unless you've got a warrant. If you harass me once more I'm going to call my embassy in Paris and have them take the matter up with your bosses at the Quai d'Orsay. Including the phoney wine your co-operative's pedalling too. Am I coming through loud and clear?'

Chasselas took a step closer to Ezra. His lips were pursed and he was breathing heavily through his nose.

'I strongly advise you to leave Haut St Antoine, Monsieur,' said Chasselas acidly. 'Unpleasant things happen when you are around.'

'I can't be out of here soon enough for my liking,' stormed Ezra. 'Good day.'

As he crossed the square to Le Sarment d'Or, Ezra began formulating his plan of attack. He would call upon Jean-Michel Parent, Verrier's neighbour, and find out if he could help him get the necessary documentation for the Beaujolais Nouveau. Then he would drop Marie-Claire's envelope off to Théophile Mirze. He would pack, have dinner and then pick up the wine from Verrier's cellar. He would have to sacrifice the idea of bringing back a barrel. A case of a dozen bottles would have to suffice but at least it would be easier to handle.

At midnight he would join the race using Farmiloe's route north. He would arrange to meet Connie west of Paris, leave the car at the dock in Calais, take the ferry to Dover and then on by train and taxi to the embassy in London. He made a mental note to call ahead the London bureau to ensure that there was a photographer on the steps to record the moment.

'My key, please.'

Madame Barrière smiled at him from behind the desk. She was wearing a pink angora sweater which made her look as if she were thrusting herself forward as a candidate for the next printing of French banknotes.

'You have a message, Monsieur,' she said, as she slid the key across the counter. 'It's from your wife.'

'May I have it?' he said irritably.

Why did everyone have to know his business before he did?

'It's in your room.'

Ezra climbed the stairs. He realized he had not thought about Connie since his meeting with Verrier. She had probably found herself a hotel near the Sorbonne and was reliving her student memories. She never spoke much about those days but she had insisted that Michael take French immersion at school when the programme had first been introduced in Toronto. After eight years Michael still refused to speak French in front of them. They had driven to Quebec City one holiday to see how he fared in Canada's other language. Ezra had sent him to ask directions from a hotel doorman. Michael had returned blushing furiously, protesting that he could not understand a word the man said.

The message, written in a microscopic hand, was brief. 'Call me between six and six-fifteen. Room number 21,' and then a Paris telephone number.

Ezra checked his watch. It was already well after six. Connie would be sitting on the edge of her bed, staring at the phone, willing it to ring. He dialled the number but the line went dead. The same thing happened at his second attempt so he called down to the desk.

Monsieur Barrière answered.

'I can't seem to get a line to Paris,' he said.

'That is because all long-distance numbers must go through this switchboard, Monsieur,' said the laconic proprietor.

Sure, thought Ezra, so you can keep track of everything that's going on.

Connie answered on the second ring.

'You're late,' she said.

Ezra sighed.

'Oh, I know that sigh. You have the most eloquent sighs of anyone I know. They speak volumes. That one said, "You have no idea what I've been through today, woman. While you've been gallivanting around Paris, I've been . . ."'

'Connie, I'm not in the mood. Where are you?'

'A little dump on the Left Bank. Rue Henri Cinq. You have no idea how expensive Paris is. You're going to die when you see my hotel bill, darling.'

'Forget about the hotel bill.'

'Well. Something really must be on your mind.'

'Derek Farmiloe's dead.'

'You mean the owner of Beaujolais Bistrol? I was just speaking to his restaurant manager. How did it happen?'

'A car crash. The brakes of his car were cut.'

'Oh my God. That's horrible.'

'What did he say?'

'Who?'

'The manager, dammit.'

'There's no need to get shirty, Ezra. I asked him if he would be serving Beaujolais Nouveau tomorrow and he said they haven't had it for five years.'

'What do you mean?'

'They haven't sold it for five years. He said they only serve the *crus* now, whatever that means.'

'The wines named after the ten villages. They're not allowed to make it *nouveau* style.'

He realized he was lecturing again and Connie had probably mentally tuned out, studying her nails until he had finished.

'Are you sure it was The Beaujolais Bistro?'

'Well, that's how the man answered the phone so I was left with the distinct impression that it was, hon. Are you still there?'

Ezra was thinking. If the bistro had not served Beaujolais Nouveau for five years what had Farmiloe been doing with the wine he had raced back to London each year?

'Did the manager say anything else?'

'Something about the customers complaining because the wine tasted funny so they never ordered it again.'

For five years Farmiloe had a special barrel made with his restaurant name stencilled on the head and yet the wine was never served from the barrel.

His silence on the end of the line unnerved Connie.

'Ezra, you've got to get out of there. Forget about the

stupid race. Just drive to Paris. You could be here in time for dinner. There's a lovely little bistro just round the corner I used to eat at when I was a student.'

'I can't.'

'Why not? Why are you being so pig-headed?'

'I have an assignment.'

'Nobody's going to think any the less of you if you don't bring back the wine. Hell, you can buy it in Paris tomorrow morning.'

'That's not the point.'

'What is the point?'

'I'm not running away. I came here to do something and I'm going to do it.'

'You have a son back in Toronto, if you haven't forgotten, and then there's me whom you once promised to cherish till death do us part. Why are you risking your life?'

'Because an innocent man is in jail. And now they're trying to implicate me.'

'All the more reason you should get out now, Ezra. Please.'

'I'll be leaving at midnight. I should make Versailles in four hours. I will meet you at the war memorial in the main square. I'll wait for you. Get a taxi out there but be sure and get a receipt.'

'Honestly, Ezra, this whole thing is childish.'

'Just do as I ask. Did you find out anything from the lawyer?'

'I called saying I was the executive assistant to a New York developer who was interested in buying a winery in

Beaujolais. I needed to find a lawyer who could make enquiries about properties for sale in Haut St Antoine. The secretary was very helpful at first. She said it was quite a coincidence because she was just typing some papers relating to that village. I asked her if she could tell me who was interested because one of my boss's competitors had got wind of his intention and wanted to get in first. She said it was a French name. Mirze. Isn't he the funny little lawyer?'

'Darling, you're wonderful.'

'Of course I am. Now please, Ezra, take care.'

'Listen. This call is costing a fortune, so I'll say goodbye and see you in Versailles.'

'Charming. Goodbye.'

So it was Théophile Mirze who was after Verrier's estate. No wonder the shifty little lawyer was making the most perfunctory of efforts to get his client released from jail. The deeper the vintner became mired in legal quicksands the more expensive his extrication would become and the more debt he would incur.

Verrier was obviously mortgaged to the hilt to pay for the new equipment in his cellar. He owed money to Montreuil for his new barrels, a debt his sister had secretly tried to settle. Was it money she had been saving for her dowry or some jewellery she had sold?

He took the envelope from his pocket and held it up to the light. It was time to visit Théophile Mirze.

The bed creaked as he rose to his feet. He slipped the envelope back into his pocket and was about to head for the door when the telephone rang.

'Monsieur?'

It was the hotel proprietor.

'Yes.'

'There is a gentleman here to see you.'

'I'll be right down.'

'He is waiting for you in the lounge.'

'Thank you.'

As Ezra descended the staircase Monsieur Barrière indicated a room along a dark corridor beyond the reception desk. Ezra had not seen it before. There was a television in one corner surrounded by an odd assortment of sofas and chairs. In the centre was a card table with an unfinished jigsaw puzzle. Standing over it with a frown of concentration on his face as he tried to fit in a piece was Paul de Blancourt.

'Ah, Monsieur!'

He greeted Ezra as if it was the first time he had seen him that day.

'What can I do for you, Monsieur de Blancourt?'

The sight of the handsome, smiling face annoyed him. There was something overly solicitous about the man as if he was practising his charm to ensure that it was firing on all cylinders.

'Do you do jigsaw puzzles? I find them very relaxing. Not as demanding as chess problems but each piece brings you closer to a solution. There is nothing more satisfying than that, don't you agree?'

'You didn't come here for jigsaw puzzles.'

'No, I have a proposition. One that may solve your problem and will help me too.'

'What's that?'

'Please, let's sit down. That's better. How shall I begin?'

'At the beginning.'

De Blancourt smiled, undaunted by Ezra's cold demeanour.

'Haut St Antoine is a little village, Monsieur. We live in each other's pockets. Like small change constantly rubbing up against each other. So naturally when something happens we all get to know about it.'

'I'm listening.'

'There is gossip, of course. Sometimes what you hear is true, sometimes not. I am hearing that you cannot take Jacques Verrier's wine out of France because you do not have the necessary papers.'

'They were stolen last night from his house.'

'Yes, I heard that too. You are probably aware of the regrettable accident that occurred earlier today. An Englishman was killed in a car crash. But then, of course, you know. It was you whom the police found at the scene.'

'You are remarkably well informed, Monsieur de Blancourt.'

'As I told you, it is a very small village.'

'So you said.'

De Blancourt nodded.

'His name was Farmiloe and he owned a restaurant in London. For many years now he used to buy a barrel of Jacques Verrier Beaujolais-Villages Nouveau. Since he is no longer in a position to join the race, I suggest that you do it for him. After all, that is why you came here, no?'

215

The suggestion caught Ezra off guard. He needed time to think. Why would de Blancourt want him to step into Farmiloe's shoes? And why did he want to ensure that Verrier's wine would reach The Beaujolais Bistro when the restaurant had not sold Beaujolais Nouveau for years? He would learn more, he decided, if he appeared to co-operate with de Blancourt.

'What about the papers?'

De Blancourt took an envelope from his pocket and handed it to Ezra. Inside was the *acquit vert* relating to the sale of one twenty-litre barrel of Verrier Beaujolais-Villages Nouveau to The Beaujolais Bistro. The papers were signed by Jacques Verrier and dated midnight, 18 November.

Ezra grappled with the implications. Marie-Claire had said that all the documentation relating to the sale of her brother's wine had been stolen. How had they come into de Blancourt's possession?

'The papers are in order, I assure you,' said the Frenchman, taking them back from Ezra. 'Come up to the château at eleven o'clock tonight. Check out of your hotel and be prepared to leave from there. Everything will be ready. You'll get the papers and the wine then.'

'My assignment is to bring back Beaujolais Nouveau for a reception at the Canadian embassy in London,' said Ezra.

'Well, that can be arranged. If you are willing to deliver the barrel to The Beaujolais Bistro then I will personally buy a case of *nouveau* for your reception. My gift to you.'

'We have an expression back home, Monsieur de

Blancourt. Not very elegant but it cuts through all the bullshit. What's in it for you?'

De Blancourt nodded.

'Let's just say it is a debt of honour. Derek Farmiloe used to come to buy wine in Haut St Antoine every year. You might say he gave his life for that. It is the least we could do to show our gratitude. As a fellow Compagnon de Beaujolais I'm sure you will agree.'

Hypocrite, said Ezra to himself.

'One other thing. If you are going to enter the race you will need a faster car than your Citroën. I would be happy to lend you my Maserati for the trip. I can have it picked up in Calais and I will make arrangements to have the Citroën returned to the rental agency. If you like I will have a car waiting for you in Dover. Will you do it?'

The idea of racing through the French countryside at night in a red Maserati had enormous appeal for Ezra. He could just picture Connie's face as he roared into the main square in Versailles at four o'clock in the morning with de Blancourt's car.

'It sounds very tempting,' he said.

'And your charming wife,' said de Blancourt. 'You will be meeting her *en route*, I suppose?'

Ezra stood up. He ignored de Blancourt's outstretched hand.

'Eleven o'clock then.'

When de Blancourt had left he sat down in an over-stuffed armchair, lost in thought. Murder, theft, fraud, vendettas, jealousies. This village was a living soap opera. Yvette

Montreuil, Farmiloe. What was the connection between their deaths and the attempts on his own life? Who had torched Bernard Montreuil's cooperage and why? Who benefited from Jacques Verrier's conviction for Yvette's murder? Who had stolen the papers from Marie-Claire and how did they come into Paul de Blancourt's possession? And why was the wealthy Frenchman so anxious for him to drive the Farmiloe's barrel to London? Was he being set up for the final betrayal?

The questions floated through his mind like helium-filled balloons. There was nothing solid to hold them down. If there were only something he could be sure of, some anchor to stop the questions multiplying. But there were no answers. No pattern emerged however hard he concentrated on what he knew of the events in Haut St Antoine. Nothing made sense any more. But there had to be something that would pull it all together, one fact that would forge the link between Verrier, the murders and the conspiracy of silence among the villagers.

Perhaps Connie was right. He should get out now before it was too late. He was out of his depth. By accepting de Blancourt's proposition he would be forced to see the matter through. But there must be a connection between every incident that had occurred since his arrival in the village.

Should he alert Inspector Chasselas? De Blancourt was in possession of stolen documents. But the police chief had dismissed Ezra's earlier allegations that his life had been threatened. Chasselas would be only too happy to see him leave Haut St Antoine to protect the good name of the village. The words Marie-Claire Verrier had uttered at the funeral came back to him: 'I don't trust any of them.'

Ezra had come to the same conclusion.

But he had to protect himself and ensure that the story would be told. He returned to his room and took the laptop computer from his suitcase. Balancing it on his knees he began to write an account of his three days in Haut St Antoine, beginning with the encounter with Yvette Montreuil as he drove into the village. On his way to see Théophile Mirze at his office in Fleurie, he would pass by the local post office and fax his story direct to his newspaper's London office. If anything should happen to him *en route* to meet Connie in Versailles they would know where to start investigating.

But when he arrived in Fleurie the post office was closed.

Théophile Mirze was just about to lock his office door as Ezra pulled up in front. He wound down the car window and called to him. The lawyer seemed discomfited by his sudden appearance, glancing up and down the street before motioning him inside.

Mirze sat down behind his desk with his overcoat on. Papers were strewn across every inch of the surface.

'I don't think you've been straightforward with me, Monsieur Mirze,' Ezra began.

'Oh?'

'Yes. And I'm sick and tired of being lied to. I want some answers. Why is Jacques Verrier still in jail? You know he's innocent.'

'The due process of law, Monsieur,' replied Mirze, visibly uncomfortable. 'There are technicalities.'

'If you mean money, then here's money,' said Ezra, withdrawing the envelope from his inside pocket and throwing it on the desk.

Mirze stared at the package but made no move to pick it up.

'Open it,' commanded Ezra.

'But it's addressed to Bernard Montreuil.'

'Just open it.'

'How did you get this?'

'Jacques' sister gave it to me. I tried to deliver it but I didn't have the opportunity. I saw Jacques this afternoon. He told me to bring it to you.'

'You saw Jacques?'

'Yes. Now open the envelope because I want a written receipt for its contents. You see, I'm learning fast around here.'

Mirze picked up the envelope, held it lengthways and tapped it against the desk. Then he tore a strip off the edge, careful to avoid ripping through the stamp. He pressed the edges until it swelled out into a concave shape and glanced inside.

'You're right, it is money.'

He withdrew a wad of banknotes secured with an elastic band. Tucked inside was an invoice. Mirze counted the bills with the expertise of a bank teller.

'There are ten thousand francs here,' he said.

Ezra picked up the invoice and read it. There was a schedule of monthly payments listed. The first, due two months ago was for eight thousand francs. The total amount was for ninety-six thousand francs. Odd, thought,

Ezra, that Marie-Claire would pay more than the monthly amount.

He handed the invoice back to Mirze who slipped it around the bills and replaced the elastic band. Then the lawyer stood up and crossed the room to a corner table. It was draped to the floor with a damask table cloth. On top was a lamp which he lifted and with his other hand he pulled back the cloth revealing a safe underneath. Placing the lamp on the floor, he knelt down and began to work the combination lock. When it clicked, he swung the heavy door open, placed the envelope inside, locked it again and replaced the cloth and the lamp. He sat down at the desk again and took a receipt book from the top drawer. With meticulous care he squared up a piece of carbon paper between the two top sheets and began to write.

Ezra had two questions he wanted to put to Mirze. He decided to lead with the more innocuous one.

'Your uncle, Eric Mirze, sold his estate to the co-operative. That's how they got started, right?'

'Yes, Monsieur.'

'He would have got a better price for it if he had sold it privately, wouldn't he?'

'Perhaps.'

'Land in Beaujolais is not easy to come by, I'm told. Families don't sell unless they have to.'

'My uncle was a socialist,' said Mirze with obvious disdain. He tore the receipt from the book and waved it three times to dry the ink.

'There you are.'

221

He handed Ezra the piece of paper.

'He's dead now, isn't he?'

'Yes, heart trouble. Three years ago.'

'There was some talk in the village that he was prescribed the wrong medicine.'

The lawyer's head jerked up sharply. The shadows thrown by the green-shaded lamp on the desk accentuated the size of his nose.

'He died in his sleep, Monsieur.'

'Then why was there a question about Dr Fournier giving him the wrong medicine?'

'Malicious gossip. No one can die a natural death in Haut St Antoine.'

'I thought you said your village was Les Versaud.'

'I was born in Les Versaud, Monsieur. My family owned property in Haut St Antoine and here in Fleurie. Now, if you will excuse me.'

'One other question before I go. You told me that someone is trying to buy Jacques Verrier's estate. I've made enquiries in Paris at the law firm. They say the anonymous buyer is a man called Mirze.'

The lawyer blanched visibly.

'Wouldn't you say that's a conflict of interest? Defending Jacques Verrier against a murder charge and trying to buy his property at the same time?'

'You do not understand, Monsieur.'

'Oh, I understand. It suits your purposes very well that he stays in jail. Well, you can damn well get him off the hook with that money or I'm going to have you disbarred. I'll take it to whatever passes for a law society in this place.'

Mirze cleared his throat and rubbed the tips of his fingers together.

'It is not what it seems, Monsieur. It is not me who is making offers on Jacques' estate. I am acting for another party in the matter.'

Mirze had begun to perspire but even under pressure he phrased his responses in legal jargon.

'Who?'

'I am not at liberty to say.'

'Jacques Verrier is not at liberty either. And I care more about that than your goddammed lawyer's confidentiality.'

He stood up and clenched his fists more as a threatening gesture than as a prelude to physical violence. The effect on Mirze was immediate and dramatic. He threw up his hands in front of his face and cowered down in his chair, gibbering with fear.

'Don't hit me! I'll tell you but please don't hit me!'

In that moment Ezra recognized the terror of a child about to be physically abused by an enraged and brutal father. He felt a wave of pity for the cowering figure in front of him as he sat down and waited for Mirze to regain his composure.

'You are right. My uncle sold land to the co-operative but he did not sell it for its full commercial value. He made a deal with them. In return for the land they would make him director-general for life. My father got nothing. When my Uncle Eric died he left money to my father in his will asking his forgiveness. He instructed him to use the bequest to buy a property of his own. My father only wanted the best. He chose Jacques' estate. I told him Jacques would never sell but he was obsessed with it. He will not stop until he gets what he wants. He made me start proceedings, conduct a search, draw up deeds of sale. Everything. I tried to keep putting him off because one day he will die. He is an old man.'

'But can't you get some psychiatric help?'

'No, Monsieur. He is my father.'

The two men sat staring at each other, not speaking. Outside in the street heavy trucks were rumbling down the main street of Fleurie. Men were shouting and the scouring sound of rollerskates on flagstones could be heard beyond the window.

Ezra wondered what was going on behind the black eyes now bright with tears. No doubt, Mirze was recalling the beatings his father had administered and the bond of terror that still bound him to the old man.

The mood was broken by the jangling of the telephone. Mirze fumbled with the instrument as he picked it up. He spoke softly into the mouthpiece. The caller seemed to be asking a string of questions because the lawyer answered in monosyllables, mostly saying 'no'. When he replaced the receiver on its cradle there was a half-smile on his lips.

'That was Inspector Chasselas,' he said. 'Jacques Verrier has escaped from jail.'

Chapter Nine

Ezra called Verrier's number but there was no reply. If Jacques had gone to the farmhouse he had probably instructed his sister not to answer the phone. He decided to drive there. Marie-Claire might tell him where Jacques was hiding and why he had escaped.

Darkness had fallen and a light mist hung over the damp earth. The air was cold but the village of Fleurie was alive with activity. The streets were choked with cars and there were people everywhere, spilling out of the cafés and *caves*, glass in hand, to celebrate the official moment of birth of the new Beaujolais.

Ezra picked his way through the crowds to the edge of the village and drove south along a winding road towards Haut St Antoine. Trucks were backing into the courtyards of the wineries along his route, preparing to load up for the midnight start.

As he drove he tried to put himself in the mind of Jacques Verrier. Why had he decided to escape at this time? He seemed relaxed to the point of indolence earlier in the day. He must have learned something that compelled him to risk his life by breaking out of jail. Did he know who killed Yvette? Was he about to take justice into his own hands and revenge himself on her killer? Or did he feel his position was hopeless and that he was going to be jailed for life as her murderer?

He glanced in his rearview mirror, wondering whether he was being followed. With all the commotion in the region it would be difficult to keep a tail on him, he decided. But he had to be careful. He would park the car out of sight of Verrier's house and walk there in case the police had it staked out, waiting for him to return.

Ezra backed the car off the road and turned out the lights. He locked the doors and began to walk up the slope to the farmhouse. The dampness in the air cut through the heavy material of his coat and he found himself shivering. He could smell the earth and the smoke rising from chimneys.

Verrier's house was in darkness. Marie-Claire would not want tourists rolling up to buy Beaujolais, he reasoned. Connie had done the same thing every Hallowe'en since Michael had passed the age when a pillowcase full of candy was the ultimate jubilation. In those years when they had participated in the annual rite they had given out raisins and peanuts and pennies much to the disgust of the neighbourhood children, donations only slightly more welcome than the toothbrushes their dentist neighbour dispensed.

Ezra stopped when he noticed a pinpoint of light flare for a moment. It illuminated the inside of a car. In the darkness he had not seen it parked in front of the house. Nor could he recognize the driver. He crouched down below the level of the wall as he heard the engine start. The sound grew louder as the car approached. He turned his face away hoping that his blue coat would meld into the darkness and he would not be seen.

He could feel the vibrations as the car accelerated down the slope and roared off at speed into the night. He looked up but only its red tail-lights were visible now. As it turned a corner the headlights lit up the ghostly vine stakes in serried rows like tombstones.

If it was Jacques Verrier he was heading in the direction of Bernard Montreuil's cooperage.

As he approached the gateway, Ezra glanced around to see if anyone was watching the house. Satisfied that he was alone, he picked his way through the muddy courtyard to the front door. He was about to raise the knocker when he remembered that Marie-Claire said she left the back door unlocked.

He felt his way around the side of the house. The stones were warm to his touch, giving up their summer heat. At the back he could see the garage in the moonlight. There was a Peugeot station wagon parked inside. If it had been Jacques driving he had not taken his own car.

Ezra worked his way around to the rear of the house. A candle was burning in the window by the back door but when he tried the handle he found it was locked. He tapped his knuckles on the wood and listened for movement inside.

Maybe Marie-Claire had gone to meet her brother

227

knowing the police would be watching the house. Or had she left in the car with the driver?

He was about to retrace his steps to the car when he heard movement behind the door. He tapped again softly, his ear to the wood.

'Jacques? Is that you? It's me. Ezra Brant. I have a receipt for the envelope you gave me,' he said, improvising quickly.

The door opened and Marie-Claire stood on the threshold, her expression a mixture of anxiety and disappointment. In her agitated frame of mind the cast in her eye seemed more pronounced.

'May I come in?'

She opened the door wide enough to let him pass and then pulled the cardigan she was wearing tightly across her chest. He went into the kitchen and sat down.

'So he hasn't been here,' said Ezra.

Marie-Claire shook her head.

'But you had visitors.'

'Inspector Chasselas and a gendarme. With a machine-gun. In my kitchen!'

She said it with a sense of outrage as if she herself had been defiled.

'What did Chasselas want?'

'He told me Jacques is in trouble. If he comes here I must tell him to give himself up.'

'Has Jacques been in touch with you yet?'

'No, Monsieur.'

He studied her face to see if she was telling the truth. Marie-Claire stared back at him, tight-lipped and defiant.

Ezra sighed and sat down at the kitchen table. She had not switched on the electricity. The only sources of light were the candle in the window and a single paraffin lamp that stood in the centre of the table. If she was telling the truth, it would not be long before Jacques did try to reach her. He would need clothes and money and maybe more.

'Tell me, Marie-Claire, and you must be honest with me if you want to help your brother, is there a gun in the house?'

'A gun?'

'Yes.'

'Jacques has a pistol. He keeps it in the drawer by his bed.'

'Will you get it for me?'

'But why, Monsieur?'

'Because I think your brother knows who killed Yvette Montreuil. That's why he broke out of jail. He might try to take matters into his own hands. And if he does, he'll make it worse for himself. You understand that, don't you?'

The woman nodded and pressed her sharp elbows against her stomach. She was shivering with cold.

'The man your brother was arguing with the morning my wife and I were here is dead.'

'The Englishman?'

'Yes, he was killed in a car crash.'

Suddenly, without warning she turned and with a little sob hurried out of the kitchen. Ezra waited for her to return. The lamp gave off a tendril of black smoke. Its wick needed trimming. He could hear her footsteps on the floor-boards above him.

Marie-Claire returned carrying the gun. She held it in the palms of both hands like an offering and placed it on the table in front of him. Ezra had expected an old army service revolver but this was a modern German Luger. He picked it up, examined the safety catch and then checked the magazine clip. It was fully loaded. He noticed that the weapon had recently been cleaned. He smelled the barrel but there was nothing to suggest that it had been fired.

'Where did he get this?'

'A German customer who comes every year traded it for some wine.'

Ezra checked the safety catch one more time before slipping it into his coat pocket.

'If Jacques should contact you, tell him that I am taking Derek Farmiloe's wine to London for him. I'm following his route up by the Solutré rock.'

Marie-Claire nodded and at the sound of a passing car her head jerked violently towards the window. But the noise died away.

'Before I go there's something I want you to show me.'

She turned towards him, frowning.

'May I see the desk where Jacques kept his papers?'

It might have been a trick of the light but Ezra was sure that Marie-Claire's colour had heightened suddenly. She picked up the oil lamp and crossed to the doorway.

'There it is.'

Ezra followed her.

'Do you mind,' he said, taking the lamp from her hands. He approached the desk and tried the handle of the roll-top. It was locked. He bent down and held the lamp close to the lock. Satisfied, he eased himself upright and returned to the kitchen. Marie-Claire had not taken her eyes off him.

He placed the lamp on the kitchen table again and studied her for a moment. 'There was no burglary, was there, Marie-Claire?' he said.

The woman turned her face in profile to him so that she could glare at him with her one good eye. She looked like an eagle in the nest protecting her young against a predator.

'Why do you say that, Monsieur?'

'You keep the desk locked. The key is still round your neck and yet there are no marks on the wood. The lock hasn't been forced.'

'Maybe I forgot to lock it.'

'I saw you lock it. You were very careful about it. But you said when you left the house to get eggs that night you didn't lock the back door. Yet tonight when you're expecting your brother the door is locked.'

He waited for her to speak but she continued to stare at him in silence. He could hear her breathing, short and sharp like a cornered animal.

'Nobody stole those documents, that's why you didn't report it to Inspector Chasselas.'

'If there was no robbery, where are the documents, Monsieur?' snapped Marie-Claire.

'Who did you give them to?'

She stood wrapped in defiant silence, arms across her

breast, hands clutching her shoulders. In the lamplight the hands looked like the claws of the rooster whose throat she had cut in her search for the truth.

Ezra sighed. He did not enjoy hectoring a defenceless woman but he knew his safety depended on the knowledge she had. He waited and when there was no reply, he said: 'You gave them to Paul de Blancourt, didn't you.'

Her shoulders sagged and she dropped her arms to her side.

'It was not like that,' said Marie-Claire. 'He came here and said he would pay me for them. I needed the money. For Jacques. To pay his debts.'

'How much did he give you?'

'I don't know. I didn't count it. He just gave me an envelope.'

'And you readdressed it to Bernard Montreuil.'

'Yes.'

'Why didn't you count it?'

'If I touched it I would have to tell the priest.'

It was too bizarre to be a lie, he thought. A woman who put her faith in a rooster as a source of information might well feel tainted if she handled money gained by subterfuge.

'What did de Blancourt say to you?'

'He told me he would pay for each *acquit vert* Jacques had signed.'

'How many were there?'

'Ten altogether.'

So he must have given her a thousand francs for each one, thought Ezra. Not bad.

232

'Did Jacques ever do business with Paul de Blancourt? Did he buy wine?'

'That was the first time I have spoken to him. He lives on the hill in the big château.'

'Did he give any reason why he wanted the papers?'

'No, Monsieur.'

'Did he tell you to come to me and say you'd been robbed?'

'Yes, Monsieur.'

Ezra felt suddenly tired. The only thing in the world that he wanted right now was to be sitting in a restaurant with Connie, far away from Haut St Antoine, a glass of wine at his elbow and the anticipation of a fine meal about to arrive. But that image blurred as a new emotion rumbled through him like thunder. He was angry. Paul de Blancourt was playing him for a fool, manipulating him for his own purposes. He could not walk away now. With Jacques Verrier a loose cannon somewhere in the countryside the situation had changed. To learn the truth he had to go along with Paul de Blancourt's scheme. But at least he was fully conscious of the dangerous predicament he had placed himself in and he now had the means to protect himself.

'If your brother comes here, tell him once I've completed my assignment for my newspaper I'll be in touch.'

'But how will I manage without him, Monsieur?'

Marie-Claire was wringing her hands; her squinting eye quivered as if trying to break out of its fixed position.

'He'll come back to you,' said Ezra gently. 'I promise.'

She ran towards him, embraced him and buried her face in his shoulder. Her body shook with sobs. He patted her back and could feel the sharp contours of her spine through the rough wool of her cardigan. As soon as he said it, he realized it was a promise he did not know how to keep.

He glanced at his watch. It was ten twenty-five p.m.

The night air fell like a naked sword. As Ezra walked back to his car he could see pockets of light illuminating the darkness of the valley. The winery parties were in full swing, the celebrants awaiting the countdown to midnight when the new wine would flow.

It amazed him how well he knew these roads now after only three days in Haut St Antoine. Even the black night, further camouflaged in veils of low-lying fog, could not confuse his sense of direction. The main thing was to avoid driving through the village whose streets were clogged with honking cars and tipsy tourists. He could hear their shouts as they called to each other in a variety of languages. How he would have liked to have been partying with them, to be laughing and joking and toasting the new vintage without a care in the world.

Looking up from the bottom of the hill towards de Blancourt's château, Ezra wondered how the night would end. The honey-coloured stones were lit up by spotlights set at the base of the wall. The play of lights draped the towers in shadow, lending them the sombre look of a Grimms' fairy-tale.

He drove slowly to postpone his arrival, trying to sort out in his mind where de Blancourt might fit into this conspiracy of murder. The smiling, handsome Frenchman, too sophisticated for a village like Haut St Antoine. Rich, poised, with too much charm for his own good. And well connected too if he could ensure that wine from a local co-op found its way onto the table of the presidential palace.

Why had he gone to such lengths to get hold of the documents? And what was his interest in Bernard Montreuil? Was he the man Yvette and Jacques Verrier argued about? The questions only seemed to pile up.

He wondered where Jacques was now. The vintner must have contacted someone he trusted. Someone who would meet him at a prearranged spot and drive him back to Haut St Antoine.

The gates to the château were open. Ezra drove in and parked the car by the fountain. Paul de Blancourt, in a tweed jacket and cavalry-twill slacks, leaned indolently against the parapet smoking a cigarette.

'Perfect timing,' he said, as he opened the car door to allow Ezra to alight. He produced a silver hip flask from his back pocket.

'Something to keep out the cold? A little Marc de Beaujolais.'

Ezra refused the offer.

'Perhaps you're wise. Even with your legendary capacity for alcohol, Monsieur Brant, you will need all your concentration for the drive. I have filled the car up for you. There are written instructions for a fast route. You'll see it traced on the map in the pouch by the driver's door. The tank is full but I advise you to top up in Dijon. That should get you to Paris. Shall we get started?'

Ezra stood immobile, scrutinizing the man who stood before him. Was this Yvette's murderer? The form he had glimpsed in the darkness from Dr Fournier's living-room? The man who had engineered the death of the English restaurateur?

'There's something I need to know before I go anywhere. How did you get hold of Derek Farmiloe's *acquit vert*?'

'Don't worry. I have one for you too. For the case of Beaujolais-Villages Nouveau I promised you.'

'But how did you get them? Marie-Claire Verrier told me they were stolen from her house.'

'They are merely pieces of paper for the functionaries, of no value in themselves. You cannot get what you want without them and neither can I. So what does it matter?'

'Two people have been murdered here, Monsieur de Blancourt, and someone has tried to kill me. But I assure you I do not intend to be a victim. My newspaper has a story ready to print if anything should happen to me. I just thought you should know that.'

The two men stood facing each other in the shadow of the walls. An image from his childhood flashed through Ezra's mind: he was in a boxing ring at his private school. He must have been eleven years old. He was facing the boy he roomed with, a friend whom he did not want to fight but Mr Mitchell, the gym teacher, who liked to feel the boys' muscles, had insisted on the bout. Mr Mitchell, wiry-haired with glasses, sang at chapel in a contratenor voice that made the boys laugh. Everyone in his class had to box and he made a special point of pitting friend against friend. 'Watch your opponent's eyes,' he used to say. 'Watch his eyes and circle away from his best punch.' It was good advice. Ezra studied de Blancourt's eyes. Even in the darkness he could see the extraordinary length of his lashes that women must have envied. Small wonder Connie had been smitten. She was always complaining that hers had as much appeal as the bristles of a nail-brush.

But behind the lashes, de Blancourt's eyes were cold and unfathomable.

'I know nothing about murders, Monsieur Brant,' he said. 'My only interest is in wine. I am preparing to make substantial investments in this village. Scandal is bad for business. I have to protect my investment and that means preserving the good name of Haut St Antoine.'

'Funny, Inspector Chasselas said the same thing,' said Ezra. 'He and I have seen a lot of each other lately.'

Ezra wanted to let him believe that the police chief would be aware of his movements but de Blancourt's expression signalled no interest. The Frenchman reached into his pocket, a sudden movement that caused Ezra to do likewise. He felt for the Luger's safety catch but before he could find it de Blancourt's hand was out of his pocket. Dangling from his fingers was a set of car keys.

'Here,' he said, handing them to Ezra. 'I will show you what has to be done.'

He took Ezra by the arm and led him across the cobbled courtyard to what appeared to be a stable. Ezra could smell rotting hay and manure. Barnyard smells, the fragrance of fine red Burgundy. De Blancourt opened a wooden door which groaned on its hinges. Inside, a naked light bulb glowing orange illuminated the shiny contours of the red Maserati. Attached to the top of the boot was a wooden cradle with heavy webbing straps.

237

'The barrel will be carried there. The weight will be evenly distributed but even so you should be careful cornering,' he said.

'Where is the barrel?' asked Ezra.

'We must collect it now. Here are the papers. One for the barrel and one for the case of wine in the back seat. It's from Dominique Piron. Do you know him? He also makes a very good Morgon.'

Ezra opened the door and reached inside the cardboard case. He pulled out a bottle and inspected the label.

'Here are instructions for you where to leave the car when you reach Calais. You will ask for a Monsieur Bages at the ferry security office. He will take the keys. I will return your car to Hertz, I assure you.'

Ezra held up the customs paper to the light. *Document d'Accompagnement Viti-Vinicole*, it read. It was date stamped 18 XI 1993, heure 0000.

'We must hurry,' said de Blancourt. 'You will want to make an early start before all the lunatics take to the road. I suggest you drive my car to get the feel of it and I will follow you in yours. Give me your keys, please.'

'Where are we going?'

'To pick up the wine, of course.'

'You mean, it's not here?'

'Of course not. The barrel is waiting for you at Bernard Montreuil's. But I must warn you. You are not to talk to him. Since the death of his wife he is not himself.'

He tapped the side of his forehead with his index finger as Inspector Chasselas had done, referring to Marie-Claire Verrier.

238

'Poor man,' continued de Blancourt. 'He tried to burn down his own business. You saw the fire. So, under no circumstances are you to deal with him. The doctor says that the sight of strangers will distress him.'

Another Fournier diagnosis, thought Ezra.

'How am I to get the barrel then?'

'The boy will help you. Now we must go.'

Ezra, curious to know why de Blancourt was so anxious to get started, decided on a delaying tactic of his own. He reached into the glove compartment of his rented car.

'You'll need my Hertz contract,' he said, handing the folder to de Blancourt.

'Of course,' smiled the Frenchman. 'It will be taken care of. For your own comfort I suggest we go now.'

'I just have to put my case in the boot,' he said. 'Which key opens yours?'

With a gesture of impatience, de Blancourt said, 'The smaller of the two.'

Ezra opened the boot of the Citroën and lifted out his black wardrobe case. He prided himself on his ability to pack so that nothing got creased. An experienced traveller, he knew what to take but always managed to return home with clothes he had not worn.

'I guess you've heard that Jacques Verrier has escaped from jail,' he said, as he laid the case in the boot of the Maserati.

From his position at the rear of the car de Blancourt's face was no longer in shadow. The dull light from the lone bulb gave it a jaundiced pallor. Connie should see him like this, he thought.

239

De Blancourt, who had made a movement towards the black Citroën, wavered in his stride. He got into the driver's seat of Ezra's rental car and wound down the window.

'An innocent man would have stayed put, wouldn't you say? Now, follow me, Monsieur Brant, and remember, you talk only with the boy. If Bernard is there I will deal with him.'

Ezra eased himself with difficulty into the driver's seat of the Maserati. He was almost prone, a driving position unfamiliar to him. He adjusted the wing mirrors, felt for the pedals and pumped the brake. He searched for the lights on the instrument panel and when he found the switch he turned them on. Satisfied that he knew where everything was, he watched de Blancourt back the Citroën around the fountain and nose it out of the château gate. He turned the ignition key and the Maserati's engine snarled like a jungle cat awakened by hunger. He put the car in gear and at the lightest touch of his foot on the accelerator the beast leapt forward. He braked violently and the car stalled.

His armpits prickled with perspiration. He had never driven such a powerful car. In front of him he could see de Blancourt's tail-lights, angry red eyes in the darkness waiting for him to pull out. He started the car once more and eased it gently over the cobblestones and out through the gates.

Every window in the façade of Bernard Montreuil's farmhouse was ablaze with lights. An orange glow emanated from the gap under the barn door of the cooperage. Ezra felt his heart pounding. Events, he sensed, were rushing to a climax. He was being swept along on a dam burst. He could only hang on to the gunwales of his rudderless boat hoping to avoid the rocks along the way. He knew that soon, somewhere along the route, everything would be made clear to him. If only he could ride the flood.

De Blancourt had parked in front of the house. As Ezra pulled into the drive he motioned for him to back the Maserati up to the barn door. Someone inside had heard the feline purr of its engine because the door swung open. Silhouetted against the light and wearing only a pair of army fatigues and a khaki singlet stood the young Bernard Montreuil, his body glistening with sweat. The weights in each hand extended his arms to their full length reaching almost to his knees.

Ezra could not hear what de Blancourt said to him but the urgency in his voice caused the boy to drop the weights which resounded like cracked bells on the cement floor.

De Blancourt appeared agitated. He glanced over his shoulder towards the house before reaching into his pocket. He took out a wad of notes and pressed them into Bernard's hand. The boy stared at the money for a moment, grinned and then pushed the bundle into his underpants.

'Quickly, Bernard,' hissed de Blancourt. 'Show the gentleman how strong you are. Get the barrel marked "Beaujolais Bistro".'

The boy turned his back and flexed his shoulders. Even

beneath the singlet Ezra could see muscles defined like thick cables. The sight recalled the plaited loaves sold in the Jewish bakery near his home where Connie bought raisin bread. The stern-looking old woman behind the counter used to smile at the way she pronounced 'chalah'.

The clock in the village church tower struck fifteen minutes before eleven. The sound resonated in the cold night air, as baleful as a ship's horn. De Blancourt's anxiety to have the barrel removed from the cooperage before the boy's father appeared became more apparent with each passing moment.

From the shadows between the rows of barrels Ezra could hear a sudden intake of breath followed by a teeth-clenching groan. Then Bernard emerged, stumbling out of the darkness, one foot placed deliberately in front of the other. Hoisted high above his head was a twenty-litre barrel. On it was stencilled in yellow spray paint the words, 'Beaujolais Bistro'.

'Good boy,' whispered de Blancourt. 'Now put it on the trestle. Gently does it.'

Bernard did a slow, clumsy pirouette, his arms locked above his head. The veins in his neck stood out with the exertion and his shoulders were trembling. But all the while he wore a fixed grin that exposed the pinkness of his gums. Slowly, he lowered the barrel and manoeuvred it until it rested on his left shoulder. He carried it to the Maserati and placed it with surprising tenderness on the wooden cradle.

The Maserati's springs squealed in complaint and the back half of the car lowered perceptibly. At least his own weight in the driver's seat would create a balance, thought Ezra. 'You always were good for ballast,' Connie used to say.

De Blancourt was busy fixing the heavy webbing straps to secure the barrel when Bernard Montreuil *père* arrived.

The stocky cooper took in the scene at a glance. He wore a black arm band and he carried a bicycle inner tube in his hands, holding it in a manner to suggest he had located a puncture hole and was about to mend it.

'What's this? What's this?' he shouted.

At the sound of his angry voice the young Bernard began to pound his fists on the wing of the car.

'The straps, finish the straps,' de Blancourt said under his breath to Ezra.

The Frenchman moved forward and placed himself between the cooper and the car. Ezra began tightening the last strap, trying to keep an eye on both father and son.

He could see de Blancourt offering the man money which he was refusing, cursing and pushing at de Blancourt, trying to get around him. His son continued to beat a tattoo on the car body which was beginning to buckle under the blows. All the while he let out a wolf-like howl.

The older Montreuil was now wrestling with de Blancourt, shouting at his son for assistance.

'Get in the car!' de Blancourt yelled in English. 'Drive! Drive!'

Ezra pulled open the car door and slithered into the driver's seat, hitting his head as he did so. He saw the boy

243

run around the front of the car and he pressed the door-lock down. The car rocked as the young Bernard began pulling at the handle. Through the windscreen he could see the cooper and de Blancourt struggling. He fumbled for the keys and turned on the ignition. The Maserati roared to life, the noise of its engine causing the three other occupants of the cooperage to stop and stand back, as if some terrible new force had suddenly been unleashed in their midst.

Ezra put the car in gear and it shot forward, grazing the doorpost and knocking off a sideview mirror as it burst from the barn. He had no time to look back because the road yawned in front of him and he had no lights. Frantically, he ran his fingers over the panel until he found the switch.

The headlights, on high beam, lit up the night, illuminating the mobile distillery of the brothers Fréjac. Ezra could see the alarm in their faces and the terror in the horse's eyes as the Maserati thundered towards them.

They seemed to fill the roadway.

Desperately, Ezra swung the wheel to the right to avoid a collision. The car swerved and skidded on the slick tarmac. The terrified horse reared up, snapping its shafts with the sudden movement and tipping the wagon on its side. The men jumped clear as copper tanks and condensers tore away from the rotting floor-boards and tumbled into the ditch.

The Maserati swung out onto a grass verge and brushed a hedge before Ezra could manoeuvre it back onto the road again.

244

His first thought was about the damage to the car and the plight of the mad brothers. But as the car sped through the night he realized he had no idea where he was going. His only instinct had been to put enough distance between himself and Haut St Antoine so that he could gather his thoughts and plan what he should do.

Once clear of the village he drove until he saw the first road sign. He stopped the car and reached into the pocket of his coat for Farmiloe's Michelin map. He studied the route outlined in red. He was going the wrong way.

Then he remembered de Blancourt had said that he had left instructions in the pouch of the driver's door. He reached down and withdrew a thick envelope. Inside was a map, not the usual tourist kind but a large-scale survey used for army manoeuvres showing individual farmhouses and bridges across streams. De Blancourt had also marked a route. Ezra compared it to the one the Englishman had drawn.

The two were identical. Except that de Blancourt had circled a feature called La Roche de Solutré. Had he intended a rendezvous here with Farmiloe?

Ezra recalled the rock from his last visit to the Mâconnais, just north of the Beaujolais area where they grew excellent Chardonnay. Here the limestone hills rise up to a dramatic escarpment shaped like a vast ski-jump. At its precipitous western end the rock falls away in a sheer cliff. Stone Age hunters used to drive herds of wild horses and deer over the edge to slaughter them and the ground below is a deep graveyard of bones. Every summer President François

Mitterand had donned his climbing gear to scale its perpendicular face in the company of his secret service-men. The French president had done it, he had read, to help him formulate his social policies. There were politicians in Ottawa Ezra would like to see tackle some overhangs in the Rockies.

He switched off the overhead light and turned the car round in the direction of Moulin-à-Vent.

Pinpoints of golden light glimmered through the fog that veiled the hills. The Maserati's headlamps illuminated a narrow corridor of highway that made the night around it all the blacker. Ezra squinted through the windscreen. Perhaps Connie was right. Maybe he did need glasses. He sighed. 'Getting old,' he murmured. Getting old, his father used to say, meant you can never find a pair of shoes that fits.

The road twisted and turned like a black ribbon fluttering in the wind but the car hugged the line as if it were on rails. Ezra felt a sudden surge of exhilaration. He wanted to sing, to shout out at the sleeping hills that he was alive. He had escaped Haut St Antoine with its dark secrets. He had left behind him the treachery, lies and deceit that seemed to be the everyday stock in trade of the villagers. His euphoria made him playful and in his mood of black humour he began to indulge in word games. 'Come to beautiful Haut St Antoine,' he crooned, 'for a saintly high. Twin city with Sodom and Gomorrah.'

Yet part of him would have liked to be back there. But for an accident of time and place he could have been sitting in a café at this moment, quaffing the new wine with other revellers, ignorant of the village's terrible secrets. Still, he had escaped in one piece. He was on his way to join Connie. They would take the ferry to London and fulfil his assignment and then it was back to Toronto and the usual round of tastings and interviews with visiting winery principals. Haut St Antoine would be an interesting memory.

But he had promised Marie-Claire he would be back and he knew that he could not just forget about what he had seen. The barrel strapped to the back of the car was a constant reminder that he could not leave without knowing who had killed Yvette Montreuil and engineered Derek Farmiloe's death. There had to be a connection between the killings.

The key, he was convinced, was the twenty-litre barrel of Jacques, Verrier's Beaujolais-Villages Nouveau that he could see through his rearview mirror. De Blancourt must have had good reasons for me to get it away from Montreuil, he said to himself. Why else would he have made it so easy for me to take Farmiloe's place? He got hold of the papers before the appointed hour. He's lent me his own car and mapped out a fast route. But why did he have to fight off Bernard Montreuil in order to get hold of the barrel when he had the proper documentation? Surely, it couldn't have been just because it was an hour before release time.

Ezra experienced a rush of dreadful excitement. He knew he had been set up by de Blancourt. The aristocratic Frenchman had told Marie-Claire to say she had been burgled after he had paid her for the documents that were meant to have been stolen.

247

But Verrier had said that he had sold Farmiloe the wine in his own barrel. 'He buys my wine in my barrel.' He was adamant about that and even angry at any other suggestion. Then why had the Englishman gone to the expense each year of having Bernard Montreuil make up a new barrel? The cooper supplied barrels to Verrier. He had seen them in the vintner's cellar. If Farmiloe wanted a special cask why didn't he have it delivered to Verrier for filling? And why put Beaujolais Nouveau in new oak barrels anyway? The whole idea of *nouveau* was to be fresh and fruity without the tannic taste that new oak would impart.

Unless Derek Farmiloe was carrying something other than wine.

According to Connie, the bistro had not served the new Beaujolais for five years now. Its clientele had complained that the wine 'tasted funny', yet Farmiloe had continued to buy it, put it in a new barrel and race it back to London.

Ezra pictured Montreuil's cooperage with its rows of neatly stacked casks. All his barrels were handmade, of course, but this one was not a usual size. And then there was the business of the missing bung-borer and the metal filings on the floor.

He decided that he would take a better look at the barrel when he stopped at La Roche de Solutré.

As he drove through the village of Leynes the road began to climb steeply. He was leaving Beaujolais now and heading into the Mâconnais. He checked the map and was thankful that there were no other cars on this route. Snaking up the hills in a series of hairpin bends he could see all the way down the valley behind him and any headlights would be visible for miles.

At the top of the hill there was a wooded area. He considered stopping here but decided against it. La Roche de Solutré was the spot de Blancourt had marked on the map and the sooner he arrived there the longer he would have to prepare himself for what might happen.

Once into the woods, the road began to sweep steeply down to Fuissé in the plain and Ezra had to slow down as he drove through the village. On the corner of the square a man was kissing a woman under a streetlight. She was wearing a summer dress, oblivious to the cold. Her skin shone orange in the light. She reminded him of Yvette Montreuil, the way she looked that morning when he had almost hit her on his way into Haut St Antoine. Shoeless and weaving drunkenly in the roadway, her red hair plastered flat to her head. An hour later she lay dead in a pool of wine, a puncture mark on the left side of her neck.

The only other mark on her body was the gash on her forehead where she must have struck a barrel as she fell. He was certain there was no blemish on her face when she had peered dazedly through his windscreen. That needle mark and the slight swelling it produced must have been the cause of her death.

A lethal injection administered from behind, one that she could not have inflicted upon herself.

A lover in a fit of jealousy would have attacked her from the front. In his rage he would have used his fists or a knife, a heavy object to hand or a gun. Not something as precise and premeditated as a needle.

Unless it was a deliberate execution. Yet no one sits passively awaiting death. Even the most timorous animal will fight when their life is threatened and flight is impossible. There were no marks on Yvette's body to suggest that she had been tied up or restrained in any way. She must have accepted the needle voluntarily from someone she trusted.

A doctor.

Yvette was within walking distance of Dr Fournier's house when Ezra first saw her. She was barefoot which could be consistent with a medical examination. But why would she have left his surgery without her shoes?

He tried to concentrate, thinking back on his conversation with the old doctor and what he had learned of him from Marie-Claire and the lawyer Mirze. Cyril Fournier's history of misdiagnoses, his possible negligence in the defective birth of young Bernard Montreuil, his wrong prescription for Mirze's uncle if local gossip were to be believed. And then there was the question of Yvette's death certificate – 'a blow to the left temple by an unknown assailant,' Chasselas had said. If the ageing doctor were true to form, Farmiloe's death would be recorded as accidental.

The moon broke through a cloud and Ezra could see above him the outline of the Roche de Solutré rock. The impressive escarpment rose in a giant step from a sheer wall of limestone like a Mohawk haircut. At its highest point it stood 493 metres above the valley floor. The shape reminded Ezra of the cut that Michael had perpetrated upon himself with an electric razor the day before his thirteenth birthday. Connie had insisted that he wear a baseball cap until his hair grew back again.

The skeletal limbs of grapevines climbed the slopes that angled steeply up to Solutré-Pouilly. The village nestled under the shadow of the dominating cliff, as prominent as a ship's prow against the black sky. In his mind's eye, Ezra imagined cavemen with flat foreheads and wild eyes, waving flint-tipped spears and lighted torches, caterwauling and leaping frenziedly as they stampeded herds of wild horses over the precipice. Overkill in both senses of the word, reminiscent of Lamb's essay on the discovery of roast pork.

He was jerked back to reality by the sensation that he was sliding across the road. The turn up to the village was sharper than he had expected. The Maserati's front wheels struck the grass verge and he felt a sickening clunk as the car hit a weathered marker stone on the passenger side. At first he thought the barrel had fallen from its trestle on the boot.

Ezra had not had an accident since he had spun his father's old Buick on the winter roads of Toronto within a week of passing his driving test. The rear end had clipped a parked Cadillac and chewed through its side panels like a can opener. The incident had cost him his entire summer-job earnings to pay the body shop.

He pulled up and sat clutching the wheel not wanting to assess the damage. Instead he picked up the map and turned on the interior light. A car passed him and he watched its tail-lights round the bend and climb towards Solutré-Pouilly. Unlike the villages of Beaujolais which were alive with partying merchants, restaurateurs and truck drivers, those of the Mâconnais slumbered in darkness.

Ezra could hear the dull pulse of the traffic on the autoroute to the west but the country roads he travelled were silent and the presence of another car was a cause for anxiety.

He checked the map once more, satisfied he could find the spot de Blancourt had circled, and put the car in gear. The church clock was striking 11.30 p.m. The cobbled road shone with dew as the moon emerged briefly from behind a curtain of fog. At the edge of the village the road became steeper as it rounded the base of the rock. It was wide enough for two cars to pass and on both sides tall hedges obscured a view of the valley below. He came to the village of Vergisson where the road suddenly began to climb in earnest.

Soon he was at the tree line and he could feel the pressure in his ears. At breaks in the forest he was surprised to see open fields like alpine pastures.

He pulled over at a point where a narrow lane joined the main road. There was a signpost at the junction pointing the way to Pierreclos and Milly-Lamartine, the next villages on his route. He parked the car and got out. The damage to the passenger door was not as bad as it had sounded from inside the car. A little panel-beating and a respray would see it right.

He walked around to the back of the car and checked the barrel to see if the straps had loosened. Was this small amount of wine the cause of two deaths?

He leant down and sniffed the new oak. It smelled of sap and faintly of cloves, or was it cinnamon? He ran his fingers over the curve of the staves. Montreuil did fine work. Ezra could hardly detect the seams where one piece of hand-shaped wood joined the next. The craftsmanship was perfect. The grain of the bung was at the requisite 45-degree angle to that of the centre stave.

His fingertips ran over the head of the barrel, reading its surface like braille. He could feel the indentations where the double-pointed nails called *gudgeons* joined together the five slats of half-inch-thick oak which Montreuil would have cut into a circle with a bandsaw. And where they joined the crevices would have been rendered watertight by slivers of reed.

At the epicentre of the head Ezra felt a round indentation and his fingers registered a different texture and a sudden coldness. He felt in his pockets for a book of matches and when he had found it, he struck one and held it close to the barrelhead. On the first upright stroke of the 'J' in Beaujolais he detected a slight curvature into a circular flatness the size of a dime. He took the corkscrew he habitually carried and with its blade began to scrape at the yellow paint.

Underneath was a metal stud. He ran his fingers over the bottom of the cask and at its centre he felt a matching circular depression. He had no idea for what reason the cooper would have used metal in the barrel. It certainly wasn't to reinforce it.

As he speculated what it might be, he became aware of a glow of light above the trees, stubby pines and mountain oaks. There was only one road up to the rock from the north, winding its way from Vergisson in a large loop.

Ezra could see the light bouncing off the forest wall now. Headlights from an approaching car.

Instinctively, he moved back, melting into the shadow of the trees. The grass was heavy with dew and he could feel the wetness seeping into his socks. He moved deeper into the trees as the lights approached, concealing himself as best he could.

He could hear the engine slowing and then the headlights were turned off. The night was black again as if a giant cloak had been thrown over the entire scene. From his vantage point some thirty yards away from the Maserati he strained to hear the sound of the approaching car.

He heard the grinding of tyres on the gravel surface and a high-pitched shriek of brakes. Then the 'thunk' of a car door opening and the crunch of footsteps.

They were too heavy and measured to be a woman's.

Somewhere, deep in the forest behind him, an owl mourned its nocturnal fate as shivering fieldmice skittered over the leaves that papered the forest floor.

Ezra could feel his breath catching in his throat. His heart thudded against his ribs. He reached into his pocket and withdrew the Luger. The click of its safety catch seemed to ring like an alarm bell in the night. The feel of its butt in his hand gave him a strange sense of reassurance. He had never fired a pistol before but at Trinity, in the Army Corps, he had been an Empire Marksman with a .303. The old bolt-action Lee Enfield rifle used in the Second World War had a kick like a rodeo stallion.

He peered through the branches trying to catch sight of the intruder. He saw a shape approaching the Maserati.

He saw the orange-yellow flame before he heard the symphony of sounds that followed: an explosion, the shattering of glass and the screams of blackbirds flapping out of the trees in terrified flight. The noise echoed off the hills to the north, rolling back across the valley, a caricature of its original power.

Ezra felt his knees go weak. He held onto the tree for support. His first thought was, 'Oh my God! He's blown out the window.' And then it occurred to him that he could have been sitting in the driver's seat.

Whoever it was appeared to hesitate. They were bending down looking inside the driver's door window. If only the moon would come out, he thought. Surely they must know I'm here somewhere. Either they're desperate or they're not afraid that I have the advantage.

There was a click as the door opened. The courtesy light went on but Ezra had no chance to see the man's face. In its soft glow he could discern a rounded back and powerful shoulders. The man was leaning across the front seat, one foot off the ground. He was rooting through the glove compartment.

Ezra made a quick decision. In this position the odds were in his favour. He moved through the trees into the open. Manoeuvring around the back of the car, he positioned himself at a point sufficiently far from the driver's door so that his quarry could not kick at him or hit him without aiming.

He held the Luger at arm's length and supported the butt

with his free hand. He could feel the wetness in his socks and an uncomfortable prickling sensation in his armpits. He could smell cordite in the air.

Keep your voice steady, he told himself. For God's sake don't show him how scared you are.

'Get out with your hands in the air!'

For one irrational moment he mentally checked his French grammar. Was he saying it correctly?

The man froze in his position, stretched out across the front seat of the car.

'You heard me. Just come out slowly.'

His face was a white disc in the moonlight.

'Jacques!'

Verrier pulled himself upright. On the floor of the car was a shotgun. There were fragments of glass strewn across the leather upholstery.

The vintner seemed surprised for a moment and then his expression changed to one of morose indifference. He just stood staring at the gun in Ezra's hands.

'You followed the car thinking I was de Blancourt, didn't you?'

'I have no quarrel with you, Monsieur Brant,' he said, wearily. 'Just give me back my gun.'

'You were going to kill him. That's why you escaped from prison.'

'That bastard, he was having an affair with Yvette. He killed her.'

'How do you know?'

'Dr Fournier came to see me after you left. He is worried about my sister's health.'

'What did he tell you?'

'Please, Monsieur. There is no need for the gun. I have nothing against you.'

Ezra lowered the Luger but did not put it back in his pocket.

'What did Fournier say?'

'He told me he had a spare room in his house. He rented it to de Blancourt. He said they used to meet there. It troubled him because he was very fond of Yvette.'

Ezra recalled the ship in the bottle he had seen in Montreuil's cooperage. Fournier must have given it to Yvette, a gift from a lonely old man to a beautiful young woman. Had he thought of her as a daughter? Her death would have been as much a loss to him as it had been for her lover.

But Yvette must have been insensitive to the workmanship of Fournier's gift as well as to the impulse behind it. She had relegated it to her husband's workshop.

'How did you get out of jail?' asked Ezra.

Verrier shrugged. 'It was crazy. The guard forgot to lock the door when he delivered my dinner. It could have had something to do with the Beaujolais Dr Fournier brought for him.'

'So what are you going to do now?'

'I will kill him,' said Verrier. 'They will call it a crime of passion. In a few years I will be out.'

'Why don't you let the police deal with it?'

'Chasselas is only interested in protecting his rear. Besides, a man like de Blancourt can buy his freedom.'

Ezra considered what Verrier had said. If de Blancourt had conducted a clandestine affair with Yvette in the doctor's house, why had he killed her? Fournier was the more likely of the two to have a syringe.

'There's something I want you to see.'

He moved to the trunk of the car.

'Feel the head of the barrel and tell me what you think.'

Verrier joined him and ran his fingers over the smooth oak.

'It's a Montreuil cask,' said Verrier, 'but there is something I don't understand.'

'Exactly,' said Ezra. He tapped the flat surface with his knuckles. 'It doesn't even sound right. I'm convinced that both Yvette and Derek Farmiloe were murdered because of this barrel. Help me get it down.'

He unfastened the leather straps and between them they lifted the barrel off its trestle.

'Find me a rock,' said Ezra, 'something to hammer in the bung.'

Verrier returned with a couple of stones and handed them to Ezra. He placed the point of one at the centre of the wooden bung and struck it sharply with the other. After a few hits the circle of wood gave way.

Ezra tilted the barrel until the wine began to belch out onto the roadway. Verrier knelt down next to him and cupped his hand under the flow. He lifted it to his mouth, took a swig and then spat it out.

'*Merde!*' he exclaimed. 'This is not my wine.'

'It *is* your wine,' said Ezra. 'But there's something else

in there. Get the tool kit from the boot. There's bound
to be something we can use to break it open. Here are the
keys.'

Ezra watched mesmerized as the wine gurgled out of the
barrel and spread in a shallow lake across the road, as black
as blood. The sight of it brought back the image of Verrier's
cellar and his discovery of Yvette Montreuil's wine-soaked
body.

Verrier opened the boot and hunted inside for the car
tools. He returned with a jack and the iron used for
unscrewing wheel nuts. He held them out mutely for Ezra
to choose. Ezra took the iron bar and inserted it into the
bung hole.

'Hold the barrel steady.'

While Verrier gripped the sides of the small cask, Ezra
put his knee on it and began to lever downwards on the bar.
The stave began to give, working loose from the metal
hoops that bound it. It tore away and he was able to slide
his hand inside.

'There's a chain,' he said, 'and a metal ball. A chain from
the top and the bottom clipped to a ball the size of a melon!'

'Bring it out,' said Verrier.

Ezra pried two more staves loose in order to remove the
ball. It was a simple matter of unhooking the links. He held
it gingerly by the eyes that had been welded to the globe at
its poles.

'What do you make of that?' he asked Verrier,
perplexed.

The vintner shrugged.

Ezra took a handkerchief from his pocket and carefully

259

dried the surface of the metal ball. It was beautifully engineered, a perfect sphere with no perceptible seams. The material felt like aluminium, its surface polished to a smooth finish.

He tested its weight and then put it to his ear, shaking it gently.

'It has to open somehow. It must unscrew.'

He held the two metal eyes and tried to turn them in opposite directions but they would not budge.

'There must be some screwdrivers in the kit.'

Verrier returned to the open boot and began to root about inside.

Ezra contemplated the object in his hand like Yorick's skull. The metal filings on the floor of Montreuil's cooperage must have come from a lathe used to fashion this ball. The cooper had put together a false barrel for Derek Farmiloe. Verrier's Beaujolais Nouveau was just a blind, a way to get the barrel past customs. There would be lots of wine coming through at the same time. Any anxiety witnessed by customs officers would be put down to the urgency of the race, all the merchants and restaurateurs vying with each other to get their wine back to London first. What an ideal cover! And all those other templates with the names of restaurants. My God, he thought, it was an international conspiracy.

Verrier handed him the tool kit. It was wrapped in oilskin fastened at the waist with two strings. It reminded Ezra of the set of fish knives and forks he and Connie had received as a wedding gift from her mother. The familiar pale blue Birks apron, with each utensil nestled in its own pocket of velveteen that rolled up and tied with a silver ribbon. They had brought it out the first time his mother-in-law had come to dinner and never used it since. An instant heirloom useless in the back of the drawer.

'Pliers,' he said, folding back the oilskin. 'Even better.'

He took out the pair of pliers and clamped the jaws around the bottom eye. He inserted a screwdriver through the top one and began to turn.

Slowly, the hemisphere came away. Apprehensive, Ezra held the object at arm's length and leaned his head away as he removed the top.

Inside, formed to the shape of the aluminium ball, was a large plastic bag that completely filled the interior of the sphere.

'Just what I thought,' said Ezra. 'Heroin. There must be at least a couple of kilos here.'

Verrier remained strangely silent. He had stood without moving, staring at the silver globe. Ezra placed a hand on his shoulder and looked into his eyes.

'You know something about this, don't you, Jacques?'

The vintner's expression contorted in silent pain.

'Yvette took drugs, didn't she? The morning of her death I saw her in the street. I saw her eyes. I thought she was drunk but it was drugs, wasn't it?'

Verrier cracked his knuckles and tears welled up in his eyes.

'I didn't believe it at first. She told me it was painkillers. Fournier prescribed them, she said. When she was on it she was like a demented woman. She toyed with everybody. Men, women, even her own son. It didn't matter. Rubbing her body up against them. It made her crazy. The night before she was murdered we had a fight. I told her I would get her help but she said it was her only escape. She wanted me to take it with her.'

'How did she use it?'

'What do you mean?'

'Did she inject it?'

'No, she was terrified of needles. I caught her once. She was drinking it mixed with water.'

'Do you know where she got it?'

Verrier shook his head.

Ezra screwed the top back carefully. He had begun to understand the connections.

Bernard Montreuil conspired with Derek Farmiloe to smuggle drugs into London every year, and to a network of restaurants throughout Europe. He made up the spherical metal containers and fixed them into his barrels. But a sleepy Beaujolais village would hardly be a source for such a quantity of narcotics. The drugs would have to have come through a centre like Paris or Marseilles. Fournier came from Marseilles and he had been a ship's doctor. He could have had a source.

Verrier said that it was Fournier who prescribed the stuff for Yvette. But why would he jeopardize such a lucrative operation by creating an addict in his own village?

And the old doctor did not seem capable of the organization needed to run a successful drug smuggling ring on an international scale.

Montreuil was a fine barrel-maker but he too could not have set up such a sophisticated operation. Only a man like

Paul de Blancourt with his money and his political connections could carry it off.

Fournier had rented a room to de Blancourt. According to Verrier, he was the other man in Yvette's life. She had died from an injection in the neck.

A lethal dose of heroin.

Verrier had just said she was terrified at the sight of a needle. But would she have been afraid if she had not seen it? If it had been administered in the back of her neck?

Ezra was so preoccupied with his thoughts that he did not hear the approaching footsteps.

The whole scene was suddenly illuminated in a blinding light. Instinctively he put one hand up to shield his eyes. In the other he held the metal ball like an orb behind his back. The beam moved away to focus on Verrier's face, then to the car and quickly back to Ezra.

'It seems I have snared two pheasants with one net,' said a voice out of the darkness.

Chapter Ten

The voice behind the white glare was calm and amused. Ezra recognized the ironic tone of Inspector Chasselas.

'Any weapons you have please place them gently on the ground in front of you.'

Ezra did as he was told. He reached into his pocket, keeping the metal globe out of sight, and placed the Luger on the ground.

'You should not have escaped, Jacques,' said Chasselas. 'By running you only confirm your guilt.'

Verrier did not reply. From the corner of his eye Ezra could see him edging towards the Maserati. The shotgun still lay on the floor.

'Jacques, don't move,' he warned.

'Good advice, Monsieur Brant. And may I ask what your intention is? All this wine. A libation to the gods, is it? Or are you just celebrating the new Beaujolais a little early?'

As his eyes became accustomed to the flashlight Ezra could see the policeman's silhouette behind its powerful beam. In his left hand he held an automatic pistol.

'There's no need to arrest Jacques, Inspector,' he said. 'I can prove he's innocent.'

'Finding Jacques Verrier here with you has saved me time, Monsieur. But it is you I have come to arrest.'

'Me! On what charge?'

'Theft.'

'I have papers for the barrel. Everything is in order, you can see for yourself.'

'Just keep your hands to your side, Monsieur Brant. I am not referring to the barrel. I have a report of a stolen car. That car,' said Chasselas, indicating the red Maserati with the barrel of his automatic pistol.

So that was how de Blancourt had set him up. He cursed himself for his stupidity. But what had the Frenchman to gain from such a transparent ploy? Unless he was trying to brand me as a drug smuggler, thought Ezra. It didn't make any sense. Chasselas was looking for Verrier and he interrupts his search to pursue a stolen car.

And how could he have made it up to the rock without my seeing him, Ezra asked himself? There was only one road to the top and he had spotted Verrier's headlights a long way off.

It must have been Chasselas' car that passed me below, he reasoned. If that was the case, why hadn't he arrested me there in the village? Unless Chasselas knew what he was transporting.

Ezra decided to play for time.

'Whoever killed Yvette and Farmiloe, Inspector, wanted this. And the others like it.'

He held up the metal sphere. The moon broke through the clouds bathing its dull patina in a silver glow.

'If that is evidence Monsieur Brant I would appreciate it if you did not handle it.'

'The only fingerprints you'll find on it are mine.'

'Then kindly place it on the ground in front of you. Not near the gun, if you please.'

Ezra made no move. Something Chasselas had said when they had first met came back to him. 'It is not often the air is so clear.' He had been talking about the photograph of Marseilles. The shot he had taken himself. He must have lived in the city to have made a statement like that. Fournier and Chasselas, both from Marseilles.

And this was the first time Ezra had seen the policeman on duty without a back-up. Where was the gendarme with the machine-gun who had accompanied him at the arrest of Jacques Verrier and had been with him to investigate the scene of Farmiloe's death? Marie-Claire had said there was a gendarme in her kitchen with a machine-gun when Chasselas had come looking for Verrier and yet, in this potentially more dangerous situation, the Inspector was alone.

'I said, put it on the ground.'

Chasselas' voice had hardened. The mocking, ironic tone was gone.

'It's heroin, you know,' said Ezra, tossing the aluminium ball lightly in his palm. 'Your brother-in-law was smuggling it into London for Derek Farmiloe. Inside one of his barrels. But you knew that, didn't you? You know everything that goes on in Haut St Antoine.'

'You are on dangerous ground, Monsieur Brant.'

'All that bullshit about protecting the good name of the village, Inspector. You didn't want me to find out about your operation. But something went wrong, didn't it? Maybe Farmiloe got greedy and decided to leave without paying you. That's why you had to kill him. But de Blancourt crossed you up too by giving me the barrel and the papers to get it through customs.'

A frown crossed Chasselas' face.

'I am not interested in your theories, Monsieur Brant. I am here to bring back a fugitive and suspected murderer. And you are not only in possession of stolen property and a firearm, you are also aiding and abetting an escaped criminal. If you resist arrest I shall have to shoot you. Now, kindly put that ball at your feet.'

Ezra considered his position. The policeman was quite capable of killing both Verrier and himself on the spot. Once he had the drugs they were as good as dead. His only chance was to play for time in the hopes that he would be able to pick up the Luger.

'One thing I don't understand. Why did you have to kill Yvette?'

The blackness of the night intensified the silence between them. Verrier, who had been standing quite still, suddenly let out a roar and charged at the policeman. The fury of his attack caught Chasselas off guard but before the vintner could get within striking distance he let off a burst of automatic fire.

Ezra heard the sound of ripping metal as the bullets struck the wing of the Maserati and then a scream from

Verrier who collapsed, clutching his right thigh with both hands. He lay on the ground groaning in pain.

Behind Chasselas Ezra could see distant flashes of light from the valley below. Cars were coming up to the rock. He had to keep Chasselas talking.

'You injected her with heroin. The needle mark was at the base of her neck on the left. It could only have been done from behind by someone who was left-handed. Like you. She must have been sitting up waiting for it. That's the way you did it, wasn't it?'

Chasselas waved the pistol at Ezra.

'Just put the ball down, Monsieur Brant.'

'And then you'll kill me too. You tried before. That man on the motor bike was you. And what about the co-operative? Was that you too? How much did you have to pay the fork-lift driver?'

'No, that was an accident. I can't take credit for that.'

The lights behind Chasselas grew more intense. Desperately, Ezra kept talking to distract him.

'But why did you have to kill her?'

'She was blackmailing me, Monsieur Brant. She found the stuff and began using it. Bernard got careless. We had to move it to Dr Fournier's surgery for safekeeping.'

'So the price of her silence was to keep her supplied. She met you at the surgery and you would give her a shot because she couldn't bear to do it herself. You were the man she used to meet. And Jacques thought she had a lover.'

'She became like an animal,' said Chasselas, with

disgust. 'She wanted more and more. She threatened to ruin everything.'

The lights from the approaching cars lit up the tops of the trees and Chasselas could now see the leaping shadows they created.

'Knowledge is a dangerous thing, my friend. Now I will have to kill you.'

Ezra closed his fingers around the metal ball. Planting all his weight on his right foot he drew back his shoulder and hurled it as far as he could into the trees.

Chasselas watched its trajectory until it was lost in the night. They could hear the sound of the cars clearly now and the policeman turned off his flashlight.

'That was very foolish for such an intelligent man,' said Chasselas. 'Now you will be my shield. Turn round.'

Ezra could hear the sound of car doors opening and running footsteps. He turned round.

'Are you going to shoot me in the back, Inspector?'

'Shut up and do as I say.'

He felt the stab of the pistol into his left kidney. Almost immediately the whole area blazed with light. A voice crackled over a loudhailer.

'Put down your weapon, Chasselas, and step forward with your hands in the air.'

'I have the Canadian,' Chasselas shouted back. 'I am walking to my car. If you try to stop me I will kill him.'

'Release your prisoner,' called the voice. 'You cannot escape.'

Chasselas fired a burst into the air.

'The next one is into his back. Now, tell your men to

stand aside. We're coming through. Move,' he whispered to Ezra, 'and don't try to be a hero.'

Ezra began to walk slowly towards the blinding wall of lights. Whose bullet would kill him? One from Chasselas or one from an over-anxious gendarme. He thought of Connie waiting for him in Versailles, of Michael in Toronto and Steppenwolf. He thought of Verrier lying wounded on the forest floor. The Beaujolais Nouveau would go undelivered and his column would no longer appear. At least not under his byline. The novel he had written in his head for the last ten years would go unpublished and he would never have visited Thailand. There would be a brief obituary in his newspaper and none in the rival *Globe & Mail*. And maybe a memorial service where his colleagues and friends would gather to comfort Connie. A minister who didn't know him would read a list of his achievements, exaggerating for effect. And then oblivion.

The man with the loudhailer stepped out into the road, silhouetted by the bank of lights.

'You should know better than anyone you cannot get away,' he called.

Ezra recognized the voice now. It was Paul de Blancourt.

Chasselas continued walking slowly towards them, angling Ezra's large frame so that it protected him from the police at the road block.

'Police have been radioed throughout the department, Inspector. All the roads will be blocked.'

'But I have my flesh-and-blood passport,' shouted Chasselas. 'Move back I tell you.'

The phalanx of uniformed men parted like the Red Sea. Ezra could hear the crackle of police radios inside the cars. Every sound and image seemed magnified as if his senses knew instinctively this was the last time they would be exercised.

He could smell the Beaujolais Nouveau that ran like blood under his feet mingling with the scent of pines and woodsmoke. He could see across the sleeping valley to the Mont de Pouilly, a huge black breast in the moonlight. In front of him the exhaust from the car engines rose in plumes like ostrich feathers. It was curious how ageing Riesling smelled like gasoline, he thought. He would never taste it again.

He heard the blast and waited for the pain. Behind him Chasselas gave a grunt and slumped into him. He stumbled and both of them fell. Chasselas dropped his pistol and rolled over on his back, glasses askew, his eyes wide open.

Lying in the road behind them was Jacques Verrier. He lowered the smoking shotgun and began to weep.

'I'm sorry about your car,' said Ezra, running his fingers over the bullet holes in the metal and the crumpled mudguard.

Jacques Verrier had been laid out on the back seat of a police car and was already being driven back to hospital in Mâcon.

Paul de Blancourt smiled.

'Don't worry, Monsieur Brant. The French taxpayer will foot the bill.'

'What do you mean?' asked Ezra.

'It's rented, like the château. Do you think I could afford all that on the salary of a civil servant?'

'Civil servant?'

'But of course. I am the assistant director of Internal Security at the Elysée Palace. I moved to Haut St Antoine six months ago to try to infiltrate a drug ring. For that I had to pose as a wealthy man.'

Ezra leaned again the car. With the realization came the anger.

'You mean, you knew all along and you used me to smoke Chasselas out?'

'We are very grateful to you, Monsieur Brant. Without you we would never have been able to do it.'

'You son of a bitch! You could have got me killed.'

De Blancourt was unprepared for the blow and it caught him on the side of the face. He fell to the ground and looked up at Ezra who towered over him, his hands still clenched in fists.

'I suppose I deserved that,' he said, easing himself to his feet and brushing the dirt from his coat. 'But think of it this way. You have a better story now. There is more to life than wine, my friend. And before you try to hit me again tell me if you didn't enjoy the chase.'

Ezra would not admit it to the Frenchman but he felt more alive than he had ever done before.

'And after all,' continued de Blancourt, 'as a Compagnon de Beaujolais did you not swear before St Vincent to uphold the traditions of hospitality, wisdom and good humour of the region? Where is your sense of humour now?'

'Thanks a bunch. Now what am I supposed to do?'

'I have your car here. The keys are in the ignition and there is a case of Beaujolais Nouveau in the trunk. A gift from the people of Haut St Antoine. Now you are free to go and join your wife.'

De Blancourt took Ezra by the arm and led him along the road to where the rented Citroën was parked.

'Tell me one thing,' said Ezra. 'The fire at the cooperage. What was that all about?'

'It was a warning to Montreuil. Chasselas suspected his brother-in-law of stealing some of the drugs and selling them directly to Farmiloe. But really it was Farmiloe who was trying to cut Chasselas out. He didn't need him any more. He had discovered the Inspector's contacts in Marseilles and he decided to deal directly with them. Chasselas found out and fixed his brakes so that he would have an accident.'

'And you needed someone to drive the barrel to London before he could get hold of it. That's why you wanted to avoid Montreuil.'

'Exactly.'

'And where did Dr Fournier fit into the picture?'

'It was Fournier who knew the dealers in Marseilles. As a ship's doctor he was an ideal courier. But he made the mistake of trying some himself. It nearly destroyed him. So he came to Haut St Antoine to leave it all behind. Chasselas was in the Marseilles police at the time. He followed him to the village and used his contacts to establish a smuggling ring there.'

No wonder Chasselas was concerned about the doctor's

drinking, thought Ezra. It must have been the Inspector he had seen from Fournier's living-room the night of the induction dinner.

'By the way,' said de Blancourt, 'my men have not been able to locate the drugs. I do hope you are not intending to go into business on your own account.'

'You'll find them somewhere in the woods,' said Ezra, climbing into the driver's seat. 'In a metal ball. I threw them as far as I could.'

'Good luck, Monsieur Brant. And please give my regards to your charming wife.'

Ezra scanned the handsome features in the moonlight. He turned the ignition key and the engine coughed to life.

'We have an expression in English,' he said, as he turned on the headlights and slipped the car into gear. 'The shoemaker should stick to his last.'

'What does that mean?' asked de Blancourt.

'You're an undercover cop and I'm a wine writer. We shouldn't trespass onto each other's territory.'

'I don't understand.'

'The wine you recommended for your President, the Beaujolais from the village co-operative. Try it again some time. I hope your President likes Italian wine.'

Ezra let out the clutch and turned the car round ready for the descent to Vergisson.

He had no recollection of the drive from La Roche de Solutré to Versailles. Enveloped in the night, he drove oblivious to everything but the thoughts in his head. He was trying to reconstruct what had happened in Haut St

Antoine. Yvette, Farmiloe and now Chasselas. All dead. And soon Dr Fournier and Bernard Montreuil would be in jail. He wondered what would happen to the cooper's son, motherless and soon to be without a father. Could he run the cooperage without his father? And then he thought of his own son. How would Michael cope without him and Connie? If he had been killed, or worse, both of them, there would be no relatives in Toronto to take him in.

But he was alive. He had come through and Connie would be waiting for him in the square at Versailles.

How was he going to write his story? The wine column was no place for murder and drug smuggling. What would he say at the embassy dinner in London as he raised his glass to toast the new wine?

These questions danced in his head as the autoroute signs flashed by: Saulieu, Avallon, Chablis, Auxerre. The headlights of passing cars created shadows in the trees and ghostly farmhouses suddenly appeared in the blackness of the fields.

How would he explain it all to Connie? So much had happened since she had boarded the train for Paris.

She was waiting for him in the square as he knew she would be, her suitcases by her side. He pulled up in front of her five minutes before the appointed hour. The square was deserted. The streetlights made the wet pavement shine.

He leaned across the seat and opened the door from the inside. Connie bent down and studied him in the light before getting in.

'Are you sure you should be driving? You look like hell.'

'Is that all you can say to me?'

'I thought maybe you'd been celebrating too much.'

'Put your luggage in the back seat, Connie. It's been a long night.'

Sliding into the seat, she kissed him lightly on the cheek.

'Well, at least I can rely on you to be on time ... Ezra, what's the matter?'

He had slumped forward, his forehead touching the steering-wheel. She could see his shoulders trembling.

'Are you sick?'

She put her arms around him and he lay back, his eyes closed.

'It's all over, Connie.'

She drew back from him in alarm.

'What are you saying?'

'The murders, the lies, it's all over.'

Connie stroked his hair. 'Tell me what happened.'

'Chasselas is dead. It's finished.'

Exhaustion and relief mingled with a curious sense of anticlimax. He felt empty and dull but he owed her an explanation.

'Dead?' said Connie.

Sitting in the car in the empty square he began to tell her the story. Haltingly at first, staring straight ahead into the night, and then the words came pouring out. Connie took his hand, only interjecting to ask a question when she did not understand.

'Chasselas killed Yvette because she found out he was the leader of the drug ring. He planned her murder to implicate his partners. He had to get rid of her, otherwise

277

she would have destroyed the whole business. So he decided to give her an overdose and then dump her body in Jacques Verrier's cellar to make it look as if she had been killed on his premises. Everyone knew they were lovers and that they had quarrelled the night before. But Chasselas had to make sure that the cellar was empty when he dropped the body in. That's why he needed Farmiloe. When I was in the cellar Marie-Claire came to call Verrier away to meet him. Farmiloe didn't know I was still down there.'

'But we saw Yvette that morning.'

'Yes, she was on her way to see Dr Fournier to get more drugs. He was the weak link. He salved his conscience by giving her money from the profits he made from the smuggling operation. The rest he sank into buying antique books. A country doctor couldn't afford a collection like that on his salary.'

'But why did he give her money?'

'Because he butchered the birth of her son. At the delivery the cord was wrapped round his neck cutting off oxygen. The boy was born retarded and Fournier felt responsible. But Yvette wanted more than money when she got hooked on the drugs she found in her husband's cooperage. Fournier warned Chasselas and that was her death warrant. The morning we saw her she was on her way to Fournier's surgery. She had already taken a little but she needed more. It was then Chasselas and Farmiloe must have picked her up in Farmiloe's car. Chasselas probably injected her in the back seat. She must have thrown up because there was a large stain on the leather which had been recently cleaned, and there were strands of her hair caught in the door handle.'

'But what about the bung-borer? Why would Chasselas have gone to all that trouble?'

'In case outside police were brought in he had to incriminate others. He took the tool from Montreuil's cooperage and used it as a handle to open the trapdoor.'

'Why did Chasselas have to kill Farmiloe then?'

'He must have panicked after Yvette's murder. He wanted out but he also wanted the drugs so he tried to get the barrel from Bernard Montreuil's son and make a run for it. Chasselas found out and made sure he didn't leave.'

'And Paul de Blancourt wasn't the rich playboy he pretended to be,' said Connie, trying to keep the disappointment out of her voice.

'De Blancourt is number two in the Department of Internal Security. He was sent down to Haut St Antoine to flush out Chasselas. He's an unscrupulous son of a bitch. He doesn't care whom he uses. He had Marie-Claire tell me she had been robbed of the papers I needed. Then he set me up as bait. He wanted me to drive the barrel to London to smoke out Chasselas. Luckily, Jacques got to me first.'

'But how did Jacques get out of jail?'

'Chasselas engineered it. He's a cop after all. He set it up so that Jacques could break out. That way when he caught him he could kill him without arousing suspicion.'

'But why would Jacques want to escape?'

'Dr Fournier went to see him after I did. Chasselas must have told him that it was de Blancourt who killed Yvette. Jacques wanted revenge.'

'Then Chasselas must have suspected Paul.'

Ezra's concentration was broken by her use of the man's first name. He glanced sideways at her.

'He must have, mustn't he?' said Connie.

'Yes. It would have solved all his problems if Jacques had been able to get to de Blancourt and shoot him. Only it was me who was driving his car. De Blancourt had reported it stolen to make sure Chasselas would come after me, knowing that I had the barrel.'

'Well, at least you're safe,' said Connie, settling back in her seat. 'Now let's go home, Ezra.'

'We're going to London,' he said.

'You know what I mean. Are you all right to drive?'

'Yes,' he said.

Ezra consulted the map and then started the car. Street cleaners were already at work in the square although the sky was still dark. They drove in silence until they were in open country again, each wrapped in their own thoughts.

'Tell me something,' he said. 'That afternoon you spent with de Blancourt. Did anything happen?'

Connie shifted her weight in the seat and clutched her handbag tightly to her stomach.

'I wondered when you were going to cross-examine me about that.'

'You haven't answered my question.'

'What is your question?'

'You heard me.'

'Ezra, we've been married for eighteen years. Why do you want to know that?'

'I suppose I'd rather not know.'

280